Fires of the Past

FIRES OF

THIRTEEN CONTEMPORARY

THE PAST

FANTASIES ABOUT HOMETOWNS

Edited by

Anne Devereaux Jordan

ST. MARTIN'S PRESS   NEW YORK

Design by Glen M. Edelstein

Library of Congress Cataloging-in-Publication Data
Fires of the past : thirteen contemporary fantasies about hometowns / Anne Devereaux Jordan, editor.
   p. cm.
  ISBN 0-312-05433-5
   1. Fantastic fiction, American. 2. City and town life—Fiction. 3. Home—Fiction. I. Jordan, Anne Devereaux.
  PS648.F3F57 1991   90-49312
  813'.08766081732—dc20   CIP

First Edition: March 1991
10 9 8 7 6 5 4 3 2 1

For David, and for Lisa, Gretchen, Holly,
and Mandy

CONTENTS

$\mathcal{A}$CKNOWLEDGMENTS

I wish to thank Gordon Van Gelder, of St. Martin's Press, without whose support, enthusiasm, direction, and editorial acumen this book might not have been written.

ℐNTRODUCTION

'Mid pleasures and palaces though we
    may roam,
Be it ever so humble, there's no place
    like home;
A charm from the skies seems to hallow
    us there,
Which sought through the world is ne'er
    met with elsewhere.

> —"Home Sweet Home"
> John Howard Payne, 1823

Corny as this old song is, there is an ele-
ment of truth in it that tugs our heart-
strings whether or not we wish to admit
it. The idea of home is a powerful concept, emotionally and intellectually. Our
homes and hometowns are the magical
places that defined us, which we carry
with us over time and distance. Margaret
Hamilton, made famous by her role in
The Wizard of Oz (a film whose entire
thrust was returning home), aptly said,
"The structure may disappear, but its essence is forever with us. Home has as

many different expressions as there are people to recognize them, and there is no other word which conveys to us the same emotion. . . . We can always return to that which holds our hearts—to home."[1]

In *Fires of the Past*, each author was asked to create a story set in his or her hometown or adopted hometown—the place that holds *their* hearts. Ironically, a number of authors found they first had to decide where their hometowns *were*; they had moved about so often in their lives and so many places had had an impact upon them. Some of the choices are intriguing. Joe Haldeman, who has lived all over the United States, including Alaska, finally settled on the stars and space. In all his travels, he explained, the sky—space—was the one constant place, the place to which he always returned. The result is his poignant, haunting narrative poem, "Homecoming." Lew Shiner's "home" is in Texas, but the actual place where he feels he has spent most of his time, he notes, is on the highway between Dallas and Austin. His story, "Wild For You," is a bizarre little tale spanning one afternoon on that highway. Kit Reed, although born in Connecticut, was reared in St. Petersburg, Florida, and her chilling "Calling Hours" reflects how she felt being a young person growing up surrounded by the old. As these stories show, often our hometowns are not the places in which we were born, but rather the places that have influenced us the most.

That influence is also captured by the well-known artist Ron Walotsky in his cover painting for this anthology. Ron Walotsky has been in the field of illustration for almost twenty-three years and during that time has provided hundreds of exciting, vibrant, and imaginative cover illustrations for the major fantasy and science fiction magazines as well as holding a number of one-man shows of both representational and abstract paintings. Much of that work has been done in East Atlantic Beach, New York, the area in which he grew up and currently lives. In fact, the middle house in the cover painting is his home and, if one looks closely, he can be seen through its window, hard at work. "I thought I'd put myself in," he said, "because I've spent so much time sitting and painting in that window." He commented that, as with the writers included in *Fires of the Past*, many of his ideas have come from his hometown. "I use the things that surround me—when they're not moving—that I haven't tried before or looked at from a new point of view."

Currently, in addition to revisiting his hometown for this cover, he is revisiting the past in his other work, a collection of his illustrations and paintings to be published in 1992.

Just as setting plays a significant role in the cover painting and in each of the tales here, each writer's feelings toward that setting also enriches each story, as does the *time* of the story. One's hometown yesterday and today may be very different tomorrow. Robert Silverberg, although born and reared in the eastern United States, considers San Francisco his adopted hometown. In his story, "The Last Surviving Veteran of the War on San Francisco," he gives us a wry and perceptive look at the future of "his" city. Connie Willis grew up and still lives in the Denver area and in "Cibola" not only do we share her humorous affection for Denver, we come to see, through her eyes, its magical qualities. This feeling for place—past, present, or future—has contributed to the creation of a collection of stories that are among the best written today.

Thomas Wolfe wrote, "You can't go home again," but he was wrong. One can return, as Harlan Ellison says, through "memory and art." That is what each of these writers—and illustrator Ron Walotsky—has done. *Fires of the Past* is thirteen "different expressions of home," all unique, all enthralling, all superb.

Welcome Home.

—Anne Devereaux Jordan

---

1. "There's No Place Like Oz," *Children's Literature*, Vol. 10. New Haven: Yale University Press, 1982, p. 155.

Harlan Ellison
JANE DOE #112

Since running away from home at the age
of thirteen, Harlan Ellison, like Ben Laborde in "Jane Doe #112," has led many
lives. A writer, screenwriter, editor, lecturer, and film and television critic, the
success of Harlan's "lives" can be seen in
the numerous books, movies, short stories, and teleplays he has written, and in
the multitude of awards his work has gar-
nered for him. Most recently, his short
story collection *Angry Candy* received the
1989 World Fantasy Award and was se-
lected by the *Yearbook* of the *Encyclopedia
Americana* as one of the "Major Works of
American Literature for 1988." In 1990,
his collection of critical essays on film,
Harlan Ellison's Watching, won the Bram
Stoker Award.

Harlan's writing, whether for film or
literature, is uniquely rich in language,
imagery, and levels. Beneath the surface
of his many stories are counterpoints that
speak to us all. In "Jane Doe #112" the
theme of returning home is balanced
against the idea of escaping that same

home and the past; sin of a very different sort is juxtaposed against redemption. All combine to create a tale that is deeply persuasive and moving, a story of one man's going home.

"In the case of 'Jane Doe #112,' " Harlan writes,

I began with New Orleans because that was where I was sitting when I began writing it, and it seemed only fair. But the scenes in other locales were drawn from memory. I have been to, passed through, lived in all of the places that appear in this story. I returned to them by way of recollection as inexorably as the protagonist returns to his home. They never change. They are imprinted clearly, ready to provide me with a vast Baedeker for any story I care to tell.

So in that way, more truly than by returning physically to the town or street where one grew up—now changed, plowed under, turned into a heartless mini-mall, filled with strangers too young or too old to remember you—I go back endlessly. Not to the place called Painesville on maps of Ohio, which bears no relation to the little stage of my youth, but to the Painesville and Evanston and Madison, Indiana, of memory, where all is as it was then.

Can you go home again? Yes, if you travel exclusively on the freeways and dirt roads of memory and art.

ℐANE ᗝOE #112
ℋarlan ℰllison

S HADOWS OF LIVES UNLIVED, as milky as opal glass, moved through the French Quarter that night. And one begged leave, and separated from the group to see an old friend.

Bourbon Street was only minimally less chaotic than usual. It was two days till the Spring Break deluge of horny fraternity boys and young women seemingly unable to keep their t-shirts on.

The queue outside Chris Owens's club moved swiftly for the last show. Inside, the entertainer was just starting the third chorus of "Rescue Me" when she looked out into the audience and saw the pale shadow of a face she hadn't seen in twenty years.

For a moment she faltered, but no one noticed. She had been a star on Bourbon Street for twenty years; they wouldn't know that the face staring up palely at her was that of a woman who had been dead for two decades.

Doris Burton sat in the smoky center of a cheering mob half-smashed on Hurricanes; and she stared up at Chris Owens with eyes as quietly gray and distant as the surface of the moon. The last time Chris had seen those eyes, they had been looking out of a newspaper article about the car crash over in Haskell County, when Doris had been killed.

Her parents wouldn't let her go over to the funeral. It was a piece of Texas distance, from Jones County over to Haskell. She had never forgotten Doris, and she had always felt guilty that she'd never gotten to say goodbye.

Now she felt the past worming its way into her present. It couldn't possibly be. She danced to the edge of the stage and looked directly at her. It *was* Doris. As she had been twenty years ago.

The woman in the audience was almost transparent in the bleed of light from the baby spots and pinlights washing Chris as she worked. Trying to keep up with the beat, Chris could swear she could see the table full of Kiwanis behind Doris. It threw her off . . . but no one would notice.

Doris moved her lips. *Hello, Chris.*

Then she smiled. That same gentle smile of an awkward young woman that had first bound them together as friends.

Chris felt her heart squeeze, and tears threatened to run her makeup. She fought back the sorrow, and smiled at her dead friend. Then Doris rose, made a tiny goodbye movement with her left hand, and left the club.

Chris Owens did not disappoint her audience that night. She never disappointed them. But she was only working at half the energy. Even so, they would never know.

That night, the Orleans Parish Morgue logged in its one hundred and twelfth unknown female subject. The toe was tagged JANE DOE #112 and was laid on the cold tile floor in the hallway. As usual, the refrigerators were full.

Ben Laborde took his foot off the accelerator as he barreled north on the I-10 past St. Charles Parish, and kicked the goddamned air conditioner one last time. It was dead. The mechanism on the '78 Corollas had been lemons when they were fresh off the showroom floor, and twelve years of inept service had not bettered the condition. Now it had given out totally; and Ben could feel the sweat beginning to form a *tsunami* at his hairline. He cranked down the window and was rewarded with a blast of mugginess off the elevated expressway that made him blink and painfully exhale hot breath. Off to his left the Bonnet Carré Spillway—actually seventeen miles of fetid swamp with a name far too high above its station—stretched behind him as an appropriate farewell to New Orleans, to Louisiana, to twenty-two years of an existence he was now in the process of chucking. The blue Toyota gathered speed again as he punched the accelerator, and he thought, *So long, N'wallins; I give you back to the 'gators.*

Somewhere north lay Chicago, and a fresh start.

When he thought back across the years, when he paused to contemplate how fast and how complexly he had lived, he sometimes thought he had been through half a dozen different existences. Half a dozen different lives, as memorable and filled with events as might have been endured by a basketball team with one extra guy waiting on the bench.

Now he was chucking it all. Again. For the half-dozenth time in his forty-one years.

Ben Laborde had run off when he was ten, had worked the crops across the bread basket of America, had schooled himself, had run with gangs of itinerant farm laborers, had gone into the army at nineteen, had become an MP, had mustered out and been accepted to the FBI, had packed that in after four years and become a harness bull in the St. Bernard Parish Sheriff's Department, had been promoted to Detective, and had had his tin pulled two years ago for throwing a pimp through the show window of an antique shop on Rue Toulouse. The pimp had been on the muscle with someone in the Department, and that was that for Detective Benjamin Paul Laborde.

He had become a repairman for ATMs, but two years fixing the bank teller machines had driven him most of the way into total craziness. And then, there was that group of pale gray people that kept following him . . .

He looked in the rearview. The expressway was nearly empty behind him. If he was being tracked, they had to be very good; and very far behind him. But the thought had impinged, and he cranked up the speed.

There had been six of them for the last year. Six men and women, as pale as the juice at the bottom of a bucket of steamed clams. But when he had seen them out of the corner of his eye the night before last, moving through the crowd on Bourbon Street, there had only been five.

He couldn't understand why he was so frightened of them.

He had thought more than once, more than a hundred times in the past year, that he should simply step into a doorway, wait for them to catch up, then brace them. But every time he started to do just that . . . the fear grabbed him.

So he had decided to chuck it all. Again. And go.

He wasn't at all certain if not having the Police Positive on his hip made any difference.

The nagging thought kept chewing on him: would a bullet stop them?

He ran, but the Corolla didn't have anything more to give. Still, it wasn't fast enough.

Chicago was dark. Perhaps a brownout. The city lay around him as ugly and desperate as he felt. The trip north had been uneventful, but nonetheless dismaying. Stopping only briefly for food and gas, he had driven straight through. Now he had to find a place to live, a new job of some menial sort till he could get his hooks set, and then . . . perhaps . . . he could decide what he wanted to be when he grew up.

As best he could discern, he hadn't been followed. (Yet when he had pulled in at a bar in Bloomington, Indiana, and had been sitting there nursing the Cutty and water, he had seen, in the backbar mirror, the street outside. And for a moment, five sickly white faces peering in at him.)

(But when he had swiveled for a direct look, only the empty street lay beyond the window. He had paid up and left quickly.)

Laborde had never spent much time in Chicago. He barely knew the city. A few nights around Rush Street, some drinking with buddies in an apartment in a debutante's condo facing out on the Shore Drive, dinner one night in Old Town. But he had the sense that staying in the center of the city was not smart. He didn't know why, but he felt the push to keep going; and he did. Out the other side and into Evanston.

It was quieter here. Northwestern University, old homes lining Dempster Street, the headquarters of The Women's Christian Temperance Union. Maybe he'd take night courses. Get a job in a printing plant. Sell cars. Plenty of action and danger in those choices.

He drove through to Skokie and found a rooming house. It had been years since he'd stayed in a rooming house. Motels, that was the story now. Had been for forty years. He tried to remember where he'd last lived, in which town, in which life, that had provided rooming houses. He couldn't recall. Any more than he could recall when he'd owned a Studebaker Commander, the car that Raymond Loewy had designed. Or the last time he had heard The Green Hornet on the radio.

He was putting his underwear in the bureau drawer as these thoughts wafted through his mind. Studebaker? The Green Hornet? That was over when he'd been a kid. He was forty-one, not sixty. How the hell did he remember that stuff?

He heard footsteps in the hall. They weren't the halting steps of the woman who owned the hostel. She had been happy to get a boarder. But not even a need to accommodate her new tenant could have eliminated the arthritic pace she had set as she climbed the stairs ahead of him.

He stood with his hands on the drawer, listening.

The footsteps neared, then stopped outside his door. There was no lock on the door. It was a rooming house, not a motel. No chain, no double-latch, no security bolt. It was an old wooden door, and all the person on the other side had to do was turn the knob and enter.

He barely heard the tapping.

It was the rapping at a portal of something composed of mist and soft winds.

Laborde felt a sharp pain as he realized he had been clenching his teeth. His jaw muscles were rigid. His face hurt. Whatever he wanted to do, it was not to go over and open that door to the visitor.

He watched, without breathing, as the knob slowly turned, and the door opened, a sliver of light at a time.

The door opened of its own weight after a moment, and Laborde saw a woman standing in the dimly-lit hallway. She looked as if she were made of isinglass. He could see through her, see the hallway through her dim, pale shape. She stared at him with eyes the color of an infirmary nurse's uniform.

Isinglass? How could he remember something like that? They had used isinglass before they'd started putting real glass in car windows.

The woman said, "Jessie passed through in New Orleans. She was the oldest of us. She was the one wanted to find you the most."

His mouth was dry. His hands, still on the dresser drawer, were trembling.

7

"I don't know any Jessie," he said. The voice seemed to belong to someone else, someone far away on a mountainside, speaking into the wind.

"You knew her."

"No, I never, I've *never* known anyone named Jessie."

"You knew her better than anyone. Better than her mother or her father or any of us who traveled with her. You knew the best part of her. But she never got to tell you that."

He managed to close the drawer on his underwear. He found it *very* important, somehow, just to be able to close the drawer.

"I think you'd better let the landlady know you're here," he said, feeling ridiculous. How she had gotten in, he didn't know. Perhaps the old woman had let her in. Perhaps she had asked for him by name. How could she know his name?

She didn't answer. He had the awful desire to go to the door and *touch* her. It was continuing strange, the way the light shone through her. Not as if there were kliegs set off in the distance, with radiance projected toward her; but rather, as if she were generating light from within. But what he saw as he looked at her, in that plain, shapeless dress, her hair hanging limp and milky around her shoulders, was a human being made of tracing paper, the image of the drawing behind shadowing through. He took a step toward her, hoping she would move.

She stood her ground, unblinking.

"Why have you been following me, all of you . . . there are six of you, aren't there?"

"No," she said, softly, "now there are only five. Jessie passed through." She paused, seemed to gather strength to speak, and added, "Very soon now, we'll *all* pass through. And then you'll be alone."

He felt an instant spike of anger. "I've *always* been alone!"

She shook her head. "You stole from us, but you've never been without us."

He touched her. He reached out and laid his fingertips on her cheek. She was cool to the touch, like a china bowl. But she was real, substantial. He had been thinking ghost, but that was ridiculous; he'd *known* it was ridiculous all along. From the first time he had seen them following him in New Orleans. Passersby had bumped into them, had acknowledged their existence, had moved

8

aside for them. They weren't ghosts, whatever they were. And whatever it was, he was terrified of them . . . even though he knew they would not harm him. And, yes, a bullet would have done them.

"I'm leaving. Get out of my way."

"Aren't you curious?"

"Not enough to let you keep making me crazy. I'm going out of here, and you'd better not try to stop me."

She looked at him sadly; as a child looks at the last day of summer; as the sun goes down; as the street lights come on before bedtime; one beat before it all ends and the fun days retreat into memory. He thought that, in just that way, as she looked at him. It was the ending of a cycle, but he had no idea how that could be, or what cycle was done.

He moved a step closer to her. She stood in the doorway and did not move. "Get out of my way."

"I haven't the strength to stop you. You know that."

He pushed her, and she went back. He kept his hand on her sternum, pressing her back into the hall. She offered no resistance. It was like touching cool eggshell.

"This time you leave even your clothes behind?" she asked.

"This time I shake you clowns," he said, going down the hall, descending the stairs, opening the curtained front door, stepping out into the Illinois night, and seeing his car parked across the street. Surrounded by the other four.

As fragile as whispers, leaning against the car. Waiting for him.

Oh, Christ, he thought, *this isn't happening.*

"What the hell do you *want* of me?" he screamed. They said nothing, just watched. Three men and another woman. He could see the dark outline of his car through them.

He turned right and began running. He wasn't afraid, he was just frightened. It wasn't terror, it was only fear.

Abandon the underwear in the drawer. Lose the past life. Jettison the car. Get out of this existence. Forget the deposit on the room. Run away. Just . . . run away.

When he reached the end of the block, he saw the lights of a mini-mall. He rushed toward the light. Dark things have no shadows in sodium vapor lights.

9

Behind him, the milky figure of the fifth one emerged from the rooming house and joined her traveling companions.

They caught up with him only three times in the next year. The first time in Cleveland. There were four of them. Three months later, he stepped off a Greyhound Scenicruiser at the Port Authority Terminal in Manhattan, and they were coming up the escalator to meet the bus. Two of them, a man and the woman who had confronted him in the rooming house in Skokie.

And finally, he came full circle. He went home.

Not to Chicago, not to New Orleans, not as far back as he could remember, but as far back as he had come. Seven miles south of Cedar Falls, Iowa—on the thin road out of Waterloo—back to Hudson. And it hadn't changed. Flat cornfield land, late in September after the oppressive heat had passed, into the time of jackets and zipping up.

Where his house had stood, now there was a weed-overgrown basement into which the upper floors had fallen as the fire had burned itself out. One wall remained, the salt box slats gray and weathered.

He sat down on what had been the stone steps leading up to the front porch, and he laid down the cheap plastic shoulder bag that now contained all he owned in the world. And it was there that the last two of those who had dogged him came to have their talk.

He saw them coming down the dirt road between the fields of freshly-harvested corn, the stalks creaking in the breeze, and he gave it up. Packed it in. No more getting in the flow, chasing the wind. No more. He sat and watched them coming up the road, tiny puffs of dust at each step. The day was on the wane, and he could see clouds through them, the horizon line, birds reaching for more sky.

They came up and stood staring at him, and he said, "Sit down, take a load off."

The man seemed to be a hundred years old. He smiled at Ben Laborde and said, "Thanks. It's been a hard trip." He slumped onto the stone step below. He wiped his forehead, but he wasn't perspiring.

The woman stood in front of him, and her expression was neither kind nor hard. It was simply the face of someone who had been traveling a long time, and was relieved to have reached her destination.

"Who are you?"

The woman looked at the old man and said, "We were never a high school girl named Doris Burton, who was supposed to've died in a car accident in West Texas, but didn't. We were never an asthmatic named Milford Sterbank, who worked for fifty years as a reweaver. And we never got to be Henry Cheatham, who drove a cab in Pittsburgh."

He watched them, looking from the man to the woman, and back. "And which ones are you?"

The woman looked away for a moment. Laborde saw the setting sun through her chest. She said, "I would have been Barbara Lamartini. You passed through St. Louis in 1943."

"I was born in '49."

The old man shook his head. "Much earlier. If you hadn't fought with the 2nd Division at Belleau Wood, I would have been Howard Strausser. We shared a trench for five minutes, June 1st, 1918."

"This is crazy."

"No," the woman said wearily, "this is just the end of it."

"The end of what?"

"The end of the last of us whose lives you've been using. The last soft gray man or woman left on a doorstep by your passing."

Laborde shook his head. It was gibberish. He knew he was at final moments with them, but what it all meant he could not fathom.

"For godsakes," he pleaded, "hasn't this gone on long enough? Haven't you sent me running long enough? What the hell have I ever done to you . . . any of you? I don't even know you!"

The old man, Howard Strausser, smiled sadly and said, "You never meant to be a thief. It isn't your fault, any more than it's our fault for finally coming after you, to get our lives back. But you did, you stole, and you left us behind. We've been husks. I'm the oldest left. Barbara is somewhere in the middle. You've been doing it for several hundred years, best we've been able to tell. When we found one another, there was a man who said he'd been panning gold at Sutter's Mill when you came by. I don't know as I believe him; his name was Chickie Moldanado, and he was something of a liar. It was the only memorable thing about him."

The woman added, "There's nothing much memorable about any of us."

"That's the key, do you see?" Howard Strausser said.

"No, I *don't* see," Laborde said.

"We were never *anything*. None of us."

He let his hands move helplessly in the air in front of them. "I don't know what any of this means. I just know I'm tired of . . . not of running . . . tired of, just, I don't know, tired of being *me.* "

"You've never been you." Howard Strausser smiled kindly.

"Perhaps you can be you now," Barbara Lamartini said.

Laborde put his hands over his face. "Can't you just tell it simply? Please, for godsakes, just *simply.*"

The woman nodded to the old man, who looked to be a hundred years old, and he said, "There are just some people who live life more fully than others. Take, oh, I don't know, take Scott Fitzgerald or Hemingway or Winston Churchill or Amelia Earhart. Everybody's heard their names, but how many people have read much Hemingway or Fitzgerald, or even Churchill's—" He stopped. The woman was giving him that look. He grinned sheepishly.

"There are just some people who *live* their lives at a fuller pace. And it's as if they've lived two or three lifetimes in the same time it takes others to get through just one mild, meager, colorless life, one sad and sorry—"

He stopped again.

"Barbara, you'd better do it. I've waited too long. I'm just running off at the mouth like an old fart."

She put a hand on his thin shoulder to comfort him, and said, "You were one of the passionate ones. You lived at a hotter level. And every now and then, every once in a while, you just leached off someone's life who wasn't up to the living of it. You're a magpie. You came by, whenever it was, 1492, 1756, 1889, 1943 . . . we don't know how far back you go . . . but you passed by, and someone was wearing a life so loosely, so unused, that it just came off; and you wore it away, and added it on, and you just kept going, which way it didn't matter, without looking back, not even knowing.

"And finally, the last of us followed the thread that was never broken, the umbilicus of each of us, and we came and found you, to try and get back what was left."

"Because it's clear," said Howard Strausser, "that you're tired of it. And don't know how to get out of it. But—"

They sighed almost as one, and Barbara Lamartini said, "There isn't enough of either of us left to take back. We'll be gone, passed through very soon."

"Then you're on your own," Howard Strausser said.

"You'll be living what portion has been allotted to you," the woman said, and he could see through the holes where her milky eyes had been.

And they sat there into the deepening twilight, in Hudson, Iowa; and they talked; and there was nothing he could do for them; and finally, the woman said, "We don't blame you. It was our own damned fault. We just weren't up to the doing of it, the living of our own lives." What was left of her shrugged, and Laborde asked her to tell him all she could of the others they had known, so he could try to remember them and fit to their memories the parts of his own life that he had taken.

And by midnight, he was sitting there alone.

And he fell asleep, arms wrapped around himself, in the chilly September night, knowing that when he arose the next day, the first day of a fresh life, he would retrace his steps in many ways; and that one of the things he would do would be to return to New Orleans.

To go to the Parish Coroner, and to have exhumed the body of Jane Doe #112; to have it dug out of the black loam of Potter's Field near City Park and to carry it back to West Texas; to bury the child who had never been allowed to be Doris Burton where she would have lived her life. Pale as opal glass, she had passed through and whispered away, on the last night of the poor thing that had been her existence; seeking out the only friend she had been allowed to have, on a noisy street in the French Quarter.

The least he could do was to be her last friend, to carry her home by way of cheap restitution.

John Kessel
BUFFALO

In "Jane Doe #112," Harlan Ellison pre-
sents us with the view that home is a
physical refuge to which one can flee in
times of trouble, but home is also a refuge we carry with us, that shapes us and
teaches us as we go, as we see here in
John Kessel's "Buffalo." "Buffalo" is a
story that makes an extremely strong
statement about what it means to go
home—if only in your mind.

Born in Buffalo, New York, tall, lean
John Kessel is a professor of English at
North Carolina State University and a
writer of short stories and novels that
transcend the everyday. In 1983 he received the Nebula Award for his novella
"Another Orphan," and, more recently,
his novel *Good News From Outer Space*
was nominated for the Nebula Award for
best novel of the year.

John is a superb writer and "Buffalo" is
one of his finest stories. "My father often
talked to me about the Depression," John
said, "and when I started thinking about
a 'hometown' story, I thought of that.

14

Add the irony of H. G. Wells and my father being in Washington, D.C., at the same time (although, in reality, they never met) and the result is this fantasy.

"In turning Buffalo into a metaphor, I may sound harder on the city than I intended. For me, Buffalo is quintessentially American. In his autobiography, written soon after the visit to the U.S. that I describe in this story, H. G. Wells described the state of the world in terms that sum up the way I feel about the city and country I grew up in:

> The truth remains that nothing stands in the way of the attainment of universal freedom and abundance but mental tangles, egocentric preoccupations, obsessions, misconceived phrases, bad habits of thought, subconscious fears and dreads and plain dishonesty in people's minds. . . . We who are Citizens of the Future wander about this present scene like passengers on a ship overdue, in plain sight of a port which only some disorder in the chart room prevents us from entering.

"I keep thinking I can see that port, and I only wish the people I love and grew up with in Buffalo, and the rest of us, could find some way to reach it."

"Buffalo" is a poignant and ironic story of hope and memories, of things past; all the things that greet us when we travel home.

$\mathscr{B}$UFFALO
$\mathscr{J}$ohn $\mathscr{K}$essel

I N APRIL 1934 H. G. Wells made a trip to the United States, where he visited Washington, D.C., and met with President Franklin Delano Roosevelt. Wells, sixty-eight years old, hoped the New Deal might herald a revolutionary change in the U.S. economy, a step forward in an "open conspiracy" of rational thinkers that would culminate in a world socialist state. For forty years he'd subordinated every scrap of his artistic ambition to promoting this vision. But by 1934 Wells's optimism, along with his energy for saving the world, was waning.

While in Washington he asked to see something of the new social welfare agencies, and Harold Ickes, Roosevelt's Interior Secretary, arranged for Wells to visit a Civilian Conservation Corps camp at Fort Hunt, Virginia.

It happens that at that time my father was a CCC member at that camp. From his boyhood he had been a reader of adventure stories; he was a big fan of Edgar Rice Burroughs, and of H. G. Wells. This is the story of their encounter, which never took place.

In Buffalo it's cold, but here the trees are in bloom, the mocking-birds sing in the mornings, and the sweat the men work up clearing brush, planting dogwoods and cutting roads is wafted away by warm breezes. Two hundred of them live in the Fort Hunt barracks high on the bluff above the Virginia side of the Potomac. They wear surplus army uniforms. In the morning, after a breakfast of grits, Sergeant Sauter musters them up in the parade yard, they climb onto trucks and are driven by forest service men out to wherever they're to work that day.

For several weeks Kessel's squad has been working along the river road, clearing rest stops and turnarounds. The tall pines have shallow root systems, and spring rain has softened the earth to the point where wind is forever knocking trees across the road. While most of the men work on the ground, a couple are sent up to cut off the tops of the pines adjoining the road, so if they do fall, they won't block it. Most of the men claim to be afraid of heights. Kessel isn't. A year or two ago back in Michigan he worked in a logging camp. It's hard work, but he is used to hard work. And at least he's out of Buffalo.

The truck rumbles and jounces out the river road, which is going to be the George Washington Memorial Parkway in our time, once the WPA project that will build it gets started. The humid air is cool now, but it will be hot again today—in the eighties. A couple of the guys get into a debate about whether the feds will ever catch Dillinger. Some others talk women. They're planning to go into Washington on the weekend and check out the dance halls. Kessel likes to dance; he's a good dancer. The fox trot, the lindy hop. When he gets drunk he likes to sing, and has a ready wit. He talks a lot more, kids the girls.

When they get to the site the foreman sets most of the men to work clearing the roadside for a scenic overlook. Kessel straps on a climbing belt, takes an ax and climbs his first tree. The first twenty feet are limbless, then climbing gets trickier. He looks down only enough to estimate when he's gotten high enough. He sets himself, cleats biting into the shoulder of a lower limb, and chops away at the road side of the trunk. There's a trick to cutting the top so that it falls the right way. When he's got it ready to go he calls down to warn the men below. Then a few quick bites of the ax on the opposite side of the cut, a shove, a crack and the top starts to go. He braces his legs, ducks his head and grips the trunk. The treetop skids off and the bole of the pine waves ponderously back and forth, with Kessel swinging at its end like an ant on a metronome. After the pine stops swinging he shinnies down and climbs the next tree.

He's good at this work, efficient, careful. He's not a particularly strong man—slender, not burly—but even in his youth he shows the attention to detail that, as a boy, I remember seeing when he built our house.

The squad works through the morning, then breaks for lunch from the mess truck. The men are always complaining about the food, and how there isn't enough of it, but until recently a lot of them were living in Hoovervilles—shack cities—and eating nothing at all. As they're eating, a couple of the guys rag Kessel for working too fast. "What do you expect from a Yankee?" one of the southern boys says.

"He ain't a Yankee. He's a Polack."

Kessel tries to ignore them.

"Why'n't you lay off him, Turkel?" says Cole, one of Kessel's buddies.

Turkel is a big blond guy from Chicago. Some say he joined the CCCs to duck an armed robbery rap. "He works too hard," Turkel says. "He makes us look bad."

"Don't have to work much to make you look bad, Lou," Cole says. The others laugh, and Kessel appreciates it. "Give Jack some credit. At least he had enough sense to come down out of Buffalo." More laughter.

"There's nothing wrong with Buffalo," Kessel says.

"Except fifty thousand out-of-work Polacks," Turkel says.

"I guess you got no out-of-work people in Chicago," Kessel says. "You just joined for the exercise."

"Except he's not getting any exercise, if he can help it!" Cole says.

The foreman comes by and tells them to get back to work. Kessel climbs another tree, stung by Turkel's charge. What kind of man complains if someone else works hard? It only shows how even decent guys have to put up with assholes dragging them down. But it's nothing new. He's seen it before, back in Buffalo.

Buffalo, New York, is the symbolic home of this story. In the years preceding the First World War it grew into one of the great industrial metropolises of the United States. Located where Lake Erie flows into the Niagara River, strategically close to cheap electricity from Niagara Falls and cheap transportation by lakeboat from the Midwest, it was a center of steel, automobiles, chemicals, grain milling and brewing. Its major employers—Bethlehem Steel, Ford, Pierce Arrow, Gold Medal Flour, the National Biscuit Company,

Ralston Purina, Quaker Oats, National Aniline—drew thousands of immigrants like Kessel's family. Along Delaware Avenue stood the imperious and stylized mansions of the city's old money, ersatz-Renaissance homes designed by Stanford White, huge Protestant churches, and a Byzantine synagogue. The city boasted the first modern skyscraper, designed by Louis Sullivan in the 1890s. From its productive factories to its polyglot work force to its class system and its boosterism, Buffalo was a monument to modern industrial capitalism. It is the place Kessel has come from—almost an expression of his personality itself—and the place he, at times, fears he can never escape. A cold, grimy city dominated by church and family, blinkered and cramped, forever playing second fiddle to Chicago, New York and Boston. It offers the immigrant the opportunity to find steady work in some factory or mill, but, though Kessel could not have put it into these words, it also puts a lid on his opportunities. It stands for all disappointed expectations, human limitations, tawdry compromises, for the inevitable choice of the expedient over the beautiful, for an American economic system that turns all things into commodities and measures men by their bank accounts. It is the home of the industrial proletariat.

It's not unique. It could be Youngstown, Akron, Detroit. It's the place where my father, and I, grew up.

The afternoon turns hot and still; during a work break Kessel strips to the waist. About two o'clock a big black De Soto comes up the road and pulls off onto the shoulder. A couple of men in suits get out of the back, and one of them talks to the Forest Service foreman, who nods deferentially. The foreman calls over to the men.

"Boys, this here's Mr. Pike from the Interior Department. He's got a guest here to see how we work, a writer, Mr. H. G. Wells from England."

Most of the men couldn't care less, but the name strikes a spark in Kessel. He looks over at the little potbellied man in the dark suit. The man is sweating; he brushes his mustache.

The foreman sends Kessel up to show them how they're topping the trees. He points out to the visitors where the others with rakes and shovels are leveling the ground for the overlook. Several other men are building a log rail fence from the treetops. From way above, Kessel can hear their voices between the thunks of his ax. H. G.

Wells. He remembers reading "The War of the Worlds" in *Amazing Stories*. He's read *The Outline of History,* too. The stories, the history, are so large, it seems impossible that the man who wrote them could be standing not thirty feet below him. He tries to concentrate on the ax, the tree.

Time for this one to go. He calls down. The men below look up. Wells takes off his hat and shields his eyes with his hand. He's balding, and looks even smaller from up here. Strange that such big ideas could come from such a small man. It's kind of disappointing. Wells leans over to Pike and says something. The treetop falls away. The pine sways like a bucking bronco, and Kessel holds on for dear life.

He comes down with the intention of saying something to Wells, telling him how much he admires him, but when he gets down the sight of the two men in suits and his awareness of his own sweaty chest make him timid. He heads down to the next tree. After another ten minutes the men get back in the car, drive away. Kessel curses himself for the opportunity lost.

That evening at the New Willard hotel, Wells dines with his old friends Clarence Darrow and Charles Russell. Darrow and Russell are in Washington to testify before a congressional committee on a report they have just submitted to the administration concerning the monopolistic effects of the National Recovery Act. The right wing is trying to eviscerate Roosevelt's program for large-scale industrial management, and the Darrow Report is playing right into their hands. Wells tries, with little success, to convince Darrow of the shortsightedness of his position.

"Roosevelt is willing to sacrifice the small man to the huge corporations," Darrow insists, his eyes bright.

"The small man? Your small man is a romantic fantasy," Wells says. "It's not the New Deal that's doing him in—it's the process of industrial progress. It's the twentieth century. You can't legislate yourself back into 1870."

"What about the individual?" Russell asks.

Wells snorts. "Walk out into the street. The individual is out on the street corner selling apples. The only thing that's going to save him is some coordinated effort, by intelligent, selfless men. Not your free market."

Darrow puffs on his cigar, exhales, smiles. "Don't get exasperated, H.G. We're not working for Standard Oil. But if I have to choose between the bureaucrat and the man pumping gas at the filling station, I'll take the pump jockey."

Wells sees he's got no chance against the American mythology of the common man. "Your pump jockey works for Standard Oil. And the last I checked, the free market hasn't expended much energy looking out for his interests."

"Have some more wine," Russell says.

Russell refills their glasses with the excellent Bordeaux. It's been a first-rate meal. Wells finds the debate stimulating even when he can't prevail; at one time that would have been enough, but as the years go on the need to prevail grows stronger in him. The times are out of joint, and when he looks around he sees desperation growing. A new world order is necessary—it's so clear that even a fool ought to see it—but if he can't even convince radicals like Darrow, what hope is there of gaining the acquiescence of the shareholders in the utility trusts?

The answer is that the changes will have to be made over their objections. As Roosevelt seems prepared to do. Wells's dinner with the president has heartened him in a way that this debate cannot negate.

Wells brings up an item he read in the *Washington Post*. A lecturer for the Communist party—a young Negro—was barred from speaking at the University of Virginia. Wells's question is, was the man barred because he was a Communist or because he was Negro?

"Either condition," Darrow says sardonically, "is fatal in Virginia."

"But students point out the university has allowed Communists to speak on campus before, and has allowed Negroes to perform music there."

"They can perform, but they can't speak," Russell says. "This isn't unusual. Go down to the Paradise Ballroom, not a mile from here. There's a Negro orchestra playing there, but no Negroes are allowed inside to listen."

"You should go to hear them anyway," Darrow says. "It's Duke Ellington. Have you heard of him?"

"I don't get on with the titled nobility," Wells quips.

"Oh, this Ellington's a noble fellow, all right, but I don't think you'll find him in the peerage," Russell says.

"He plays jazz, doesn't he?"

"Not like any jazz you've heard," Darrow says. "It's something totally new. You should find a place for it in one of your utopias."

All three of them are for helping the colored peoples. Darrow has defended Negroes accused of capital crimes. Wells, on his first visit to America almost thirty years ago, met with Booker T. Washington and came away impressed, although he still considers the peaceable coexistence of the white and colored races problematical.

"What are you working on now, Wells?" Russell asks. "What new improbability are you preparing to assault us with? Racial equality? Sexual liberation?"

"I'm writing a screen treatment based on *The Shape of Things to Come*," Wells says. He tells them about his screenplay, sketching out for them the future he has in his mind. An apocalyptic war, a war of unsurpassed brutality that will begin, in his film, in 1939. In this war, the creations of science will be put to the services of destruction in ways that will make the horrors of the Great War pale in comparison. Whole populations will be exterminated. But then, out of the ruins will arise the new world. The orgy of violence will purge the human race of the last vestiges of tribal thinking. Then will come the organization of the directionless and weak by the intelligent and purposeful. The new man. Cleaner, stronger, more rational. Wells can see it. He talks on, supplely, surely, late into the night. His mind is fertile with invention, still. He can see that Darrow and Russell, despite their Yankee individualism, are caught up by his vision. The future may be threatened, but it is not entirely closed.

Friday night, back in the barracks at Fort Hunt, Kessel lies on his bunk reading the latest *Astounding Stories*. He's halfway through the tale of a scientist who invents an evolution chamber that progresses him through fifty thousand years of evolution in an hour, turning him into a big-brained telepathic monster. The evolved scientist is totally without emotions and wants to control the world. But his body's atrophied. Will the hero, a young engineer, be able to stop him?

At a plank table in the aisle a bunch of men are playing poker for cigarettes. They're talking about women and dogs. Cole throws in his hand and comes over to sit on the next bunk. "Still reading that stuff, Jack?"

"Don't knock it until you've tried it."

"Are you coming into D.C. with us tomorrow? Sergeant Sauter says we can catch a ride in on one of the trucks."

Kessel thinks about it. Cole probably wants to borrow some money. Two days after he gets his monthly pay he's broke. He's always looking for a good time. Kessel spends his leave more quietly; he usually walks into Alexandria—about six miles—and sees a movie or just walks around town. Still, he would like to see more of Washington. "Okay."

Cole looks at the sketchbook poking out from beneath Kessel's pillow. "Any more hot pictures?"

Immediately Kessel regrets trusting Cole. Yet there's not much he can say—the book is full of pictures of movie stars he's drawn. "I'm learning to draw. And at least I don't waste time like the rest of you guys."

Cole looks serious. "You know, you're not any better than the rest of us," he says, not angrily. "You're just another Polack. Don't get so high-and-mighty."

"Just because I want to improve myself doesn't mean I'm high-and-mighty."

"Hey, Cole, are you in or out?" Turkel yells from the table.

"Dream on, Jack," Cole says, and returns to the game.

Kessel tries to go back to the story, but he isn't interested anymore. He can figure out that the hero is going to defeat the hyperevolved scientist in the end. He folds his arms behind his head and stares at the knots in the rafters.

It's true, Kessel does spend a lot of time dreaming. But he has things he wants to do, and he's not going to waste his life drinking and whoring like the rest of them.

Kessel's always been different. Quieter, smarter. He was always going to do something better than the rest of them; he's well spoken, he likes to read. Even though he didn't finish high school he reads everything: *Amazing*, *Astounding*, *Wonder Stories*. He believes in the future. He doesn't want to end up trapped on some factory his whole life.

Kessel's parents emigrated from Poland in 1911. Their name was

Kisiel, but his got Germanized in Catholic school. For ten years the family moved from one to another middle-sized industrial town, as Joe Kisiel bounced from job to job. Springfield. Utica. Syracuse. Rochester. Kessel remembers them loading up a wagon in the middle of the night with all their belongings in order to jump the rent on the run-down house in Syracuse. He remembers pulling a cart down to the Utica Club brewery, a nickel in his hand, to buy his father a keg of beer. He remembers them finally settling in the First Ward of Buffalo. The First Ward, at the foot of the Erie Canal, was an Irish neighborhood as far back as anybody could remember, and the Kisiels were the only Poles there. That's where he developed his chameleon ability to fit in, despite the fact he wanted nothing more than to get out. But he had to protect his mother, sister and little brothers from their father's drunken rages. When Joe Kisiel died in 1924 it was a relief, despite the fact that his son ended up supporting the family.

For ten years Kessel has strained against the tug of that responsibility. He's sought the free and easy feeling of the road, of places different from where he grew up, romantic places where the sun shines and he can make something entirely American of himself.

Despite his ambitions, he's never accomplished much. He's been essentially a drifter, moving from job to job. Starting as a pinsetter in a bowling alley, he moved on to a flour mill. He would have stayed in the mill but he developed an allergy to the flour dust, so he became an electrician. He would have stayed an electrician except he had a fight with a boss and got blacklisted. He left Buffalo because of his father; he kept coming back because of his mother. When the Depression hit he tried to get a job in Detroit at the auto factories, but that was plain stupid in the face of the universal collapse, and he ended up working up in the peninsula as a farmhand, then as a logger. It was seasonal work, and when the season was over he was out of a job. In the winter of 1933, rather than freeze his ass off in northern Michigan, he joined the CCC. Now he sends twenty-five of his thirty dollars a month back to his mother and sister back in Buffalo. And imagines the future.

When he thinks about it, there are two futures. The first one is the one from the magazines and books. Bright, slick, easy. We, looking back on it, can see it to be the fifteen-cent utopianism of Hugo Gernsback's *Popular Electrics*, which flourished in the midst

24

of the Depression. A degradation of the marvelous inventions that made Wells his early reputation, minus the social theorizing that drove Wells's technological speculations. The common man's boosterism. There's money to be made telling people like Jack Kessel about the wonderful world of the future.

The second future is Kessel's own. That one's a lot harder to see. It contains work. A good job, doing something he likes, using his skills. Not working for another man, but making something that would be useful for others. Building something for the future. And a woman, a gentle woman, for his wife. Not some cheap dance-hall queen.

So when Kessel saw H. G. Wells in person, that meant something to him. He's had his doubts. He's twenty-nine years old, not a kid anymore. If he's ever going to get anywhere, it's going to have to start happening soon. He has the feeling that something significant is going to happen to him. Wells is a man who sees the future. He moves in that bright world where things make sense. He represents something that Kessel wants.

But the last thing Kessel wants is to end up back in Buffalo.

He pulls the sketchbook, the sketchbook he was to show me twenty years later, from under his pillow. He turns past drawings of movie stars—Jean Harlow, Mae West, Carole Lombard, the beautiful, unreachable faces of his longing—and of natural scenes—rivers, forests, birds—to a blank page. The page is as empty as the future, waiting for him to write upon it. He lets his imagination soar. He envisions an eagle, gliding high above the mountains of the West that he has never seen, but that he knows he will visit some day. The eagle is America; it is his own dreams. He begins to draw.

Kessel did not know that Wells's life has not worked out as well as he planned. At that moment Wells is pining after the Russian émigrée Moura Budberg, once Maxim Gorky's secretary, with whom Wells has been carrying on an off-and-on affair since 1920. His wife of thirty years, Amy Catherine "Jane" Wells, died in 1927. Since that time Wells has been adrift, alternating spells of furious pamphleteering with listless periods of suicidal depression. Meanwhile, all London is gossiping about the recent attack published in *Time and Tide* by his vengeful ex-lover, Odette Keun. Have his mistakes followed him across the Atlantic to undermine his purpose? Does Darrow think him a jumped-up cockney? A moment of doubt overwhelms him. In the end, the future depends as much on the open-mindedness of men like Darrow as it does on a reorganization of society. What good is a guild of samurai if no one arises to take the job?

Wells doesn't like the trend of these thoughts. If human nature lets him down, then his whole life has been a waste.

But he's seen the president. He's seen those workers on the road. Those men climbing the trees risk their lives without complaining, for minimal pay. It's easy to think of them as stupid or desperate or simply young, but it's also possible to give them credit for dedication to their work. They don't seem to be ridden by the desire to grub and clutch that capitalism demands; if you look at it properly that may be the explanation for their ending up wards of the state. And is Wells any better? If he hadn't got an education he would have ended up a miserable draper's assistant.

Wells is due to leave for New York on Sunday. Saturday night finds him sitting in his room, trying to write, after a solitary dinner in the New Willard. Another bottle of wine, or his age, has stirred something in Wells, and despite his rationalizations he finds himself near despair. Moura has rejected him. He needs the soft, supportive embrace of a lover, but instead he has this stuffy hotel room in a heat wave.

He remembers writing *The Time Machine*, he and Jane living in rented rooms in Sevenoaks with her ailing mother, worried about money, about whether the landlady would put them out. In the drawer of the dresser was a writ from the court that refused to grant him a divorce from his wife Isabel. He remembers a warm night, late in August—much like this one—sitting up late after Jane and her mother had gone to bed, writing at the round table before the open window, under the light of a paraffin lamp. One part of his mind was caught up in the rush of creation, burning, following the Time Traveller back to the Sphinx, pursued by the Morlocks, only to discover that his machine is gone and he is trapped without escape from his desperate circumstance. At the same moment he could hear the landlady, out in the garden, fully aware that he could hear her, complaining to the neighbor about his and Jane's scandalous habits. On the one side, the petty conventions of a

26

crabbed world; on the other, in his mind—the future, their peril and hope. Moths fluttering through the window beat themselves against the lampshade and fell onto the manuscript; he brushed them away unconsciously and continued, furiously, in a white heat. The Time Traveler, battered and hungry, returning from the future with a warning, and a flower.

He opens the hotel windows all the way but the curtains aren't stirred by a breath of air. Below, in the street, he hears the sound of traffic, and music. He decides to send a telegram to Moura, but after several false starts he finds he has nothing to say. Why has she refused to marry him? Maybe he is finally too old, and the magnetism of sex or power or intellect that has drawn women to him for forty years has finally all been squandered. The prospect of spending the last years remaining to him alone fills him with dread.

He turns on the radio, gets successive band shows: Morton Downey, Fats Waller. Jazz. Paging through the newspaper, he comes across an advertisement for the Ellington orchestra Darrow mentioned: it's at the ballroom just down the block. But the thought of a smoky room doesn't appeal to him. He considers the cinema. He has never been much for the "movies." Though he thinks them an unrivaled opportunity to educate, that promise has never been properly seized—something he hopes to do in *Things to Come*. The newspaper reveals an uninspiring selection: *Twenty Million Sweethearts*, a musical at the Earle; *The Black Cat*, with Boris Karloff and Bela Lugosi at the Rialto; and *Tarzan and His Mate* at the Palace. To these Americans he is the equivalent of this hack, Edgar Rice Burroughs. The books I read as a child, which fired my father's imagination and my own, Wells considers his frivolous apprentice work. His serious work is discounted. His ideas mean nothing.

Wells decides to try the Tarzan movie. He dresses for the sultry weather—Washington in spring is like high summer in London—and goes down to the lobby. He checks his street guide and takes the streetcar to the Palace Theater, where he buys an orchestra seat, for twenty-five cents, to see *Tarzan and His Mate*.

It is a perfectly wretched movie, comprised wholly of romantic fantasy, melodrama and sexual innuendo. The dramatic leads perform with wooden idiocy surpassed only by the idiocy of the screenplay. Wells is attracted by the undeniable charms of the young heroine, Maureen O'Sullivan, but the film is devoid of intellectual

27

content. Thinking of the audience at which such a farrago must be aimed depresses him. This is art as fodder. Yet the theater is filled, and the people are held in rapt attention. This only depresses Wells more. If these citizens are the future of America, then the future of America is dim.

An hour into the film the antics of an anthropomorphized chimpanzee, in a scene of transcendent stupidity which nevertheless sends the audience into gales of laughter, drive Wells from the theater. It is still midevening. He wanders down the avenue of theaters, restaurants and clubs. On the sidewalk are beggars, ignored by the passersby. In an alley behind a hotel Wells spots a woman and child picking through the ashcans beside the restaurant kitchen.

Unexpectedly, he comes upon the marquee announcing DUKE ELLINGTON AND HIS ORCHESTRA. From within the open doors of the ballroom wafts the sound of jazz. Impulsively, Wells buys a ticket and goes in.

Kessel and his cronies have spent the day walking around the Mall, which the WPA is relandscaping. They've seen the Lincoln Memorial, the Capitol, the Washington Monument, the Smithsonian, the White House. Kessel has his picture taken in front of a statue of a soldier—a photo I have sitting on my desk. I've studied it many times. He looks forthrightly into the camera, faintly smiling. His face is confident, unlined.

When night comes they hit the bars. Prohibition was lifted only last year and the novelty has not yet worn off. The younger men get plastered, but Kessel finds himself uninterested in getting drunk. A couple of them set their minds on women and head for the Gayety Burlesque; Cole, Kessel and Turkel end up in the Paradise Ballroom listening to Duke Ellington.

They have a couple of drinks, ask some girls to dance. Kessel dances with a short girl with a southern accent who refuses to look him in the eyes. After thanking her he returns to the others at the bar. He sips his beer. "Not so lucky, Jack?" Cole says.

"She doesn't like a tall man," Turkel says.

Kessel wonders why Turkel came along. Turkel is always complaining about "niggers," and his only comment on the Ellington band so far has been to complain about how a bunch of jigs can make a living playing jungle music while white men sleep in barracks and eat grits three times a day. Kessel's got nothing against the colored, and he likes the music, though it's not exactly the kind of jazz he's used to. It doesn't sound much like Dixieland. It's darker, bigger, more dangerous. Ellington, resplendent in tie and tails, looks like he's enjoying himself up there at his piano, knocking out minimal solos while the orchestra plays cool and low.

Turning from them to look across the tables, Kessel sees a little man sitting alone beside the dance floor, watching the young couples sway in the music. To his astonishment he recognizes Wells. He's been given another chance. Hesitating only a moment, Kessel abandons his friends, goes over to the table and introduces himself.

"Excuse me, Mr. Wells. You might not remember me, but I was one of the men you saw yesterday in Virginia working along the road. The CCC?"

Wells looks up at a gangling young man wearing a khaki uniform, his olive tie neatly knotted and tucked between the second and third buttons of his shirt. His hair is slicked down, parted in the middle. Wells doesn't remember anything of him. "Yes?"

"I—I been reading your stories and books a lot of years. I admire your work."

Something in the man's earnestness affects Wells. "Please sit down," he says.

Kessel takes a seat. "Thank you." He pronounces "th" as "t" so that "thank" comes out "tank." He sits tentatively, as if the chair is mortgaged, and seems at a loss for words.

"What's your name?"

"John Kessel. My friends call me Jack."

The orchestra finishes a song and the dancers stop in their places, applauding. Up on the bandstand, Ellington leans into the microphone. "Mood Indigo," he says, and instantly they swing into it: the clarinet moans in low register, in unison with the muted trumpet and trombone, paced by the steady rhythm guitar, the brushed drums. The song's melancholy suits Wells's mood.

"Are you from Virginia?"

"My family lives in Buffalo. That's in New York."

"Ah—yes. Many years ago I visited Niagara Falls, and took the train through Buffalo." Wells remembers riding along a lakefront of factories spewing waste water into the lake, past heaps of coal, clouds of orange and black smoke from blast furnaces. In front of dingy rowhouses, ragged hedges struggled through the smoky air. The landscape of laissez-faire. "I imagine the Depression has hit Buffalo severely."

"Yes sir."

"What work did you do there?"

Kessel feels nervous, but he opens up a little. "A lot of things. I used to be an electrician until I got blacklisted."

"Blacklisted?"

"I was working on this job where the super told me to set the wiring wrong. I argued with him but he just told me to do it his way. So I waited until he went away, then I sneaked into the construction shack and checked the blueprints. He didn't think I could read blueprints, but I could. I found out I was right and he was wrong. So I went back and did it right. The next day when he found out, he fired me. Then the so-and-so went and got me blacklisted."

Though he doesn't know how much credence to put in this story, Wells's sympathies are aroused. It's the kind of thing that must happen all the time. He recognizes in Kessel the immigrant stock that, when Wells visited the U.S. in 1906, made him skeptical about the future of America. He'd theorized that these Italians and Slavs, coming from lands with no democratic tradition, unable to speak English, would degrade the already corrupt political process. They could not be made into good citizens; they would not work well when they could work poorly, and given the way the economic deal was stacked against them would seldom rise high enough to do better.

But Kessel is clean, well-spoken despite his accent, and deferential. Wells realizes that this is one of the men who was topping trees along the river road.

Meanwhile, Kessel detects a sadness in Wells's manner. He had not imagined that Wells might be sad, and he feels sympathy for him. It occurs to him, to his own surprise, that he might be able to make *Wells* feel better. "So—what do you think of our country?" he asks.

"Good things seems to be happening here. I'm impressed with your President Roosevelt."

"Roosevelt's the best friend the working man ever had." Kessel pronounces the name "Roozvelt." "He's a man that"—he struggles for the words—"that's not for the past. He's for the future."

It begins to dawn on Wells that Kessel is not an example of a class, or a sociological study, but a man like himself with an intellect, opinions, dreams. He thinks of his own youth, struggling to rise in a class-bound society. He leans forward across the table. "You believe in the future? You think things can be different?"

"I think they have to be, Mr. Wells."

Wells sits back. "Good. So do I."

Kessel is stunned by this intimacy. It is more than he had hoped for, yet it leaves him with little to say. He wants to tell Wells about his dreams, and at the same time ask him a thousand questions. He wants to tell Wells everything he has seen in the world, and to hear Wells tell him the same. He casts about for something to say.

"I always liked your writing. I like to read scientifiction."

"Scientifiction?"

Kessel shifts his long legs. "You know—stories about the future. Monsters from outer space. The Martians. *The Time Machine*. You're the best scientifiction writer I ever read, next to Edgar Rice Burroughs." Kessel pronounces Edgar "Eedgar."

"Edgar Rice Burroughs?"

"Yes."

"You *like* Burroughs?"

Kessel hears the disapproval in Wells's voice. "Well—maybe not as much as, as *The Time Machine*," he stammers. "Burroughs never wrote about monsters as good as your Morlocks."

Wells is nonplused. "Monsters."

"Yes." Kessel feels something's going wrong, but he sees no way out. "But he does put more romance in his stories. That princess—Deja Thoris?"

All Wells can think of is Tarzan in his loincloth on the movie screen, and the moronic audience. After a lifetime of struggling, a hundred books written to change the world, in the service of men like this, is this all his work has come to? To be compared to the writer of pulp trash? To "Eedgar" Rice Burroughs? He laughs aloud.

At Wells's laugh, Kessel stops. He knows he's done something wrong, but he doesn't know what.

Wells's weariness has dropped down onto his shoulders again like an iron cloak. "Young man—go away," he says. "You don't know what you're saying. Go back to Buffalo."

Kessel's face burns. He stumbles from the table. The room is full of noise and laughter. He's run up against that wall again. He's just an ignorant Polack, after all; it's his stupid accent, his clothes. He should have talked about something else—*The Outline of History,* politics. But what made him think he could talk like an equal with a man like Wells in the first place? Wells lives in a different world. The future is for men like him. Kessel feels himself the prey of fantasies. It's a bitter joke.

He clutches the bar, orders another beer. His reflection in the mirror behind the ranked bottles is small and ugly.

"Whatsa matter, Jack?" Turkel asks him. "Didn't he want to dance neither?"

And that's the story, essentially, that never happened.

Not long after this, Kessel did go back to Buffalo. During the Second World War he worked as a crane operator in the forty-inch rolling mill of Bethlehem Steel. He met his wife, Angela Giorlandino, during the war, and they married in June 1945. After the war he quit the plant and became a carpenter. Their first child, a girl, died in infancy. Their second, a boy, was born in 1950. At that time Kessel began building the house that, like so many things in his life, he was never to entirely complete. He worked hard, had two more children. There were good years and bad ones. He held a lot of jobs. The recession of 1958 just about flattened him; our family had to go on welfare. Things got better, but they never got good. After the 1950s, the economy of Buffalo, like that of all U.S. industrial cities caught in the transition to a postindustrial age, declined steadily. Kessel never did work for himself, and as an old man was no more prosperous than he had been as a young one.

In the years preceding his death in 1945 Wells was to go on to further disillusionment. His efforts to create a sane world met with increasing frustration. He became bitter, enraged. Moura Budberg never agreed to marry him, and he lived alone. The war came, and it was, in some ways, even worse than he had predicted. He continued to propagandize for the socialist world state throughout, but with increasing irrelevance. The new leftists like Orwell considered him a dinosaur, fatally out of touch with the realities of world politics, a simpleminded technocrat with no understanding of the darkness of the human heart. Wells's last book, *Mind at the End of Its Tether*, proposed that the human race faced an evolutionary crisis that would lead to its extinction unless humanity leapt to a higher state of consciousness; a leap about which Wells speculated with little hope or conviction.

Sitting there in the Washington ballroom in 1934, Wells might well have understood that for all his thinking and preaching about the future, the future had irrevocably passed him by.

But the story isn't quite over yet. Back in the Washington ballroom Wells sits ashamed, a little guilty for sending Kessel away so harshly. Kessel, his back to the dance floor, stares humiliated into his glass of beer. Gradually, both of them are pulled back from dark thoughts of their own inadequacies by the sound of Ellington's orchestra.

Ellington stands in front of the big grand piano, behind him the band: three saxes, two clarinets, two trumpets, trombones, a drummer, guitarist, bass. "Creole Love Call," Ellington whispers into the microphone, then sits again at the piano. He waves his hand once, twice, and the clarinets slide into a low, wavering theme. The trumpet, muted, echoes it. The bass player and guitarist strum ahead at a deliberate pace, rhythmic, erotic, bluesy. Kessel and Wells, separate across the room, each unaware of the other, are alike drawn in. The trumpet growls eight bars of raucous solo. The clarinet follows, wailing. The music is full of pain and longing— but pain controlled, ordered, mastered. Longing unfulfilled, but not overpowering.

As I write this, it plays on my stereo. If anyone has a right to bitterness at thwarted dreams, a black man in 1934 has that right. That such men can, in such conditions, make this music opens a world of possibilities.

Through the music speaks a truth about art that Wells does not understand, but that I hope to: that art doesn't have to deliver a message in order to say something important. That art isn't always a means to an end but sometimes an end in itself. That art may not be able to change the world, but it can still change the moment.

Through the music speaks a truth about life that Kessel, sixteen years before my birth, doesn't understand, but that I hope to: that life constrained is not life wasted. That despite unfulfilled dreams, peace is possible.

Listening, Wells feels that peace steal over his soul. Kessel feels it too.

And so they wait, poised, calm, before they move on into their respective futures, into our own present. Into the world of limitation and loss. Into Buffalo.

for my father

George Alec Effinger
WHO DAT

Although the old cliché tells us that "It's not whether you win or lose, it's how you play the game," for George Alec Effinger, and in "Who Dat," it *is* whether you win or lose. In sending this story, he noted, "The poor guy's bad luck with professional teams is my own story. I've been all those places. It's all true!"

George may have little luck with sports, but he excels in writing. A graduate of the Clarion Workshop, his stories and novels are knowledgeable, engrossing, and often quite amusing. In 1988, his novelette "Schrödinger's Kitten" received the Nebula Award and in 1989, his novel *A Fire in the Sun* was nominated for the Hugo Award, as was his novelette "Everything But Honor."

Unlike John Kessel, who sees in "Buffalo" home as a port to which to return, if only in one's mind, for George Alec Effinger, home is a place to be *sought*. And the search can be a single step or can span a lifetime. George himself grew up in the eastern United States, attending Yale and New York University, and then traveled throughout the country, finally finding in New Orleans, a home. Reflective of his own search, the narrator of "Who Dat" finds an end to his quest in New Orleans also and the affection George has for his adopted hometown is seen clearly through the narrator's eyes.

As he says, "New Orleans is a very lovely place. In certain places, that is."

WHO DAT
George Alec Effinger

BEFORE MY PROMOTION I was a contract agent for the Company, and at the time, there didn't seem to be much hope of advancement. I had been assigned to Operation ORCHID, which I first thought was one of the loonier of the Company's projects. In my uninformed estimation it ranked right down there with Operation BANDANNA, the attempt to perfect out-of-body intelligence gathering—spooks who *really were* spooks. That project never showed any actual success, but the word from the BANDANNA project director was always that she "was confident of significant progress Real Soon Now."

You bet.

As far as ORCHID was concerned, I could judge its importance by the type of reports I sent back to the director. The reports had green covers stamped *Exdis*, which meant that they couldn't be distributed wantonly back at the Company. If ORCHID were a vital assignment that decided the Fate of the Free World, the reports would be stamped *Nodis*, meaning No Distribution. "Burn before reading," if you know what I mean.

Anyway, the deputy director for information had a computer that he loved a lot. He patted it one day in 1985, asked it nicely to mull over all the information he'd crammed into it, and a few hours later the computer spat out a watch list of only one name. This target lived in Kansas City, Missouri.

I initiated a covert intelligence-gathering operation in Kansas City. I proceeded slowly and carefully, because I'd been told by my case officer that we could not tolerate any sort of negative blow-back from my investigation. Therefore, the whole project had to remain undercover, but it left me with four equally effective options: harassment, intimidation, deception, and disinformation.

I'm not really the harassment and intimidation type, so in Kansas City I went with deception. I'm a crafty kind of guy.

The target's name was Nick Ginsberg. When I began, all I knew about him was that he worked at Middleton Lanes, unjamming pinspotters and polishing the alleys. I began casually, not even looking at Ginsberg on the three nights a week that I bowled. When I started, I averaged about 140. Weeks later, when I felt it was time to initiate direct activity, my average had climbed to 185, which is pretty respectable, if you ask me. The secret to bowling is consistency, and the secret to consistency is practice. I mentioned this improvement to my case officer once, and he responded with a complete lack of interest.

One evening, after bowling four lines—including one exhilarating game of 220—I casually asked Ginsberg how I'd go about joining one of the weekly leagues that tied up most of the lanes every night. We talked about a few other things after that, and then I steered the conversation to the topic of the lanes themselves. I told Ginsberg that he maintained them better than any other bowling alley I'd ever seen.

He smiled. "Thank you," he said. "It's a heavy responsibility. I have a definite idea about how the lanes must be waxed. You'll notice in most bowling alleys, the left-handers have a distinct advantage, because there's fewer of them, and so the wax on their side of the lane doesn't get worn away as quickly as the right-handers'. I've created a method of waxing that automatically compensates for that."

I raised my eyebrows. "That's wonderful," I said. I feigned admiration. That was all right, because it was part of the process of guarding the security of the United States of America.

I cultivated Ginsberg's friendship over the course of the next few months. My average settled at the 185 level, but sometimes I turned in scores of 240 or better. My case officer reminded me that my prowess at bowling was *not* contributing to the nation's security, so I turned my attention entirely to getting the intelligence I sought from Ginsberg.

We'd reached phase three, and I was now having a few beers in the lounge with my subject, gradually extracting the relevant data, when disaster struck: the Kansas City Royals made it into the World Series against the St. Louis Cardinals. The so-called I-70 Series. It became immediately clear to me that Kansas City was a dead end. I packed my belongings, sent terminal reports on the Kansas City intrusion to my case officer and the director of Operation ORCHID, and got on the next plane to Virginia. It took almost four years for the DDI's computer to select another target, and in the meantime I worked on a few other top-secret operations. Finally, though, the computer came up with a name and address in Detroit.

I'd never been excited about the Motor City as a place to spend a few months, but my preferences weren't at all important. The new target was Sheila Giff, a white female aged twenty-two, with brown eyes and naturally brown hair which was subject to change, who worked as an image coordinator in a beauty shop called The Hairport in Royal Oak.

The Hairport was in a large mall, and so I browsed through the bookstores and software shops for half an hour, making a few small purchases. Then I went into The Hairport on the pretext of getting my hair cut and styled. A television was on in the shop, and some of the staff and customers were watching an NBA basketball game. The Detroit Pistons were playing the San Antonio Spurs. I watched for a while, and then I began to feel a warning prickling at the back of my neck.

Sheila Giff cut and styled my hair, and I praised her work. Giff kept up a running conversation, mostly on her own because I couldn't hear a word above the obnoxious whine of her blow-drier. When she turned the machine off, she said, "Are you a basketball fan?"

"Not really," I said.

"Well," said Giff, "you must be excited by how well the Pistons are doing this year."

I laughed. "Lions and Tigers and Pistons, oh my. They'll fold. They always fold."

She just raised her eyebrows at me and went back to her clipping. Later, though, I would go into the men's room and comb my hair back the way I usually wore it.

Well, the truth of the matter is that the Pistons didn't fold. They went all the way, defeating the Los Angeles Lakers for the NBA championship. It was a good thing I hadn't wasted more time getting to know Sheila Giff. Once again I wrote my terminals and cabled them to the section. I went back to the office a few days later and caught up on paperwork while the DDI's computer considered its next choice.

It only took the computer a year to identify the next target. His name was Earl P. Lasson, and he lived in New Orleans. New Orleans! I had a good feeling about Lasson from the very beginning.

I landed at New Orleans International Airport on May 12, 1990. It was overcast and windy, and the shock of the damp air hit me as soon as I crossed from the plane to the walkway. I felt as if I'd been squeezed from a tube into a pot of water at the simmer. Near ninety degrees, near ninety percent humidity.

There was a peculiar smell in the air; it took me a while to identify it, but when I did I added a new nickname to New Orleans's collection. Already there was The Big Easy and The City that Care Forgot. I added The Mildew Capital of the World to the list. In time, I knew, I'd adapt to the heat and humidity. It was not a goal I was looking forward to achieving.

I grabbed a cab and gave him the address of the safe house the New Orleans section was letting me use. It took about twenty-five minutes to get there, and in the meantime I removed my suit coat, then my tie, then I rolled up my sleeves, and then I grumpily squirmed in the backseat trying to unstick the sodden shirt from my back.

The house was on Prytania Street, near the intersection of Napoleon Avenue. It was a beautiful part of town, quiet and peaceful, with many wonderful old houses and plenty of tall, arching palm trees. It was almost like being in some Caribbean port—until you heard the speech of the locals. I passed a gentleman on the sidewalk carrying two brown paper bags filled with groceries. I nodded to him and he said, "Where you at, Cap?" He sounded as if he'd been born and raised in Brooklyn, but I'd soon learn that was the *real* New Orleans accent; nobody here sounded like fugitives from *Gone with the Wind*.

Most of the afternoon lay ahead of me, and I decided to change my shirt and tie and pay a visit on old Earl P. Lasson. The New

Orleans section had thoughtfully left me a Ford LTD in the drive-way. The keys were in the cookie jar, as usual.

I unfolded a large map of the New Orleans area and found Esteban Street in a suburb called Arabi. All the way to Lasson's house the same tune kept running through my head: "I'm the sheik of Arabi. I'm as weird as weird can be." And so forth. My future as a lyricist appeared dim, but my covert agent's sixth sense predicted that I'd soon find what Operation ORCHID was looking for. If so, I was in for rewards and citations and pats on the back from all sorts of anonymous middle-echelon file clerks.

The Earl P. Lasson estate was a comfortable one-story white house with green trim and green shutters. There was a young palm tree on the lawn and sharp Spanish dagger plants like a skirt around the house. I followed a flagstone walk leading to a three-step stoop, where I pressed the doorbell and waited.

In a little while, a harried-looking woman came to the door, with a little boy clutching one of her legs and a pretty blond girl with chocolate streaked all over her face clutching the other. "Yes?" said the woman warily.

"Hello," I said. "Is this the Earl P. Lasson residence?"

"Yes, it is, but he's not here right now."

I nodded. "When do you expect him home?"

The woman gave a sad sniffle. "Not for months," she said. "Maybe not for years." A single tear rolled slowly from the corner of her left eye.

Well, you can bet that wasn't an answer I was prepared for. Quickly, I reviewed my options. Neither harassment nor intimi-dation was indicated here. Deception and disinformation were like-wise unattractive choices. I decided that based on my gut feelings about poor Mrs. Lasson and her missing husband and smeary-faced kids. This looked like the time for that most terrifying option of all: individual initiative. It was something I'd never before tried. I'd been told in the sixth grade that I was creative and possessed of a remarkable imagination. However, this was the first time in my adult life that I called on those qualities.

Dismissing the four regulation approaches, I decided to go with a startling new technique—truth! I gave Mrs. Lasson one of my Company cards and waited a few seconds. Finally, she looked up at me in confusion. "No need to worry, Mrs. Lasson," I said. "I'm a covert agent looking for your husband."

Her eyes opened wide. "Why do you want Earl?" she said fearfully.

I chuckled in a friendly way. "We think Earl might be able to help us. I assure you, if he decides to go along with our plan, he will be a great hero and a defender of the American Way."

"Won't . . . won't you come in, Mr. Smith?" That's the name I had on my card. John Smith.

I smiled again and plucked the card out of her hand. "Could you just tell me where I could find Earl?" I asked.

Mrs. Lasson just shrugged. "I suppose he's down by the Superdome. That's where he usually is this time of day."

"The Superdome," I said. It made a kind of sense. I thanked Mrs. Lasson for her help and went back to my car. Later, when I cabled my report back to the DDI, I was reprimanded for employing truth, but all demerits were suspended pending the outcome of my experiment.

I decided that I'd done enough work for one day. I drove myself back to the safe house on Prytania Street. Along the way I stopped and got myself half a dozen of those little square hamburgers and a root beer float. Some people call those burgers "sliders," but after I'd gulped down four of them I recalled what we used to call them as kids. We used to call them "deathballs." They were great going down, but then they'd wreak heavy vengeance on your digestive tract. I ate the last two burgers rather than throw them out, and then I stretched out on the bed and watched a couple of movies on cable. Tomorrow would be soon enough to search out Mr. Earl P. Lasson.

I awoke the next morning early, but I eased into the day in a leisurely way. No hurry, no urgency, nothing to ruffle my calm exterior. I wanted to appear to Lasson as a friendly, helpful, confident new acquaintance. I wanted to do a selling job on him that would make every used-car dealer in the world jealous.

From late spring to late fall, New Orleans has the same weather report every day. It goes something like this: Highs in the nineties, humidity around 80 to 90 percent, a 50 percent chance of rain. Day after day after day. But I did get used to it, and soon I wasn't even noticing the weather anymore. I've gotten to like flat cities with palm trees. Except Phoenix. There's no excuse for Phoenix.

42

About noon, I got in the LTD and drove toward the Louisiana Superdome, the 2,124th Wonder of the World, ranking just after some monstrous Islamic mosque that some sheik is building on some coast somewhere. I had to stop and get directions, but I found the Dome easily enough. It was hard to miss. The building's so big you could put the Houston Astrodome inside on the floor. Of course, you couldn't get the Astrodome through the doors, so you'd have to disassemble it first and rebuild inside the Superdome, and then after all that work, what would you have? Well, maybe the 2,125th Wonder of the World.

Anyway, I spotted what I believed to be the target's vehicle, an elderly blue Chevy Vega with big dents in all of its doors and most of the external area covered with primer. A rear window had been broken and the space was now covered with gray duct tape. The bumpers were covered with stickers proclaiming the owner to be a fan to the Tulane Green Wave, as hapless a team as any. One corner of the rear window was covered by an orange sign that said, "Who Dat Say Dey Gonna Beat Dem Saints?" The answer, apparently, was "Most of the teams in the NFL."

The car was parked in the middle of a gigantic parking lot. It was all alone. There wouldn't be an event in the Superdome for at least three days. I drove into the lot and parked my car about fifty yards away from my target. Then I got out, removed my suit coat and stretched, and ambled in a friendly, helpful, confident way toward the Chevy.

When I was about ten yards from it, a man opened the driver's door and looked at me. He had long, greasy hair and a thick black beard. "You a cop?" he asked me.

"Nope," I said, smiling. Well, I wasn't, not in the way he meant. "You Earl P. Lasson?"

"You a collection agent? You from the Superdome management again? Want to boot my car or tow it away?"

I waved a hand. "None of that," I said.

"Sure," said Lasson, shaking his head. He pulled his door shut, revved his engine, and screamed out of the parking lot.

I stood there, feeling like a fool. As he was pulling out onto Poydras Street, I shouted, "I'll be back!" And I would, too. I don't think he heard me, though.

I decided to wait a few days before I confronted Lasson again, just to keep him off balance. I did some sightseeing around New Orleans instead. The first evening, I strolled up and down Bourbon Street, a skewer of beef chunks in teriyaki sauce in my left hand, and a paper cup containing a quart of beer in my right. I listened to music blaring out of the nightclubs. There was even one intersection with a club on each corner, and they were all struggling to make themselves heard with four different kinds of music.

I went into a strip club that advertised topless and bottomless dancers. I didn't see any. One of the women came over and sat next to me. "Where are the topless and bottomless dancers?" I asked.

"That's us," she said. "Except for the pasties, we're topless, and except for the G-strings, we're bottomless."

She asked me to buy her a champagne cocktail, and I bought her a Coke. She thanked me and moved away.

I must've gotten pretty drunk that night, because I don't remember going home. When I woke up, I felt fine. I decided to spend the day in Audubon Park. I brought a few slices of bread for the ducks in the lagoon, who were all glad to see me. Across from where I was feeding the hungry birds was a small island. On the island was an old live oak tree, its great limbs overspreading the water. There was a goose sleeping on one of those limbs, and the noise of the duck feeding frenzy must have awakened it. It had apparently forgotten where it had fallen asleep, because it rolled just a little to its left and plummeted into the water below. Then it shook its head and long neck like a wet dog. It looked around to see if anything had noticed its fall, and I swear it was the first time I've ever seen a goose look embarrassed.

I walked through Audubon Park to St. Charles Avenue. Across the street were Tulane and Loyola Universities. I waited by the yellow sign and caught the streetcar to Canal Street. I sat with my face pressed against the window, staring at the gorgeous mansions in the Uptown and Garden District areas. I enjoyed the old-fashioned feel of the streetcar as it rolled and lurched its way to the end of the line. And the driver had a bell that she clanged. It was like being in an old movie with Judy Garland.

When I got to Canal Street, I realized that I'd left my car up by the park, so I paid another fare and relaxed. It's a shame so many tourists never see any of the city except Bourbon Street, because New Orleans is a very lovely place. In certain places, that is.

Two days later, I made the second approach. I parked my car in a lot on Poydras Street and walked a few blocks to the Superdome parking area. It was very hot, and I took off my suit jacket. The hot weather would last for months, but I decided I'd rather endure the heat than put up with cold winters. I shoveled enough snow when I was a kid. It was okay by me if I never saw the stuff again.

I tried to look casual and nonthreatening as I walked up to my target's car. When I got there, I leaned down and rested one arm alongside his open window. "Sure is hot, isn't it?" As soon as I spoke the words, I realized I should've said "ain't it?"

"Plenty hot," said Lasson.

"You got air conditioning in this car?"

"Nope."

"What you doing in there, then?"

"Sufferin' like a stuck pig," said Lasson. "What you doin' out there?"

I gave him a well-controlled little chuckle. "See, when you zoomed off the other day, you never gave me the chance to explain myself. I'm from the Census." I hated to lie. It was the part of my job that made me the most uneasy. I still remember Reverend Sawicki in my confirmation class telling us we should never lie, under any circumstances. I wonder if he'd forgive me if he understood that my lie was necessary to safeguard the liberty of all freedom-loving Americans—safeguard their very *lives*, worst come to worst.

"The Census, huh?" said Lasson dubiously.

"Yes, sir," I said.

My target looked me over slowly. "Census, huh?" he said.

"You bet." My face was getting tired of smiling.

"So where's your clipboard?"

That came out of nowhere. "Huh?" I said.

"You ain't got a clipboard. I don't even see a pencil. How you gonna interview me, no clipboard and no pencil?"

"Well—" I didn't get to say anything more, because he put his car in gear and raced out of the parking lot, just as he'd done the first time. It was just as Reverend Sawicki always said, there is no profit in deceit.

I waited another three days. I wasn't discouraged by my failure so far. Most operations begin with frustrations. Like a homicide detective, I had to look at my target from different angles, hoping I'd find the right approach sooner rather than later. I spent the time thinking hard and watching movies on cable. A cop in one of the films said something that gave me an inspiration.

I used my contacts to get me an appointment with the New Orleans chief of police. He was very helpful, and we brainstormed for a few minutes and came up with what we agreed was a bulletproof plan. Well, Lasson had never brandished a weapon, but I was speaking metaphorically.

We waited until Monday morning to spring the trap. I rode in the LTD, leading the way for four others, We cruised to the Superdome, and when we were near enough, all five units turned on their sirens and flashing blue lights. When we got to the parking lot, I saw Earl P. Lasson in his car, just sitting quietly as usual. I directed my driver to pull over beside the exit, and I waited while the other four units roared into the lot. They squealed to a stop around my target, one patrol car in front of his blue Chevy Vega, one on each side, and one behind him. He was caught now, and he'd have to listen to me.

I got out of my white, unmarked Ford LTD and strolled toward Lasson's car. I had a good feeling. I believed that Operation ORCHID would soon rack up its first success. I leaned against the unit parked to my target's left. The sirens were off, but the blue lights on the units' roofs were still flashing.

"Knew you was a cop," said Lasson, spitting out the window near my feet.

"Mr. Lasson," I said in a cold voice, "I am not a police officer. I've told you that before."

"Then who are all these guys in the blue shirts? Eagle Scouts?"

"I've brought them with me," I said, "because on the previous two attempts to interview you, you proved to be recalcitrant."

"What's that mean?"

"Stupid," I said, my expression like stone. "You were stupid, only this time I'm not going to let you have a chance to be stupid again."

"Well, I sure do feel stupid, sittin' here with these cops all around me."

I nodded and reached into the patrol unit for the radio. I gave orders that the unmarked car should block the exit, and all the police officers in the other cars should move away. I needed to be alone with my target.

"That better?" I asked him.

Lasson gave a bitter laugh. "Not so's you'd notice," he said. "I can't move an inch."

"Well, you've got two choices as I see it. You can relax and let me interview you, or you can get booted so you won't be able to move, even after the cops leave."

"Want to interview me, huh. From a TV station or *New Orleans Magazine* or something?"

"None of those."

"If I don't help you out, you gonna boot my car?" said Lasson with a frown. "So's I can't drive away? And I'll be stuck here night and day till I cooperate?"

"Exactly."

"You moron!" Lasson cried. "Sittin' here night and day is what I been doin' for the last three years! I don't care 'bout your goddamn boot!"

I thought about what he'd said, and I realized that he was correct. "Well, along with booting your car, we have a few other tricks up our sleeves that I hoped we wouldn't have to use."

He shook his head. "What you mean? Like beatin' me senseless here in the parking lot of the Superdome?"

"We're beyond all that," I said. "We could put a potato in your exhaust pipe. We could pour sugar in your gas tank. We could let the air out of all your tires."

"Oh. Terrorism."

"In Operation ORCHID, we don't use the word terrorism. We prefer to think of these methods as essential covert ways and means."

"What are you?" asked Lasson. "FBI?"

I showed him my Company identification, and he gave a little gasp. "May I get in your car and ask a few questions?"

"Don't know how. These cop cars are parked pretty damn close on all sides."

"I'm thin enough to squeeze in through the passenger door, I think."

Lasson shrugged. "Okay, then. Try it."

I was able to open the car door several inches, and for a few moments I was afraid I'd scrape loose certain of my more promontory body parts. I did manage at last to squeeze through the narrow opening and into the blue Vega. I was breathing hard when I sat beside my target.

"You made it," said Lasson. "I'll give you credit for that."

"Give the credit to the excellent training program the Company provides."

"Sure, what you say. Now, what's this all about? And don't give me no story about the Census."

I nodded. "I have to admit that I tried deception on you last time. You were very clever to see through my disguise. Still, I had several other options including intimidation and harassment. I could get the IRS to pay you a visit here in this parking lot. Or I could threaten physical intimidation on you or your lovely wife. I met her several days ago, and I'd hate to have to resort to harming her."

My target's eyes grew larger, and he snarled, "You saw my wife? You stay away from her, Cap. She ain't involved in this at all."

I smiled politely. "I know that. Her charming innocence is what makes her vulnerability so poignant." I thought about concluding that point with a darkly meaningful chuckle, but my sense of restraint persuaded me that enough was enough.

"What you know about Anna Marie?" he said quietly.

I shrugged. "I suppose the company has a separate 201 file on her. But please understand: Anna Marie is not our target. You are. If you decide to be uncooperative, we'll have to use your wife as a wedge. An unfortunate, disposable wedge. If you catch my meaning."

Lasson closed his eyes and rubbed his forehead. "And this is mental intimidation, right?"

"Exactly," I said happily. "It's good that you're familiar with our techniques."

"All right, all right, I give up. I know I'm beat. You got too many men on your side. What you want to know?"

"First, tell me a little something about yourself."

My target sighed. "Starting when?"

"Well, when you were a kid. Where were you born?"

"Cleveland," said Lasson. "I was born in Cleveland in 1947. That was way back when the town called itself The Best location in the Nation. Then it turned into The Mistake by the Lake, but lately Cleveland's gone through a kind of face-lift, and everybody there calls it The North Coast. I still wouldn't use the beaches along the lakefront, though."

"How long did you live in Cleveland?"

He leaned back from the wheel and stretched. "I got out of there soon as I could, right after I graduated high school. The city's a Mistake, all right, and it's better as a place to be *from* than a place to be livin' *in*. You get it?"

"I think so." It was hot and stuffy in the car, and he had the front seat pulled so far forward that my chin was almost jammed into my knees.

"I left Cleveland and went to Las Vegas, where I made a pretty good living bettin' on big-league baseball, basketball, and football games."

"Hardly a community-conscious profession," I said. I couldn't keep the disapproval out of my voice.

"You're wrong," said Lasson. "If the community's Las Vegas, you're wrong. The city counts on that gamblin' money."

"You say you were making some good money?"

"Yeah. Then I met Anna Marie, and she hated Las Vegas. We got married and moved to a nice neighborhood in Queens, New York."

I didn't think all this was getting us anywhere useful. "Does all that tie together to explain what you're doing here in this parking lot?"

He nodded sadly, then he reached under his seat. My hand immediately went to the police special I had in my jacket, but Lasson just came up with a cellophane package. He'd eaten one Twinkie, but the second one had been mashed flat and forgotten. It had gotten all moldy, and it looked horrible. " 'Like the sands of an hourglass,' " Lasson intoned, " 'so are the days of our lives.' " Then Lasson tossed the Twinkie out his window; it hit the patrol car beside us and plopped to the ground.

"You watch that show, too?" I asked with some interest.

"Not so much the last couple of years. My old black and white set died a while back. Say, did Steve and Kayla ever get married?"

"Yeah," I said enthusiastically, "and they had a daughter but she's been kidnapped."

"Uh-huh," said Lasson with a shrug, "just like Kim and Shane's kid got kidnapped. I swear they only got five plots there. They got the kid getting kidnapped plot, they got the five-day coma plot, they got the innocent person tried for murder plot, they got the evil twin plot, and they got the amnesia plot. Ever know anybody that got amnesia? On TV, you're not a real character till you get amnesia at least once."

Well, I was enjoying the conversation, but it wasn't helping me get at the truth. "Now, Earl," I said, "can you tell me briefly what the hell you're doing here all the time?" I called him by his first name to foster confidence. That was a Company-approved technique.

" 'Cause long as I'm out here, I'll pretend the ball ain't come down."

That told me nothing, zero, zip. And the hard part was that I didn't believe for a second that he was being purposefully evasive. He just had a back-assward way of talking about things.

"I don't understand what you mean, Earl," I said in a friendly way.

He took a deep breath and let it out slowly. "It all started in 1983. It was the last game of the season for the Saints. Now, you gotta remember that the Saints had been around for seventeen years and they'd never had a winning season. They had the worst cumulative winning percentage in history. Not one time did they ever end a year winning more games than they lost."

I stroked my chin, radiating understanding and acceptance, even though I still didn't have the faintest idea what the hell he was talking about. "All right," I said thoughtfully, "we're in 1983 and the Saints are losing."

He got very excited. "That's just it! The last game of the season, the Saints were playin' the Los Angeles Rams, and if the Saints won, it'd be the first winning season for them, and the Saints would've made the playoffs for the first time. Every other team had been in the playoffs except the Saints, including crummy newcomers like Tampa Bay. You know the Buccaneers started off their first couple of years with an amazing losing streak? And guess who they finally beat for their first-ever win? The Saints!"

"Well," I said slowly, "I see you're a passionate Saints fan, but I still don't see why you're living your life in self-enforced solitude here in this hot parking lot."

"Here comes the hard part," said my target, looking me squarely in the eye. "In the fourth quarter, the Saints were ahead 24–23. All they got to do was run out the clock. No such luck. The Rams got the ball back and marched down the field like nobody's tryin' to stop 'em. Maybe that was the truth. Maybe the Saints were as good as nobody. Anyway, there's only five or six seconds left in the game, and the Rams decide they're in field goal range. Soon as they call time to get set up for the kick, I jumped up and ran out of the Superdome. I didn't want to watch it. I didn't want to be a part of it. I went to my car and sat there. While later, crowds came out of the Dome, all lookin' kind of glum."

"Uh-huh," I said.

"Don't you see?" said Lasson fiercely. "I can guess that Mike Lansford made that forty-two-yard field goal, and the Rams won 26–24, and the Saints settled for a .500 season. I can imagine that's what happened, but I have no hard *evidence*. Far as I know, the ball might still be in the air, as if real life stopped the second Lansford's foot touched the ball. Sittin' here in this lot is my protest. I'll stay here, living in the car, eatin' the food my wife brings me, goin' places if I need to do something, till the Saints not only make the playoffs, but go to the Super Bowl. They don't even have to win the big game—I'll be satisfied if they just make it that far."

That was just plain screwy. "You might have a long wait," I said.

He nodded. "I know, but I sworn my oath."

"That's a hell of a commitment you've made."

Lasson sighed again. "What else can a poor man do?"

That might be just the angle I needed. "How are you living and supporting your family?"

"We been livin' on my savings from the good years in Las Vegas. But the savings are runnin' a little thin right about now."

He was so crazy, he just might have been the man I was looking for. "Have you always been such a devoted fan?"

"Devoted? *Devoted?*" he cried. "I'll start at the beginning and tell you how devoted I been. I was born in Cleveland, right? In 1947, so I was seven years old in 1954."

He looked at me as if those words were especially significant. I didn't know what he meant.

He saw my blank look and went on. "In 1954 my hometown team, the Cleveland Indians, won the pennant. The whole city was excited. I never paid much attention to baseball before, but in '54 I couldn't get away from it. I still remember those great players: Vic Wertz and Larry Doby and Al Rosen. And the starting pitchers were brilliant: Mike Garcia, Bob Feller, Early Wynn, and Bob Lemon. It was a thrilling time, and at the age of seven I never been thrilled before."

"That's what first interested you in sports, huh?"

"Sure. It was the Curse of Doom."

"Why do you call it that?" I asked.

His face flushed red. "Because the damn Indians went to the World Series and lost it four games in a row. And the next couple of years they finished second, and then they finished sixth, and pretty soon they were in their famous slide down into the pit of losers. They ain't never won another goddamn pennant in better'n thirty-five years."

"But you moved away from Cleveland. Why are you so upset about the Indians?"

His expression conveyed anguish. "Can't help it! Every year I cheer for the Indians, and every year they break my heart. I tried to cure it by movin' to New York with Anna Marie. I got there in '66, just in time to catch the Mets' ninth-place finish. I even turned to the Yankees for some relief, but they were even worse, and ending up tenth out of ten. In '67, they traded places, the Mets goin' to tenth place, and the Yankees grimly improving to ninth. It got a little better for the Yanks the followin' year. They finished in fifth, but the Mets were stuck in ninth."

"What did you do? Sit in your car outside Shea Stadium?"

He squinted his eyes and said, "What are you, makin' fun of me?"

I raised both hands. "Not at all. I want to know what you did do."

Lasson spat out the window again. "Let Anna Marie talk me into moving south, that's what I did. Now, I love New Orleans, and

Anna Marie's mama still lives here. But they lied to me. They told me fifteen years ago that when they opened the Superdome, we'd have a major league team move here any minute. It never happened. So I started followin' football and basketball."

"This was in 1969?" I said.

"Yeah," Lasson said dreamily, "the year of the Miracle Mets, who waited until I left town to win the World Series. And now here, without a local baseball team, I watch the Cubs on cable."

"The Cubs?" It made me shudder. "What about basketball and football?"

My target laughed without humor. "We *had* a basketball team here, the Jazz. Was an expansion team, so it wasn't very good the first couple of seasons. We had Pete Maravich, though, and he was wonderful to see. Then the management got fed up and moved the team from the Dome to Salt Lake City. 'The Utah Jazz,' ain't that crazy? I mean, Chicago is the toddlin' town. I don't think there's a single person in Salt Lake City who knows how to toddle."

"When that team left New Orleans, it must have hurt."

Lasson thumped himself on the chest. "My inside's been torn up so many times by these goddamn teams, I should be used to it by now. But I'm not. It's not anything you can get used to. Your hopes go up early in the season, and then you hang on to the bitter end, and you hope Maybe Next Season. Since 1954, I've never had a good Next Season."

I thought I detected a tear about to fall from his left eye. "And so now all you've got are the Saints, and your car, and your oath."

He took a deep, sad breath. "And a terrific wife who understands and supports me."

There was silence in the car after that, and I let it go on longer, to deepen the mood of despair. Then I said, "You know, it almost sounds as if your presence—or even your fannish interest—is enough to jinx these teams."

He nodded glumly. "I'd go somewhere else, 'cause I know as soon as I do, the Saints'll have a terrific year and get to the Super Bowl. I'd do it for them, but I didn't want to curse some other team."

"Maybe you don't have to," I said. "Maybe I can help you out."

He looked at me dubiously. "What you mean?"

I took out some folded papers from the inside pocket of my suit coat. "Look," I said, flattening the pages against my knees. "I represent a small, supersecret branch of the Company. We've been working on Operation ORCHID for several years now. First we correlated sports results with the movements of certain citizens. We've identified a few other people who have your negative talent, but just as I was about to recruit them, their teams suddenly blossomed into winners. You're the first field contact I've made who appears the real thing."

"You want to recruit me?" said Lasson. "What for?"

I showed him the papers and let him read for himself. One page was a simplified, censored account of the history of Operation ORCHID. Another was a waiver form he'd have to sign before we could do an in-depth background check on him and his wife. There were some medical forms, too. "Don't hesitate to ask any questions you might have," I told him.

"Well, I'm smart enough to see that you want me and Anna Marie to work for you. I wouldn't mind takin' a job from the government. What kind of job?"

I clasped his shoulder firmly with my left hand. "You can take this job and be a national hero, although a secret national hero, or you can decline and I'll take the next plane out of New Orleans."

Lasson nodded and repeated, "What *kind* of job?"

"We want you to go live in Moscow," I said. "Or Peking, or Havana. We'll pay you a good salary—by American standards—and we'll pick up one hundred percent of your living expenses. Furthermore, we'll import any kind of American food and clothes and toys, as long as you remain an agent. You'll be able to join the American community in these capital cities, and you'll be able to live there without giving up a bit of the quality of life you cherish here."

Lasson kind of goggled at me for a moment. "You mean it?"

"You'll be free to follow whatever interests you have. And when your kids are old enough, you can send them to any university you like and the Company will pay all their expenses."

Lasson leaned back and stared through the windshield. "Sounds too good to be true," he said.

I smiled. "The Company would really like to have a good jinx in place under the Kremlin's nose. But don't give me an answer now. Take the papers home and discuss it all with Anna Marie. There's no danger involved, because you won't be spying."

"And if I say no, will your Company waste us? Just for knowing about all this?"

I lifted a hand. "All that kind of stuff is just in the movies. We wouldn't kill you, we're your *country!*" I gave him my card with my telephone number on it, and got out of his car, and directed the police units to let him through. He started his blue Chevy and headed for the exit. I waved the unmarked car away, and Lasson headed home. I felt certain I'd hear back from him, and I was also sure that Operation ORCHID had its first recruit.

A few days later, after I'd gotten his call of acceptance, I packed my bags and headed to the airport. I was going on to Atlanta. Atlanta's sports teams are about as pitiful as one could hope. They had a contest recently to choose a slogan for the baseball Braves. One of the favorite entries read "Go Braves! And take the damn Falcons with you!"

Atlanta. My kind of town.

Lewis Shiner
WILD FOR YOU

Lew Shiner likes to try his hand at a variety of things—and he inevitably does
them well; his most recent science fiction
novel, *Deserted Cities of the Heart*, was
nominated for a Nebula Award. He also
writes realistic fiction (his latest realistic
novel is *Slam*), dabbles in horror, edits
anthologies, and is currently working on
a series of comic books. This diversity of
interests represents a unique talent and
perspective, a perspective that is reflected
in his ideas about home.

As George Alec Effinger showed, some
people can spend their entire lives looking for a home, and in "Wild For You,"
Lew Shiner points out that home may be
right beneath our feet and we may not
even realize it. Home is the place where
we have spent most of our time. For Lew,
that place is not the "freeways and dirt
roads of memory" of which Harlan Ellison speaks, but an actual, literal highway. Of "Wild For You," a slightly
shorter version of which appeared in *Isaac
Asimov's Science Fiction Magazine*, Lew

says, "I've driven between Austin and Dallas since 1968, since I lived in Dallas and my high school friends all went to college at the University of Texas. Now I live in Austin and drive back to Dallas to visit my mother. It's two hundred miles of the most boring interstate in creation. Sometimes the drive seems to take your entire life."

WILD FOR YOU
Lewis Shiner

I T WAS A PONTIAC FIREBIRD with a custom paint job, a metal-flake candy-apple red. The personalized plates said WILD4U.

I was right behind her on that big cloverleaf that slopes down off Woodall Rogers onto I-35. The wind caught a hank of her long blond hair and set it to fluttering outside her window. I saw her face in her own rearview as she threw her head back. Laughing, or singing along with the radio, or maybe just feeling the pull as she put the pedal down and scooted into the southbound lane.

She was a beauty, all right. Just a kid, but with a crazy smile that made my heart spin.

I whipped my pickup into fourth but I couldn't get past this big white Caddy coming up on me from behind. The two lanes for Austin were fixing to split off in half a mile. An eighteen-wheeler filled up one of them and the Caddy had the other. I eased off the gas and watched her disappear over the horizon, a bright red promise of something beyond my wildest dreams.

It was midafternoon, sunny with a few clouds. The weather couldn't decide if it was summer or winter, which is what passes for fall in Texas. I wasn't but a kid myself, with my whole life in front of me. I put Rosanne Cash on the tape deck and my arm out the window and let those white lines fly by.

I was at the Fourth Street Shell station in Waco, halfway home, when I saw that little red car again. I'd just handed my credit card to the lady when the squeal of brakes made me look up. There it was, shiny and red, rocking back and forth by the Super Unleaded.

I kept one eye on it while I signed the receipt. The driver door opened and this guy got out. He was in jeans and a pearl-button shirt and a black cap. I can't say I liked the looks of him. She got out the passenger side and leaned across the top of the car, watching the traffic. I couldn't hardly see her because of the pump. I hung around the ice cream freezer, hoping she'd come inside. Instead the guy came in to pay cash for five dollars' worth.

I followed him out. She turned to get back in the car and I felt a chill. Her hair was shorter than it had been, just barely past her collar. And her face looked older too.

I couldn't figure what the hell. Maybe she'd got her hair cut? She'd had time, as fast as she'd been driving, and as long as we'd been out. I felt like I'd already spent half my life on the road. Or maybe this was her older sister had borrowed the car somehow.

Weird, is what it was. I got back in the truck and hit it on down the highway. About two miles on they came up behind me to pass, and that's when I saw the license had changed. Now it said MR&MRS.

Right as they pulled up next to me I looked over at her. She was staring out the window, right at me. She pointed a finger, like kids do when they're making a pretend pistol. And smiled, that same crooked smile.

For some reason that really got to me. I don't think I'll ever forget it.

Some things are just Mysteries, and you don't expect to understand them. When I passed that car south of Belton, there were different people in it. The woman driving looked like the blond girl, but was old enough to be her mother. There was a dark-haired girl in the passenger seat, maybe thirty years old, and two little kids in back. The dark-haired girl was turned around to yell at them. The speed limit had gone back up to 65, but they chugged along at 60. The plates were standard Texas issue and there was a bumper sticker that said ASK ME ABOUT MY GRANDBABY.

Tell the truth, I was too tired to think much of it anymore. The sun had started to set and I had this pinched kind of pain between my shoulders. About thirty miles on I saw a roadside rest stop and pulled in.

59

I might have slept a quarter of an hour. The sky had clouded over and the sunset lit everything up pretty spectacular. It was being thirsty woke me and I gimped over to the water fountain on stiff legs.

Luck or something made me look back at the highway. That metal-flake red Firebird pulled off at about 30 miles an hour, just barely rolling. The old lady was by herself again. While I watched she hung a left turn under the interstate and disappeared.

I had my drink of water, remembering that pointing finger and crooked smile. I got back in the pickup and followed. When I came out on the northbound access, I saw the car pulled over in the Johnson grass at the side of the road. I parked behind it and eased out of the truck.

There was nobody inside. An ambulance screamed onto the northbound entrance ramp, siren going and lights flashing. After a few seconds the lights went out and it crested a hill, headed back the way we'd come.

Karen Haber
3 RMS, GOOD VIEW

Just as many people spend their lives
trying to find a home, an equal number
of people spend their time trying to return home. But home is sometimes a
place that lives only in the past, a place
we can visit only in our memories, memories enhanced by time and distance. For
Karen Haber, however, one may be able
to visit it—in the future. Karen writes

The concept of the past as a suburb of
the present has always intrigued me as a
rich science-fictional conceit. I caught
the germ of this particular story while I
was getting a check validated at the supermarket. As the electronic device
buzzed and bleeped over my check, I
wondered if other supermarkets in other
locales had this nifty machine. I
decided, perhaps a bit chauvinistically,
that California supermarkets probably
contained state-of-the-art check-validat-
ing machinery and that the rest of the
country was years behind. In fact, so far

behind that my mother, in Florida, was probably living in 1984. And Grandma in 1962.

Other elements of the story developed from the San Francisco Bay Area's charming but narcissistic penchant for celebrating its recent history, emphasizing, of course, the heady days of the Sixties. I wanted a protagonist who not only wasn't interested in time travel, but didn't know much or care about the Sixties. She, of course, would be the perfect lens through which to view the era.

Karen, dynamic and witty, is a transplanted easterner living in Oakland, California. Karen grew up in the New York City area but gravitated to the West Coast in the early 1970s, and later made it her adopted home. In "3 Rms, Good View," Karen looks at the California she first encountered, and at the California that may come to be.

Although Karen is fairly new to the field of science fiction, she has had a number of superb stories published in the major magazines, and is also busy at work on a series of four books, of which the first two, *The Mutant Season* and *The Mutant Prime* have been published by Doubleday. Karen is married to Robert Silverberg, who also appears in this anthology. They have several cats, one of whom "closets" himself during earthquakes.

3 RMS, GOOD VIEW

Karen Haber

"APARTMENT FOR RENT," the faxxad said. "3 rms, gd view, Potrero Hill area, $1200 a month, utilities pd."

I stared at it in disbelief. It sounded like a dream. Most apartments in the city had waiting lists for their sublease waiting lists.

"Southern exp. Pets OK."

Better and better. Then I found the catch. The apartment was available, all right: in 1968.

I almost didn't take it.

Don't misunderstand me. I've always wanted to live in San Francisco. Kind of felt like it was my hometown—the one I'd always been meant to live in, instead of the sprawling metroplex of Greater Los Angeles. I first came north in 1997 on a family expedition to the Pan Pacific Exposition, when I was thirteen. The fair was fun, but what I loved was San Francisco: the sunswept hillsides, the streets lined with flower boxes, the ding-a-ling of the street cars floating in the cool air, the fog creeping in at dusk—it was heaven. And I knew I would come back. It took me seventeen years and a divorce, but I did it. Right after I graduated from Boult and passed the bar.

Unfortunately, housing was tight—more than tight. The city had instituted severe building restrictions back in 2003 and got what it asked for: all residential construction not only halted but vanished, gone eastward to the greener pastures of Contra Costa County.

I got on the waiting list of every real estate agent in the Bay Area, but the best digs I could find was a studio apartment—more like a large walk-in closet with stucco walls—in a renovated duplex in Yuba City. Add on a three-hour commute to my job in San Francisco's financial district, and we're not exactly talking about positive quality of life.

So when I saw the ad, I jumped. And stopped in midair. I'm not one of those sentimental people who long to travel back in history. I like realtime, always have. It's a peculiar trait, considering my family.

My grandmother lives in 1962, and has for the last ten years. She said it was the last time that America was great—and convinced of it. "Loosen up, Christine," she said to me before she left. "You should be more flexible. There's nothing wrong with the past."

My brother lives in 1990, has shaved his head, and dyed it in concentric circles of red and black. Every now and then I get a note from him through e-mail: "Come visit. We'll hit the after-hours clubs. Don't you ever take a vacation?"

Mom likes 1984 but she always had an odd sense of humor. I haven't heard from her in five years.

Pardon me if I like realtime best. I've always had my feet planted firmly in the present. Practical, sturdy Christine. In the lofty hierarchy of Mount Olympus, I'd be placed just to the left of Zeus in the marble frieze. In the Athena position, that is. Yes, I even have the gray eyes and brown hair to go with the no-nonsense attitude. I'm tall and muscular, as befits your basic warrior-goddess/business-attorney type. My stature is useful too—who wants an attorney who doesn't look efficient and imposing?

And I've never wanted to go backward. I remember the first reports of problems and glitches associated with time travel—Sheila, one of my prelaw classmates at Berkeley, wanted to spend her Christmas break in the village where her French great-great-great-grandmother lived. But a power surge from Sacramento sent her to the fourteenth century instead. Talk about your bad neighborhoods. If she hadn't gotten her shots before she left—complaining all the way—she'd probably have come back sporting buboes the size of nectarines.

After Sheila's brush with the Black Death, I told myself I was immune to the allure of era-hopping. I ignored the faxxads for

64

Grand Tours: the Crucifixion and sack of Rome package, $1,598. Dark Ages through the Enlightenment, two weeks for $2,100, all meals and tips included. (These packages are especially popular with the Japanese, who have become time-travel junkies. And why not? They can go away and come back without losing any realtime at work.) Even when the Koreans made portable transport units for home or office, I shrugged and stuck by realtime. But when I saw the listing in the paper, I looked around the stucco walls of my apartment/cell and threw all my sturdy, practical notions to the wind. An apartment on Potrero Hill? Sure: Pallas Athena transmuted into impulsive, inquisitive Mercury.

Hands trembling with excitement and impatience, I faxxed my credit history to Jerry Raskin, the real estate agent listed, and received an appointment to view the apartment.

We met at Raskin's office in the Tenderloin. He was a short man, barely reaching my shoulder, with thinning dark hair and a doughy nose that looked like a biscuit. A matte black–enameled time transport unit sat behind his desk.

I stared at it uneasily.

"Want to look over the premises?" he asked. He gestured toward the unit.

"Uh, yes. Of course." I took a deep breath and stepped over the threshold of the transport.

There was a sudden fragmentation of color, of sound. I was in a high white space, falling. I was stepping into an apartment on Potrero Hill, shaking my head in wonder.

Even before the shimmering transport effect had diminished, Jerry had launched into his sales pitch. "It's a gem," he said proudly. "I hardly ever get this kind of listing." He flicked an invisible piece of lint from the shoulder of his blue tweed suit. "Once every five years."

It *was* perfect. Big sunny rooms paneled in pine, full of light, ready for plants. Hardwood floors. There was even a little balcony off the bedroom where I could watch the fog drift in over Twin Peaks in the summer afternoons.

All wound up, oblivious to my rapture, Jerry rattled on. "You can install a transport unit in the closet for your morning and evening commute to realtime. It's a steal. What's your rail commute now from Yuba City?"

I didn't need much convincing. "I'll take it."

"Two year lease," he said. "Sign here." Then he brandished a yellow contract. "This too."

"What is it?" I was Pallas Athena again, staring down suspiciously from my lofty legal height onto the sweaty center of his bald spot. "If this is a pet restriction clause, I'm going to protest. Your ad didn't say anything about this. I've got a cat." I kept MacHeath at work—there was more room there than at home. But where I went, he went.

"Sure, sure," he said. "You can keep your kitty as long as you pay a deposit. This is just your standard noninterference contract."

"Noninterference contract?"

He looked at me like I was stupid. It rarely happens, but when someone does that, I really don't like it.

"You know," he said, and recited in a singsong voice, " 'Don't change the past or the past will change you.' The time laws. You lawyers understand this kind of thing." He pointed a thick finger at my chin. "You, and you alone, are responsible for any dislocation of past events, persons or things, et cetera, et cetera. Read the small print and sign."

A sudden chill teased my upper vertebrae. Noninterference? Well, why would I interfere with the past? The morning sunlight streamed in through the big window in the front room. High clouds scudded over the hillside. I shook off the shivers and signed.

A week later, I took up residence, hanging my tiny collection of photos, putting down rugs, and glorying in my privacy. MacHeath didn't care for the transport effect, but he approved of his new home, and after sniffing every corner of it, spent most of his days following the sunlight from window to window, the better to admire his orange stripes before snoozing.

Life's pendulum swung between work and home, uptime and downtime, in an easy arc. Thanks to the transport, I could leave the house at any time of day and return a moment later. This made for a great deal of quality time spent snuggled with MacHeath on the red corduroy sofa. And on my own, in the heart of a smaller, cozier city where I wandered gratefully along the waterfront, bought sourdough bread and lingered over coffee in North Beach jazz clubs. And everywhere there was color and life and music: garish psychedelic posters printed in what I think were called Day-Glo colors announcing musical groups with odd names like The Jacksons' Airplane. Shaggy-haired, brightly dressed, friendly people lived in casual groups on the street, in buses, and in the old houses lining Haight Street and Ashbury. I fell in love with the past—at least, with San Francisco's past.

At work, they asked me how I could stand to watch history go by without comment.

"Don't you ever want to warn somebody?" Bill Hawthorne, the senior partner, said. "Don't you ever want to call up Martin Luther King or Bobby Kennedy and warn him? Say 'Stay off of hotel room balconies' or 'Don't go in the kitchen'?"

"Shame on you, Bill," I said. I smiled. "You know that's against the law."

In fact, I watched, agog, as the alarming parade of assassinations and demonstrations took place. History on the hoof. I began to see why people get hooked on the past. It's like participatory video.

And during the year I lived in 1968, Martin Luther King was assassinated in Memphis, and Robert Kennedy, in Los Angeles. And somebody moved into the downstairs apartment.

It had remained empty for so long that I'd begun to think of it as part of my domain. Oh, I'd assumed an uptime renter would appear one morning, strangely dressed, keeping to him-or-herself. I'd seen one or two folks in the neighborhood I suspected of being residential refugees from uptime, but I'd avoided them, and if they'd noticed me at all, they'd carefully ducked me. We all played the game with discretion.

I was out of town, uptime, when the people downstairs moved in. The first sign I had of their presence was the primal beat of rock music reverberating through my lovingly stained floorboards, occasionally punctuated by the high manic whine of amplified electric guitars. Boom-boom-bah. Boom-boom-bah. For five hours I considered various legal strategies showing just cause for murder: Sorry, Your Honor, but it was self-defense. Their music made me psychotic and if I hadn't stopped it, the entire neighborhood would have been at risk and all history would have been changed so I had to do it, don't you see? About three in the morning, somebody turned off the music.

The next day, as I was blearily putting out my garbage, I met my downstairs neighbor. He was sitting in the backyard, smoking a sweet-smelling cigarette. The pungent smoke curled up above his head in lazy circles. Long wavy blond hair fell to the middle of his back. He was wearing jeans and a brown suede vest but aside from that, his interest in clothing seemed minimal. His toenails were black with grime.

"Name's Duffy," he said. He jerked his head at a hefty woman in a long muslin skirt and peasant blouse who stood in the doorway, smiling spacily at me. Her strawberry-blond hair was gathered into two fat braids that fell past her knees. She was wearing metal-rimmed glasses whose lenses caught the light and flashed prismatic reflections on the grass. I stared, fascinated. I'd forgotten that in this era people used external devices to correct their vision.

"This is my old lady, Seashell."

The head jerked again, this time toward an urchin with a dirty face, stringy blond hair, and big blue eyes. "This is our little girl, Peacelove."

Peacelove wiped her nose against the back of her hand and stared at me. All three of them stared at me, at my burr haircut, severe business suit, dark shoes, glossy pigskin briefcase. I realized that to my new hippie neighbors I must have looked like some kind of strange male impersonator.

"Hi," I said. "Nice to meet you." I climbed the stairs.

"Far out," Duffy said, staring at my briefcase. "You some kind of secretary or actress or something?"

"Something," I said, and as I smiled, I closed my door.

Weekends, I took long walks through Golden Gate Park. It was green, beautiful, and filled with people who could have been Duffy's close relatives.

"Peace," they said, and I nodded.

"Love."

I smiled.

"Could you lay a little bread on me, please?"

I shook my head and walked away, confused—why did they think I'd just come from a bakery?

For trips to the grocery store, I bought a lime-green Volkswagen with a dented purple fender, third-hand, and after some abrupt, bucking rides down the block, mastered the quaint antique stick shift and clutch.

As for clothing, well, I found used jeans in the neighborhood

Army-Navy store and a loose-fitting top of muslin tie-dyed in pink and red. The shirt itched a bit when I wore it and turned my underwear gray-pink when I washed it, but it was good camouflage. I tied a red bandanna around my head to cover my short hair and tried to be inconspicuous. I almost succeeded.

I learned my neighbors' schedule quickly. They stayed up all night, vibrating my apartment, and slept all day. Apparently, the little girl didn't go to school. Once, I glanced out my window to see her staring up hungrily at my place. I tried not to see her. I really tried.

One night, late, as the guitars whined and I was about to switch on my noise dampers, there was a knock at the door.

"Who is it?"

"Duffy."

I opened the door a crack. "What's up?"

He peered at me from bloodshot eyes whose lids were at half mast. "Thought you might want to come to a party," he said, and smiled muzzily.

"No thanks," I said. "I need my sleep."

"C'mon, don't be a hard lady," he said. "Seashell's gone to see her folks. Just you 'n' me."

I almost laughed. Men rarely looked at me the way he was looking at me now. While I might have welcomed it from one or two of the attorneys I knew in realtime, I was not interested in this dirty, lazy, antediluvian jerk.

"That's too small a party for me. No thanks."

"Hey, Seashell won't mind. Whatever goes down is cool with her."

"Congratulations. Hope you know a good lawyer when things warm up." I shut the door.

The apartment was blissfully quiet after that—in fact, I didn't hear any of Duffy's music for at least a week. Didn't see him or Seashell. Once, when I was putting out the garbage, Peacelove appeared at the front window, pressed her little hands against the pane, and stared out at me. I smiled. She didn't smile back. When she turned to walk away, I saw that her hands had left dirty smudges on the glass.

I spent a week in realtime on an important case, and when I got back discovered I had new neighbors.

Duffy and his family were gone. In their place were two skinny guys in their twenties with long dark hair, beards, and the same interest in the same kind of music. They barely acknowledged my presence, which was fine.

One night, I heard a child crying, late, after the music had ended, when the noise dampers had cycled and shut down. It was the high, keening, hopeless sound of one who doesn't expect to be comforted. It was the kind of sound no child should ever have to make.

I got out of bed, listened, heard it again, opened the front door. Then I couldn't hear it anymore. The night was silent save for the creaking floorboards under my feet. Was I imagining things? MacHeath yawned elaborately as I got back into bed and made his sleepy, inquisitive, querching sound.

"It's nothing," I said. "Bad dream."

The next night I heard it again—the sound of a child crying hopelessly, long after everybody else in the world was asleep.

Two days later, I saw her.

She was standing in the backyard, weaving back and forth. Her eyes were half-closed as though she were stoned.

I took a step toward her. "Honey, are you all right?"

She opened her eyes. The pupils were massive, almost engulfing the blue irises.

"Peacelove, where's your mommy?"

"Mommy?" She looked at me, her face crumpled into tears, and she ran into the house.

I didn't hear the crying again after that.

But I did meet one of Peacelove's babysitters. He was waiting outside one morning as I brought out the garbage.

"Hey, sister."

I ignored him, thinking about torts, about deed restrictions. About Peacelove.

Suddenly, there was a hand on my shoulder. "Hey. You deaf?" Another hand attached itself to my ass.

I leaned toward him, feinted, grabbed his arm and pulled him past me, shoving him headfirst into the metal garbage can. He landed with a crash. For a moment, I thought I'd killed him. Then he groaned and rolled over onto his side. He lay there, stunned, peering up at me.

"Hands off," I said, enunciating carefully, showing my strong white teeth. "I don't know you. I don't want to." I kicked the can beside his head to emphasize the point. He winced and nodded.

After that, he left me alone. But I came home one night to find that the door to my apartment had been vandalized: somebody had tried to force the lock. Good thing I'd brought a security sealer from uptime and installed it. Whoever had attempted the deed had contented themselves with carving the word BITCH into the wood just above the doorknob.

Damn straight, I thought. And don't you forget it.

I left the graffito exactly where it was.

The crying at night resumed. I began to wonder if I should call somebody. But who? Where were Duffy and Seashell? Were they really even her parents? And what kind of child welfare agencies were available in the 1960s? Could Peacelove hope for anything better than what she had right now? And the time laws were explicit. No interference.

I didn't know what to do, so I waited. And she who hesitates, kills.

I transported home one night into a smoke-filled apartment. It was eleven P.M. I felt the floor—hot, too hot. I called the fire department, grabbed MacHeath, and was halfway out the door before I remembered the transport unit. Cursing, I disconnected it, threw it into my briefcase and ran down the stairs, arms full of squirming orange cat.

By the time I got to the pavement, the lower apartment was completely engulfed, the flames roaring like an insane animal. The upper story caught and I watched the flames dance up the curtains and past my front window. Imagined them licking and consuming my rugs, quilts, clothing. My life. I could hear the screams of sirens as fire trucks raced down the street.

Lights came on in houses up and down the block and sleepy faces peered through windows, through open doors. Tears were running down my cheeks, matting MacHeath's fur. He struggled furiously, trying to get away from the strange sounds, the dark, the people. Finally, I stowed him in my car.

Red-coated firemen kicked in the door downstairs. The thick rubber hose they carried spewed gallons of water into the inferno.

The roaring faltered, subsided, diminished into an ugly hissing. In half an hour, the remains of the house were smoldering, smoking, but the fire was dead.

Shivering, I watched as the bodies were carried out: charred and blackened beyond recognition as once-living things. Nine bodies—had there really been that many people living there? And one more, smaller than the rest. The last to be brought out.

Peacelove.

"Found her by the back window," the fireman said. His voice was hoarse from smoke and emotion. "I think she was trying to open it and get out. But the damned thing was painted shut." Gently, he set down the small corpse. "Jesus, I've got two at home around her age."

I turned around, walked away, spent the night at a neighbor's house. The next morning, I waited until the good Samaritan had left for work at the shipyards, then plugged in the transport, set it for autoretrieve, and took MacHeath back to realtime, right into Jerry Raskin's office.

"You son of a bitch!" I grabbed him by the lapel of his checkered coat. "You knew that place was going to burn down when you rented it to me."

"What? I swear, I didn't!" He stared fearfully at my soot-stained face. "I had no idea. You've got to believe me."

I shook him until his teeth chattered. "You are required by law to do a time sweep to alert tenants to potential dangers!"

"I did. I did. The records came up clean—the former owner must have lied to the insurance company." His eyes were huge with terror now. I put him down and he backed away from me until the desk separated us. "Besides, you look okay to me. You got out all right, didn't you? I'll refund your deposit. What are you complaining about?"

I decided not to make trouble for him. I went back to Yuba City. Found a studio apartment that almost had room for me and MacHeath. Tried to forget.

By day, it was easy. The Golden Gate Bridge glistened in the sunlight. The bay was dotted by solar-powered sailboats. The cable cars went ding-a-ling. The scent of coffee and chocolate wafted up from Ghiradelli Square. Work was blessedly absorbing, as always.

At night, my dreams were filled with little girls with dirty faces and huge blue eyes, terrified little girls with their hands and faces pressed against a wall of unyielding glass as flames raced up behind them.

"Help," they cried, in my dreams. "Help. Mommy. Daddy. Christine."

I took it for two weeks.

On my way to work one morning, I glanced through the window as we pulled into Powell Station. Another train had come in on the parallel track, and in it a small girl with big blue eyes stared at me with great seriousness. Her hands were pressed against the window. I looked down at my faxxpaper. When I looked up again, she was gone. But two small handprints smudged the glass where she had been.

That night I went back.

I went back to 1968 and stood outside the house and watched as the fire gained strength. Watched, paralyzed, as the smoke billowed upward. Saw a woman—me—peer out the upstairs window with fierce, frightened eyes as she held an orange cat in her arms.

Was that tough, severe-looking woman me? Was that who I wanted to be?

Then I saw a flash at the downstairs window. A small face, eyes huge. Peacelove, struggling with the latch. The smoke filled the room behind her. She beat against the window, coughing.

I moved, then. Picked up a rock.

The fire engine sirens howled in the distance.

I saw myself coming down the stairs and darted to the side, out of sight, quickly, quickly, until I knew that I was putting MacHeath in the car with my back to the house.

Awkwardly, then, I smashed in the window. Reached through jagged glass that scratched hands and arms, grabbed the child and pulled her through. The flames chased her right up to the edge of the sill, but they couldn't have her. No. Not this time.

Peacelove clung to me, crying. I rocked her gently.

"It's okay, honey." And smeared blood and soot on her face. I didn't care. She was alive.

When she'd calmed enough to fall into an exhausted sleep, I handed her to a neighbor and hurried away before anybody noticed that there were two of me there.

When I got back to realtime, I took a long shower, bandaged

my wounds, and had two glasses of The Macallan, eighteen-year-old single malt.

The next morning, I called in a favor from Jimmy Wu at the SFPD database and had a search made for Peacelove, beginning in 1968.

There was no sign of her.

"Shit, Chrissy, they were all called Peacelove that year," Jimmy said. "Or Morning Star or Rainbow. I need a real name, like Tammy or Katie or Sarah, and a social security number. A last name would help, too."

So the trail fizzled out in the backyard of a smoldering house on Potrero Hill, forty-six years ago. And nothing anomalous ever happened that I could detect—not one ripple of difference in the time line. MacHeath remained an orange cat with particular habits. I kept my job. San Francisco glittered as always in the chilly summer sunlight. I guess some people are just throwaway people. They don't make any difference at all, in any time.

Did she survive to adulthood? Or did she overdose in some gas station bathroom near Reseda when she was ten? Did I break every time law on the books merely to postpone her fate? I don't know—but I do know that I sleep better now.

The cuts healed. The memories faded. The rhythms of routine distract and comfort, thank God.

Three days ago, I got a call from a real estate agent in the Castro.

"I got your name from Jerry Raskin," she said.

"I'm not interested in downtime apartments," I replied.

She laughed a breathy laugh. "Oh, no. I only deal in realtime estate. And I've got two places I want to show you. The first is a beauty: a three-bedroom apartment in the Potrero Hill area. Used to be a two-family unit. You've got to see it to believe it."

I saw small, dirty handprints on glass.

"I work in the Financial District," I said, when I could find my voice. "Where's the other one?"

"Near the Embarcadero." She stared at me out of the screen as though she thought I was crazy. "But it's not nearly as big. And the one on Potrero Hill has a view."

"I don't need a view," I said, "I've seen enough."

Joe Haldeman
HOMECOMING

When asked to write a story for this anthology, Joe tells me he sat down and—
rather than a story—this superb poem
demanded to be written. Joe and his
wife, Gai, currently live four months of
the year in Cambridge, Massachusetts,
where Joe teaches creative writing at
MIT, and the rest of the year in Florida
where he watches the stars and creates
stories, novels, and poetry about them.
In 1975, his novel *The Forever War* was
awarded both the Hugo and Nebula
Awards and, in 1984, he received the
Rhysling Award for his poem "Saul's
Death".

There is much of Joe Haldeman in
"Homecoming." Like his character, Joe
has lived all over the United States—including Anchorage, Alaska—and was
part of the Vietnam War. Also like his
character, Joe writes,

I've been an amateur astronomer since I
was a little kid, and in a real way I do
consider the night sky my home. (Now

I have a stupefyingly expensive "portable observatory," a Questar, that fits under an airline seat and virtually guarantees cloudy weather at my destination.) I moved to Florida at the beginning of the Apollo days, to watch the rockets go up. Nice weather and no state income tax entered the equation too, but those of us who showed up at every launch sometimes referred to ourselves as "space junkies," so I thought I'd write a story about the champion of us all.

We expect home to be a place that is unchanging, yet, as seen in Karen Haber's story, home can be changed—by time, events, or by our trickster memories. For Joe Haldeman, however, home is the stars, a place that is always with us no matter where we live. Constant, the stars bring everything together and in a very real sense are home for us all. In this poem, Joe feelingly tells of a man's obsession, his life, death, his . . . homecoming.

HOMECOMING
Joe Haldeman

His hometown was space, and he never left:
The boy who watched the Russian beeper drift
through the twilight is the old man who camped
outside the Cape to watch huge dumbos lift
their loads of metal, oxygen, water . . .
Living in the back of an ancient Ford,
showing children, at night, the starry sky
through a telescope his young hands had built,
seventy years before.
       He died the week before
they came back from Mars. But every story
ends the same way. Some extra irony
for the Space Junky. His life had twists, turns,
wives, deaths, jail, a rock. One story that he loved:
The time he gave the army back exactly
what the army gave to him. "Bend over,
Westmoreland," he'd shout in his cracky voice,
and only other oldsters would get it.
In college in Florida, just because
he could watch the rockets; the Geminis
the Apollos—roaring, flaring, straining
around the Moon . . .
       but then he was drafted.
Sent to 'Nam months after Tet. Bad timing
more ways than one. The fighting was awful,

the worst yet—but worse than that, the timing!
The year! When men first stepped down on the Moon
he was not going to be on his belly
in the jungle. He was going to be *there*.

The Space Junky was a poker player
without peer. Saved his somewhat porky ass,
this skill, just knowing when to push your cards,
and when to pass—the others always stayed
in every hand; it was like harvesting
dandelions. Almost embarrassing,
the way the money piled up—play money,
"Military Payment Certificates,"
but a shylock in Saigon would give you
five for six, in crisp hundred-dollar bills.
Kept them in a Baggie in his flak vest,
those C-notes, until he came up for "Rest
and Recreation," a euphemism,
trading the jungle for a whore's soft bed
for a week. He went to Bangkok, where girls
were lined up on the tarmac as you left
the plane. He chose a fat and kindly one,
and explained what it was he had in mind.
She took him home for two bills, made some calls.
Gave him a rapid bit of sixty-nine
(not in the deal), and put him in a cab.
A man with a printing press signed him up
in the Canadian Merchant Marine.
Seven seasick weeks later he jumped ship
in San Francisco, and made his way down
to Florida, in July of sixty-nine,
    to stand with a million others and cheer
    the flame and roar, the boom that finally broke
    the sullen surly bonds of gravity.
    And then in a bar in Cape Kennedy,
    a large silent crowd held its beery breath,
    watching a flickering screen, where craters
    swelled and bobbed and disappeared in sprayed dust,

and Armstrong said "The Eagle has landed,"
(put *that* in your pipe and smoke it, Westy!)

.

and it was tears and back-slaps and free drinks,
but the next day the Space Junky was where
he'd be for the next seven years, the night
sky hidden by layers of federal
penitentiary.
      But iron bars do not
a prison make to a man whose mind is
elsewhere. He was just a little crazy
when he went in—and when he came out
    he was the Space Junky, and not much else.
    He never missed a launch. When the Shuttle
    first flew, he pushed that old Ford from the Cape
    to California, to watch a space ship—
    a real space ship—come in for a landing.
He watched the silent robot probes go by
every planet save one (well, you can't have
everything), and an asteroid, comets,
countless rings and moons.
      In the winter cold
    he watched ill-fated Challenger explode.
Less surprised than most, shook his head, dry-eyed;
he cried years later when it flew again.
    The Space Junky saw them lift the Station
    piece by piece; saw us go back to the Moon,
    from the back of a succession of Ford
    station wagons, always old and beat up.
    He made enough with cards to get along;
    lived pretty well, cooking off a Coleman,
    sipping cola, waiting for the next launch.
After some years, they all knew who he was,
engineers, P.I. men, the astronauts
themselves. It was a Russian cosmonaut
who bent over the rusty sands of Mars,
and picked up a pebble for the Space Junky.

79

They were all sad to find he hadn't lived.
   They put the rock in a box with his ashes.
   They put the box in low orbit, falling.
     It went around the Earth just seven times,
       and sketched one bright line in the starry sky
       that was his hometown
             where he'd not been born
     and where he never visited, alive,
                 but never left.

James Patrick Kelly
POGROM

If we reject the cold constancy of the
stars as our home, we must be prepared
for changes in our hometowns, sometimes
for the worse. Time can erode places and
people no matter how much we may dis-
like this.

Durham is home for Jim Kelly and the
setting of this gripping story. In "Pogrom," Jim paints Durham's future should
the problems that beset us all go unchal-
lenged. As Jim writes,

> If they give it any thought at all, most
> Americans think that overpopulation is
> someone else's problem: too many
> Chinese, *yeah*. Those poor Ethiopians.
> But those who worry about this problem
> are concerned not because there are
> simply too many people; they are con-
> cerned about the impact of a given pop-
> ulation on the planet. Each American,
> even the poorest of us, consumes more
> resources and creates more wastes than
> a family in Bangladesh. Because we are
> so profligate, there are too many of us.

It may be that the Woodstock Nation has not yet paid the full price for its six-packs and its Pampers and its air conditioning and its vacations at Disney. And it will not be the Third World which comes to collect—it will be our children's children's children. The concerned citizens of our future hometowns.

Jim is a full-time writer and lecturer. He is perhaps best known for his perceptive yet entertaining short fiction, which has appeared in *Isaac Asimov's Science Fiction Magazine* and in *The Magazine of Fantasy and Science Fiction;* in 1987 he received the *Asimov's* Reader's Poll Award for his "Prisoner of Chillon." His first novel, *Planet of Whispers,* was published in 1984 and, in 1985, he co-authored *Freedom Beach* with John Kessel, a surrealistic novel dealing with decadence and the importance of individuality. *Look into the Sun,* his second-and-a-half novel, was published in 1989.

In "Pogrom," Jim doesn't go home, he stays home and, with a keen eye, he looks about—and ahead—to warn us all.

$\mathcal{P}$OGROM
$\mathcal{J}$ames $\mathcal{P}$atrick $\mathcal{K}$elly

MATT WAS NAPPING when Ruth looked in on him. He had sprawled across the bedspread with his clothes on, shoes off. His right sock was worn to gauze at the heel. The pillow had crimped his gray hair at an odd angle. She had never seen him so peaceful before, but then she had never seen him asleep. She had the eye zoom for a close-up. His mouth was slack and sleep had softened the wrinkles on his brow. Ruth had always thought him handsome but forbidding, like the cliffs up in Crawford Notch. Now that he was dead to the world, she could almost imagine him smiling. She wondered if there was anything she could say to make him smile. He worried too much, that man. He blamed himself for things he had not done.

She increased the volume of her wall. His breathing was scratchy but regular. They had promised to watch out for one another; there were not many of them left in Durham. Matt had given Ruth a password for his homebrain when they had released him from the hospital. He seemed fine for now. She turned out the lights he had left on but there was nothing else she could see to do for him. She did not, however, close the electronic window which opened from her apartment on Church Hill onto his house across town. It had been years since she had heard the sounds of a man sleeping. If she shut her eyes it was almost as if he were next to her. His gentle snoring made a much more soothing background than the gurgle of the mountain cascade she usually kept on the wall. She was not really intruding, she told herself. He had asked her to check up on him.

Ruth picked up the mystery she had been reading but did not open it. She studied his image as if it might be a clue to something she had been trying to remember. Matt moaned and his fingers tightened around the cast that ran from his right hand to his elbow. She thought he must have started dreaming because his face closed like a door. He rolled toward the eye and she could see the bruise on his cheek, blood blue shading to brown.

"Someone is approaching," said Ruth's homebrain.

"The groceries?"

"The visitor is not on file."

"Show me," Ruth said.

The homebrain split Matt's window and gave her a view of the front porch. A girl she had never seen before, holding two brown paper Shop 'N Save sacks, pressed the doorbell with her elbow.

She was about thirteen and underfed, which meant she was probably a drood. She had long glitter hair and the peeling red skin of someone who did not pay enough attention to the UV forecasts. Her arms were decorated with blue stripes of warpaint. Or maybe they were tattoos. She was wearing sneakers, no socks, jeans and a T-shirt with a picture of Jesus Hitler that said FOR A NICKEL I WILL.

"Hello?" said Ruth. "Do I know you?"

"Your stuff." She shifted the sacks in her arms as if she were about to drop them.

"Where's Jud? He usually delivers for me."

"C'mon, lady! Not arguin' with no door." She kicked at it. "Hot as nukes out here."

"I don't know who you are."

"See these sacks? Costin' you twenty-one fifty-three."

"Please show me your ID."

"*Lady.*" She plunked the sacks down on the porch, brushed sweat from her face, pulled a card from her pocket and thrust it toward the eye in the door. The homebrain scanned and verified it. But it did not belong to her.

"That's Jud's card," said Ruth.

"He busy, you know, so he must give it to me." One of the sacks fell over. The girl nudged a box of dishwasher soap with her sneaker. "You want this or not?" She knelt, reached into the sack and tossed a bag of onion bagels, a bottle of liquid Pep, a frozen whitefish, two rolls of toilet paper, and bunch of carrots into a pile on the middle of the porch.

"Stop that!" Ruth imagined the neighbors were watching her groceries being abused. "Wait there."

The girl waggled a package of Daffy Toes at the eye. "Gimme cookie for my tip?"

Ruth hesitated before she pressed her thumb against the print-reader built into the steel door. What was the point in having all these security systems if she was going to open up for strangers? This was exactly the way people like her got hurt. But it *was* Ruth's order and the girl looked too frail to be any trouble.

She smelled of incense. A suspicion of sweet ropy smoke clung to her clothes and hair. Ruth was tempted to ask what it was, but realized that she probably did not want to know. The latest in teen depravity, no doubt. The smell reminded her of when she was in college back in the sixties and she used to burn incense to cover the stink of pot. Skinny black cylinders of charcoal that smeared her fingers and smelled like a Christmas tree on fire. Ruth followed the girl into the kitchen, trying to remember the last time she had smoked pot.

The girl set the bags out on the counter and then sighed with pleasure. "Been wantin' all day to get into some A/C." She surveyed the kitchen as if she were hoping for an invitation to dinner. "Name's Chaz." She waited in vain for Ruth to introduce herself. "So, want me to unpack?"

"No." Ruth took her wallet out of her purse.

"Lots of 'em ask me to. They too old, or too lazy—hey, real costin' *wine*." She pulled a Medoc from the rack mounted under the china cabinet and ran her finger along the stubby shoulder. "In glass bottles. You rich or what?"

Ruth held out her cash card but Chaz ignored it.

"Bet you think I lie. You 'fraid I come here to do your bones?" She hefted the bottle of Bordeaux by the neck, like a club.

Alarmed, Ruth clutched at her chest and squeezed the security pager that hung on a silver chain under her blouse. "Put that down."

The eye on the kitchen ceiling started broadcasting live to the private cops she subscribed to. Last time they had taken twenty minutes to come.

"Don't worry." Chaz grinned. "I deliver plenty stuff before. In Portsmouth. Then we got move to Durham. Nice town you got here." She set the bottle back on the counter. "But you can't hear nothin' I say, right? You scared 'cause kids hate you but I ain't breaking your head, am I? Not today, anyway. Just wanna earn my nickel, lady."

"I'm trying to pay you." Ruth pushed the card at her.

She took it. "Place full of costin' stuff like this." She shook her head in wonder at Ruth's wealth. "You lucky, you know." She rubbed the card against the port of Jud Gazzara's Shop 'N Save ID to deduct twenty-one dollars and fifty-three cents. "Yeah, this is great, compare to dorms. You ever seen dorms inside?"

"No."

"You oughta. Compare to dorms, this is heaven." Chaz handed the card back. "No, better than heaven 'cause you can buy this but you must die to get heaven. Gimme my cookie?" she said.

"Take it and leave."

Chaz paused on the way out and peeked into the living room. "This walter what you do for fun, lady?" Matt was still asleep on the wall. "Jeez, you pigs good as dead already."

"Would you please go?"

"Wake up, walter!" she yelled at the screen. *"Hustle or die!"*

"Huh!" Matt jerked as if he had been shot. "What?" He curled into a ball, protecting his face with the cast.

"Give nasty, you get nasty." Chaz winked at Ruth. "See you next week, lady."

"Greta, is that you?"

Ruth could hear Matt calling to his dead wife as she shouldered the door shut. She braced her back against it until she felt the homebrain click the bolts into place.

"Greta?"

"It's me," she called. "Ruth." She squeezed the security pager again to call the private cops off. At least she could avoid the charge for a house call. Her heart hammered against her chest.

"Ruth?"

She knew the girl was out there laughing at her. It made Ruth angry, the way these kids made a game of terrorizing people. "Turn your wall on, Matt." It was not fair; she was no pig.

By the time Ruth got into the living room, Matt was sitting on the edge of his bed. He seemed dazed, as if he had woken up to find himself still in the nightmare.

"You asked me to check in on you," she said. "Remember? Sorry if I disturbed you." She decided not to tell him—or anyone—about Chaz. Nothing bad happened, really. So the world was full of ignorant little bigots, so what? She could hardly report a case of rudeness to the Durham cops; they thought people like her complained too much as it was. "Did you have a nice nap?" Ruth was not admitting to anyone that she was afraid of trash like Chaz.

"I was having a dream about Greta," said Matt. "She gave me a birthday cake on a train. We were going to some city, New York or Boston. Then she wanted to get off but I hadn't finished the cake. It was big as a suitcase."

Ruth had never understood why people wanted to tell her their dreams. Most of the ones she had heard were dumb. She could not help but be embarrassed when otherwise reasonable adults prattled on about their nighttime lunacies. "How are you feeling?" She nestled into her favorite corner of the couch. "Do you need anything?"

"What was funny was that Greta wouldn't help me." He had not noticed how he was annoying her. "I mean, I told her to have some cake but she wouldn't. She screamed at me to hurry up or I'd die. Then I woke up."

What had Chaz called him? A walter. Ruth had never heard that one before. "Sorry," she said. "I really didn't mean to intrude. I should let you get back to sleep."

"No, don't go." He slid his feet into the slippers next to the bed. "I'd like some company. I just lay down because there was nothing else to do." He grunted as he stood, then glanced in the mirror and combed hair back over his bald spot with his fingers. "See, I'm up."

He turned away and waved for her to follow. The eye tracked along the ceiling after him as he hobbled down the hall to his office, a dark shabby room decorated with books and diplomas. He lived in only three rooms: office, bedroom and kitchen. The rest of his house was closed down.

"I'm pretty useless these days." He eased behind the antique steel desk he had brought home from his office when they closed the university. "No typing with this cast on. Not for six, maybe seven weeks." He picked up a manuscript, read the title, dropped it back on a six-inch stack next to the computer. "Nothing to do."

Next he would get melancholy, if she let him. "So dictate."

"I'm too old to think anymore without my fingers on a keyboard and a screen to remind me what I just wrote." He snorted in disgust. "But you didn't call to hear me complain. You've been so good, Ruth. To pay so much attention and everything. I don't know why you do it."

"Must be your sunny personality, Matt." Ruth hated the way he had been acting since they released him from the hospital. So predictable. So sad. She did not know how to make him himself again. "I'm cooking my mom's famous gefilte fish. Maybe I'll bring some over later? And a bottle of wine?"

"That's sweet, but no. No, you know how upset you get when you go out." He grinned. "You just stay safe where you are."

"This is my town, too. And yours. I've lived here thirty-two years. I'm not about to let them take it away from me now."

"We lost it long ago, Ruth. Maybe it's time we acknowledged that."

"Really? Can I stop paying property tax?"

"You know, I understand the way they feel." He tapped the keyboard at random with his good hand. "The world's a mess and it's not their fault. They watch their walls and they see all the problems and they need someone to blame. So they call us pigs and we call them droods. Much simpler that way."

"So what are you going to do? Send them a thank-you note for crippling you? Breaking your arm? Wake up and listen to yourself, Matt. You shouldn't have to hide in your house like a criminal. You didn't do anything."

"Yes, that's it exactly. I didn't do anything. Maybe it's time."

"Don't start *that* again! You're a teacher, you worked hard." Ruth grabbed a pillow she had embroidered. She wanted to hurl it right through the wall and knock some sense into the foolish old man. "God, I don't know why I bother." Instead she hugged it to her chest. "Sometimes you make me mad, Matt. I mean really angry."

"I'm sorry, Ruth. I'm just in one of my moods. Maybe I should call you back when I'm better company?"

"All right," she said without enthusiasm. "I'll talk to you later then."

"Don't give up on me, Ruth."

She wiped him off the wall. He was replaced by Silver Cascade Brook up in Crawford Notch. She had reprocessed the loop from video she had shot years ago, before she had had to stop traveling. Water burbled, leaves rustled, birds sang. "Chirp, chirp," she said sourly and zapped it. Afloat on the Oeschinensee in the Alps. *Zap.* Coral gardens off the Caribbean coast of St. Lucia. *Zap.* Exotic birds of the Everglades. *Zap.* She flipped restlessly through her favorite vacations; nothing pleased her. Finally she settled on a vista of Mill Pond across the street. The town swans cut slow V's across the placid surface. In the old days, when she used to sit on the porch, she could hear frogs in the summertime. She was tempted to drag her rocker out there right now. Then she would call Matt, just to show him it could still be done.

Instead she went into the kitchen to unpack the groceries. She put the dishwasher soap under the sink and the cookies in the bread drawer. Matt was a crotchety old man, ridden with guilt, but he and she were just about the last ones left. She picked up the whitefish, opened the freezer, then changed her mind. When was the last time she had seen Margie or Stanley What's-His-Name, who lived just two doors down? Ruth closed the door again, stripped the shrinkwrap from the fish and popped it into the microwave to defrost. If she were afraid to show him, Matt would end up like all the others. He would stop calling or move or die and then Ruth would be a stranger in her own hometown. When the whitefish thawed she whacked off the head, skinned and boned it. She put the head, skin and bones in a pot, covered them with water, cut in some carrots and onion and set it on the stove to boil. She was not going to let anyone make her a prisoner in her own kitchen. She ground the cleaned fish and some onions together, then beat in matzo meal, water and a cup of ovobinder. Her mom's recipe called for eggs but uncontaminated eggs were hard to find. She formed the fish mixture into balls and bravely dropped them into the boiling stock. Ruth was going visiting and no one was going to stop her.

． ． ．

After she called the minibus, she packed the cooled gefilte fish into one tupperware, poured the lukewarm sauce into another and tucked them both into her tote bag beside the Medoc. Then she reached to the cabinet above the refrigerator, took down her blow-cuffs and velcroed one to each wrist. In the bedroom she opened the top drawer of her dresser and rooted through the underwear until she found two flat clips of riot gas, two inches by three. The slogan on the side read: "With Knockdown they *go* down and *stay* down." The clips hissed as she fitted them into the cuffs. Outside, a minibus pulled into the parking lot of the Church Hill Apartments and honked.

"Bug it!" There must have been one in the neighborhood; service was never this prompt. She pulled on a baggy long-sleeved shirtwaist to hide the cuffs and grabbed her tote.

As soon as Ruth opened the front door, she realized she had forgotten to put sunblock on. Too late now. The light needled her unprotected skin as she hurried down the walk. There was one other rider on the mini, a leathery man in a stiff brown suit. He perched at the edge of his seat with an aluminum briefcase between his legs. The man glanced at her and then went back to studying the gum spots on the floor. The carbrain asked where she was going.

"Fourteen Hampshire Road." Ruth brushed her cash card across its port.

"The fare is $1.35 including the senior citizen discount," said the carbrain. "Please take your seat."

She picked a spot on the bench across from the door. The air blowing out of the vents was hot, which was why all the windows were open. She brushed the hair out of her eyes as the mini rumbled around Mill Pond and onto Oyster River Road.

The mini was strewn with debris: wrappers, squashed beer boxes, dirty receipts. Someone had left a paper bag on the bench next to her. Just more garbage, she thought—until it jumped. It was a muddy Shop 'N Save sack with the top crumpled down to form a seal. As she watched, it moved again.

She knew better than to talk to people on the minibus, but Ruth could not help herself. "Is this yours?"

The man's expression hardened to cement. He shook his head

and then touched the eye clipped to the neckband of his shirt and started recording her.

"Sorry." She scooted down the bench and opened the bag. A bullfrog the size of her fist rose up on its hind leg, scrabbled weakly toward her and then sank back. At first she thought it was a toy with a run-down battery. Then she realized that some brain-dead kid had probably caught it down at the pond and then left it behind. Although she had not seen a frog up close in years, she thought this one looked wrong somehow. Dried out. They breathed through their skins, didn't they? She considered getting off the mini and taking it back to the water herself. But then she would be on foot in the open, an easy target. Ruth felt sorry for the poor thing, yes, but she was not risking her life for a frog. She closed the bag so she would not have to watch it suffer.

The mini stopped at an apartment on Mill Road and honked. When no one came out it continued toward the center of town, passed another minibus going in the opposite direction and then pulled into the crumbling lot in front of the Shop 'N Save plaza. There were about a dozen bicycles in the racks next to the store and four electric cars parked out front, their skinny fiberglass bodies blanching in the afternoon sun. A delivery man was unloading beer boxes from a truck onto a dolly. The mini pulled up behind the truck and shut itself off. The door opened and the clock above it started a countdown: 10:00 . . . 09:59 . . . 09:58. The man with the aluminum suitcase got off, strode down the plaza and knocked at the door of what had once been the hardware store. He watched Ruth watching him until the door opened and he went in.

The empty lot shimmered like a blacktopped desert and the heat of the day closed around her. To escape it, she tried filling the spaces with ghost cars: Fords and Chryslers and Toyotas. She imagined there was no place to park, just like when they still pumped gas, before they closed the university. 06:22 . . . 06:21 . . . 06:20. But the sun was stronger than her memory. It was the sun, the goddamned sun that was driving the world crazy. She could even hear it: the mini's metal roof clicked in its harsh light like a bomb. Who could think in heat like this?

The bag twitched again and Ruth realized she could get water from the store and pour it over the frog. She glanced at the clock. 02:13 . . . 02:12 . . . Too late now.

91

The carbrain honked and started the engine when the clock reached 00:30. Three kids trudged out of the store. Two were lugging sacks filled with groceries; the third was Chaz, who was empty-handed. Ruth shifted her tote bag onto her lap, got a firm grip on the handle and tried to make herself as small as possible.

"Destination, please?" said the carbrain.

"One Simons." A fat kid clumped up the stepwell and saw her. "Someone on already." He brushed his card across the pay port. "Lady, where you goin', lady?"

Ruth fixed her gaze on the buttons of his blue-striped Shop 'N Save shirt; one had come undone. She avoided eye contact so he would not see how tense she was. She said nothing.

The second one bumped into the fat kid. "Move, sweatlips!" He was wearing the uniform shirt tucked into red shorts. He had shaved legs. She did not look at his face either.

"Please take your seats," said the carbrain. "Current stops are 14 Hampshire Road and 1 Simons Lane. Destination, please?"

"Stoke Hall," said Chaz.

"Hey, Hampshire's the wrong way, lady. Get off, would ya?"

"Yeah, make yourself useful for a change." Red Shorts plopped his groceries onto the bench opposite Ruth and sprawled next to them. Ruth said nothing; she saw Chaz paying the carbrain.

"Wanna throw her off?"

Ruth clenched her fists and touched the triggers of her cuffs.

"Just leave her and stretch the ride." Chaz settled beside the others. " 'Less you *wanna* get back to work."

The fat kid grunted and the logic of sloth carried the day. Ruth eased off the triggers as the mini jolted through the potholes in the lot and turned back onto Mill Road. The boys started joking about a war they had seen on the wall. Even though they seemed to have forgotten her, the side of Ruth's neck prickled as if someone were still staring. When she finally dared peek, she saw Chaz grinning slyly at her, like she expected a tip. It made Ruth angry. She wanted to slap the girl.

They looped around downtown past the post office, St. Thomas More Church and the droods' mall. The mall was actually a flea market which had accreted over the years in the parking lot off Pette Brook Lane: salvaged lumber and old car parts and plastic sheeting over chicken wire had been cobbled together to make about thirty stalls. It was where people who lived in the dorms went. When the hawkers saw the mini coming, they swarmed into the street to slow it down. Ruth saw teens waving hand-lettered signs advertising rugs, government surplus cheese, bicycles, plumbing supplies stripped from abandoned houses, cookies, obsolete computers. A man in a tank top wearing at least twenty watches on each arm gestured frantically at her to get off the mini. They said you could also buy drugs and meat and guns at the mall, and what they did not have, they could steal to order. Ruth, of course, had never gone there herself but she had heard all about it. Everyone had. The cops raided the mall regularly but no one dared close it down for good.

The fat kid reached across the aisle and snatched the abandoned paper sack. "This yours lady?" He jiggled it then unrolled the top. "Oh, no." He took the frog out, holding it by the legs so that its stomach bulged at the sides. "Gonna kill the slime did this."

"Sweet," said Red Shorts. "Someone left us a present."

"It's suffocatin'." The fat kid stood, swayed against the momentum of the mini and lurched toward Ruth. "They need water to breathe, same as we need air." When he thrust it at her, the frog's eyes bulged as if they might pop. "And you just sit here, doin' nothing." Rage twisted his face.

"I—I didn't know," said Ruth. The frog was so close that she thought he meant to shove it down her throat. "I swear, I never looked inside."

"So it's dyin'," said Red Shorts. "So let's stomp it. Come on, put it out of misery." He winked at Chaz. "Grandma here wants to see guts squirt out its mouth."

"I'll do your bones, you touch this frog." The fat kid stormed down the aisle to the door. "Stop here," he said. "Let me out."

The mini pulled over. Red Shorts called to him. "Hey, sweatlips, who's gonna help me deliver groceries?"

"Piss off." Ruth could not tell whether he was cursing Red Shorts, her or the world in general.

The door opened. The fat kid got off, cut in front of the mini and headed across town toward Mill Pond. Red Shorts turned to Chaz. "Likes frogs." He was still smirking as they drove off. "Thinks he's a green."

She was not amused. "You leave it for him to find?"

"Maybe."

The mini had by now entered the old UNH campus. On-line university had killed most residential colleges; the climate shift had triggered the depression which had finished the rest. But the buildings had not stood empty for long. People lost jobs, then houses; when they got hungry enough, they came looking for help. The campuses were converted into emergency refugee centers for families with dependent children. Eight years later, temporary housing had become permanent droodtowns. Nobody knew why the refugees were called droods. Some said the word came from the now famous song, others claimed that Drood was a real person. The mini passed several of the smaller dorms and then turned off Main Street onto Garrison Avenue. Ahead to the left was Stoke Hall.

Nine stories tall, Stoke was the biggest dorm on campus. When Ruth had gone to UNH, it had housed about sixteen hundred students. She had heard that there were at least four thousand droods there now, most of them kids, almost all of them under thirty. Stoke was a Y-shaped brick monster; two huge jaws gaped at the street. Its foundation was decorated with trash dropped from windows. The packed-dirt basketball court, dug into the sloping front courtyard, was empty. The players loitered in the middle of the street, watching a wrecker hitch a tow to a stalled water truck. The mini slowed to squeeze by and Chaz slid onto the bench beside Ruth.

"Wanna get off and look?" She nodded at the dorm.

"Huh?" Red Shorts had a mouth full of celery he had stolen from one of the bags. "Talkin' to me?"

"Up there." As she leaned over to point at the upper floors, Chaz actually brushed against Ruth. "Two down, three left. Where I live."

The girl's sweaty skin caught at the fabric of Ruth's sleeve. Ruth did not like being touched. Over the years she had gotten used to meeting people electronically, through the walls. Those few she did choose to see were the kind of people who bathed and wore clean shirts. People who took care of themselves. Chaz was so close that Ruth felt sick. It was as if the girl's smoky stink were curdling in the back of her throat. She needed to get away but there was nowhere to go. She fought the impulse to blow Chaz a faceful of Knockdown, because then she would have to gas Red Shorts too.

94

And what if one of them managed to call for help? She imagined the mob of basketball players stopping the mini and pulling her off. She would be lucky if all they did was beat her the way they had beaten Matt. More likely she would be raped, killed—they were animals, she could *smell* them.

"C'mon," said Chaz. "You show your place. I show mine."

Ruth's voice caught in her throat like a bone. The mini cleared the water truck and pulled up in front of the dorm. "Stoke Hall," said the carbrain. It opened the door.

"What you say, lady?" Chaz stood. "Won't hurt."

"Much." Red Shorts snickered.

"You shut up," said Chaz.

Ruth stared at the words on her T-shirt: FOR A NICKEL I WILL. She felt for the triggers and shook her head.

"How come I gotta play lick-ass?" Chaz squatted so that her face was level with Ruth's; she forced eye contact. "Just wanna talk." The girl feigned sincerity so well that Ruth wavered momentarily.

"Yeah," said Red Shorts, "like 'bout how you pigs ate the world."

Ruth started to shake. "Leave me alone." It was all happening too fast.

"Stoke Hall," repeated the carbrain.

"Okay, okay." Chaz rose up, disgusted. "So forget it. You don't gotta say nothing to droods. You happy, you rich, so hell with me." She turned and walked away.

Ruth had not expected Chaz to be wounded and suddenly she was furious with the foolish girl. Her invitation was a bad joke. A woman like Ruth could not take three steps into that place before someone would hit her over the head and drag her into a room. This drood wanted to make friends with her after everything that had happened? It was too late, way too late.

Chaz was already in the stepwell when Red Shorts leaned forward. "You old bitch pig." Then he spat at Ruth and the gob stuck to her chin and he laughed and without thinking she thrust her fist at him and emptied a clip of Knockdown into his face.

He screamed and lurched backward against the grocery sacks, which tipped off the bench and spilled. He bounced and pitched facedown on the floor, thrashing in the litter of noodle-soup bulbs and bright packages of candy. Ruth had never used riot gas before and she was stunned at its potency. Truth in advertising, she thought, and almost laughed out loud. Chaz came down the aisle.

"Get off." Ruth raised her other fist. "Get the hell off. *Now!*"

Chaz backed away, still gaping at the boy, whose spasms had subsided to twitching. Then she clattered down the steps and ran up the street toward the basketball players. Ruth was sure at that moment she was doomed, but the carbrain closed the door and the mini pulled away from the curb and she realized that she had gotten away with it. She did laugh then; the sound seemed to come to her from a great distance.

Suddenly she was shivering in the afternoon heat. She had to do something so she grabbed Red Shorts by the shoulders and muscled him back onto a bench. She had not meant to hurt anyone. It was an accident, not her fault. She felt better as she picked up the spilled groceries, repacked them and arranged the sacks neatly beside him. He did not look so bad, she thought. He was napping; it would not be the first time someone had fallen asleep on the minibus. She retrieved an apple from under the bench.

She got so involved pretending that nothing was wrong that she was surprised when the mini stopped.

"Fourteen Hampshire," said the carbrain.

Ruth regarded her victim one last time. Since she had tried her best to put things back the way they were supposed to be, she decided to forgive herself. She grabbed her tote bag, stepped off and hurried to the front door of Matt's decaying colonial. By the time the mini rumbled off, she had pushed the unpleasantness from her mind. She owed it to him to be cheerful.

Ruth had not been out to Matt's house since last fall; usually he visited her. It was worse then she remembered. He could not keep the place up on his pension. Paint had chipped off the shingles, exposing gray wood. Some of them had curled in the sun. A rain gutter was pulling away from the roof. Poor Matt could not afford to stay, but he could not afford to sell either. No one was buying real estate in Durham. She heard him unlocking and made herself smile.

"*Ruth!* I thought I told you to stay home."

"Mr. Watson? Mr. Matthew Watson of 14 Hampshire Road?" She consulted an imaginary clipboard. "Are you the gentleman who ordered the surprise party?"

"I can't believe you did this." He tugged her inside and shut the door. "Do you have any idea how dangerous it is out there?"

She shrugged. "So, are you glad to see me?" She put down her tote and opened her arms to him.

"Yes, of course, but . . ." He leaned forward and gave her a stony peck on the cheek. "This is serious, Ruth."

"That's right. I seriously missed you."

"Don't make jokes. You don't understand these people. You could've been hurt." He softened then and hugged her. She stayed in his embrace longer than he wanted—she could tell—but that was all right. His arms shut the world out; his strength stopped time. Nothing had happened, nothing could happen. She had not realized how lonesome she had been. She did not even mind his cast jabbing her.

"Are you okay, Ruth?" he murmured. "Is everything all right?"

"Fine." Eventually she had to let him go. "Fine."

"It's good to see you," he said, and gave her an embarrassed smile. "Even if you are crazy. Come into the kitchen."

Matt poured the Medoc into coffee cups and they toasted their friendship. "Here's to twenty-six years." Actually she had been friends with Greta before she knew Matt. Ruth set the tupperware on the counter. "What should I serve the fish on?" She opened the china cabinet and frowned. Matt was such a typical bachelor: he had none of the right dishes.

"I'm glad you came over," he said. "I've been wanting to talk to you. I suppose I could tell you through the wall but—"

"Tell me?" She dusted a cracked bowl with the edge of her sleeve.

He ran his finger around the rim of the cup and shrugged uncomfortably. "You know how lonely I've been since the—since I broke my hip. I think that's my biggest problem. I can't go out anymore and I can't live here by myself."

For a few thrilling seconds, Ruth misunderstood. "Oh?" She thought he was going to ask her to live with him. It was something she had often fantasized about.

"Anyway, I've been talking to some people at Human Services and I've decided to take in some boarders."

"Boarders?" She still did not understand. "Droods?"

97

"Refugees. I know how you feel but they're people just like us and the state will pay me to house them. I have more room than I need and I can use the money."

Her hands felt numb. "I don't believe this. Really, Matt, haven't you learned anything?" She had to put the bowl down before she dropped it. "You go to the dorms to tutor and they beat you up, crippled you. So now you bring the animals into your house?"

"They're not animals. I know several families who would jump at the chance to leave the dorms. Kids, Ruth. Babies."

"Look, if it's only money, let me help. Please."

"No, that's not it. You said something this morning. I'm a teacher all right, except I have no one to teach. That's why I feel so useless. I need to—"

A window shattered in the bedroom.

"What was that?" Matt bolted from his chair, knocking his wine over.

"There are many people on the street," announced the home-brain. "They are destroying property."

Ruth heard several angry *thwocks* against the side of the house and then more glass broke. She felt as if a shard had lodged in her chest. Someone outside was shouting. Wine pooled on the floor like blood.

"Call the police." Matt could not afford private security.

"The line is busy."

"Keep trying!"

He limped to the bedroom, the only room with a window wall; Ruth followed. There was a stone the size of a heart on the bed, glass scattered across the rug.

"Show," said Matt.

The wall revealed a mob of at least a hundred droods. Basketball players, hawkers from the mall, kids from Stoke. And Chaz. Ruth was squeezing her security pager so hard that her hand hurt.

"Hey, walter, send the bitch out!"

She had been so stupid. Of course Chaz had heard the carbrain repeat Matt's address.

"Boomers. *Fat stinkin' oldies.*"

She had never understood why they were all so eager to hate people like her and Matt. It was not fair to punish an entire generation.

"Burn 'em. Send the pigs to hell!"

The politicians were to blame, the corporations. They were the ones responsible. It was not her fault; she was just one person. "Go ahead, Matt, teach them about us." Ruth pressed herself into the corner of the bedroom. "Maybe we should invite them in for a nice glass of wine?"

"What is this, Ruth?" Matt grabbed her by the shoulders and shook her. "What did you do?"

She shook her head. "Nothing," she said.

Edward Bryant
THE GREAT STEAM BISON OF CYCAD CENTER

Of all the contributors to *Fires of the Past*, Ed Bryant had the most difficult time coming up with a story, but not for lack of ideas. Just the opposite. Ed was born in New York State, grew up in Wyoming, has traveled extensively, now lives in Colorado and, when he started writing this tale, had just returned from Las Vegas which "was full of ideas." It is this ability to see a story in every place, event, object, or person that caused him difficulty but which makes Ed's stories the rich and entertaining reading that has twice earned him the Nebula Award (in 1978 for his short story "Stone" and for his story "giANTS" in 1979). In 1990, his "A Sad Last Love at the Diner of the Damned" was nominated for a Bram Stoker Award.

As do many of Ed's stories, "The Great Steam Bison of Cycad Center" mingles a variety of elements. Set in Wyoming, Ed looks at his hometown in the future, but, unlike the bleak changes of Jim Kelly's "future" hometown, Ed's hometown has changed rather . . . bizarrely. Dinosaurs now roam the town, albeit robotic dinosaurs, and murder most foul has been committed. Yet these are merely superficial changes; the most dramatic change has come to Ben Goreham, the narrator. Sometimes our hometowns are not changed by external events, but our *perception* of our home is changed. In "The Great Steam Bison of Cycad Center," Ben Goreham is trying to solve a mystery and, at the same time, seeking to adjust to himself, to life, to his hometown, and to the tragedy that has altered them all for him forever.

THE GREAT STEAM BISON OF CYCAD CENTER

Edward Bryant

IT FIGURED THAT the stego would pick Friday night to take a little nip out of Mr. Nakashima. He was a suit—some high mucky-muck from Dai-su DinoLand.

I wasn't around when the incident happened. I didn't even find out until much later. Wasn't my fault. Who could know that a robosaur would go wonky right during the high school senior class performance of *Titus Deinonychus*, an original production written by Arnie Palenque, the valedictorian? The beeper alert came in right as I was watching the prettiest of the deinonychosaurs leaping and pirouetting around the stage in pain. Her forelegs had been amputated and long, crimson, silk scarves streamed back in emulation of spurting blood. It was damned impressive. The crowd went wild.

Then I felt the vibration against my hip that said a message was coming in. I'd cut off the audible signal out of deference to the senior class.

With regret I looked back appreciatively at the dancing deino. Then I got up and mumbled apologies as I tromped on people's toes getting to the aisle.

I used the pay phone in the high school lobby, outside the principal's office. Took me a while to find a couple dimes; the rest of my change had gone into the Coke machine back at intermission.

Betty Kennedy was on duty down at the communications desk that handles both the police and the sheriff's calls. I identified myself.

"Oh, hi, Ben. Chief Denham thought you ought to know like really asap."

"Asap?" She pronounced it as one word.

"Soon as possible, abbreviation, you know?"

"What's the problem, Betty?" I could hear the music from inside the gym. Plenty of brass and drums. I felt the urge to set the phone down gently, let the receiver dangle at the end of the wrapped cord, and just tiptoe back into the play.

"Problem?"

"You keyed my beeper, remember?"

"Oh." There was a momentary silence. "Just a sec." She went off the line a second, then came back. "Sorry, Ben. The chief again. Anyhow, he wants you to come in right away."

"How come?" I said patiently.

"He wants to talk to you himself, but basically it's 'cause a dinosaur tried to eat that Mr. Nakashima, you know? The guy from the big park in Tokyo."

"Tried to *eat* him?" I said. "That's impossible."

"Come on down," said Betty. "Sooner the better."

It didn't take long to drive over to the station. After all, this is Cycad Center, and a town of four thousand people just isn't that big. I found my Cherokee in the crowded high school lot and got to my destination inside of five minutes. Shoot, I could have walked, but I'm getting lazy. That laziness shows up around my middle.

Karl Denham was waiting for me in his office, along with one very excited Asian fellow being attended to by Doc Fancher. I recognized Mr. Nakashima from the Chamber lunch I'd been to back on Monday. Karl looked grim. Mr. Nakashima didn't look too much the worse for wear other than having the right arm of his tailored Hong Kong (I was guessing) jacket torn clean off. There was some blood spattered on his shirt. Doc Fancher was bandaging up his shoulder.

"Evening, Ben," said our chief of police. Fancher nodded to me and went back to his ministrations.

"How's it going?" I said.

Mr. Nakashima seemed visibly to get a grip on himself. "One of your robosaurs attempted this evening to devour me." There was a real tone of indignation there, and I supposed I couldn't blame him, depending on what had really happened.

I glanced back to Doc Fancher. "He'll be okay," said the doctor. "Got some superficial abrasions and a few bruises." He fingered the fabric of the jacket sleeve. "Tore hell out of this, though. Great material."

"I hear it was a stego," I said to Karl. "Betty get that right?"

The chief nodded. "Mr. Nakashima says so. Happened in the gardens east of the courthouse. Tracks around him tend to confirm. I got Barney and Lil out checking it."

Barney and Lil were the two night patrol officers. "I don't get it," I said. "The stegos are set in a pattern at night to maintain the grass down at City Park. Besides, they're hardwired to have peaceful natures as purely vegetarians."

Karl Denham shrugged. "I don't know the technical side of it. But I *do* know that one of our guests near got his arm ripped off tonight. Maybe its little lizard brain went and blew a fuse."

"Robosaurs don't have fuses," I said.

"It tried to eat me," said Mr. Nakashima again. "My employers will not be pleased."

The chief and I exchanged looks. "There's goes a billion or so in expansion investment," said Doc Fancher. He taped the loose end of the bandage in place. "There you go." He clapped Mr. Nakashima on the back. "Don't take any wooden tyrannosaurs."

The Japanese man flexed his arm gingerly, the slashed sleeve hanging down forlornly, and looked at Fancher like the doc was crazy. He turned back toward Karl. "What are you going to do about this outrage?"

"At least you don't have to get rabies shots," said the chief.

"I gave him tetanus," said Fancher.

"What are you going to do?"

"Well," said Karl slowly. "We're trying to track the stego that attacked you. If we find it," he said seriously, "we will shoot it where it stands."

Mr. Nakashima looked bewildered. "Why not just immobilize it so you can examine its software?"

"That's what I meant." Karl cracked a smile my way. "How's Cycad's liability situation?"

"Fine," I said. "We'll talk about that later." He knew as well as

I that we shouldn't be talking insurance in front of someone who had just lost an expensive outfit, a night's sleep, and a little skin to a robotic stegosaurus.

"You want a ride back to your motel?" said Karl to Mr. Nakashima. "I can send you with someone. We'll worry about the formal statement in the morning."

The Japanese man nodded. "Thank you very much. That will be fine." He followed Karl toward the office door, where he turned and looked back at me. "You are the attorney, yes?"

I nodded. "The town's lawyer," I said. "I ran for public office last November and, for my sins, I was elected."

"Then you know how serious could be the repercussions of what has happened this evening."

"I'm afraid so," I answered. "Yes."

He nodded, apparently satisfied. "My employers are conservative men. We are all quite impressed with your Cycad Center and your Paleo State Park. I want nothing to happen to adversely affect our potential relationship."

"Me either," I said.

"We shall pursue this in the morning," said Mr. Nakashima. He bowed slightly to me, nodded to Doc Fancher, and closed the door after himself.

"A *billion*?" I said to the doc.

"It's the New West," he answered. "More cash than you could pack nuggets on a stagecoach."

I wondered if he was kidding. That wasn't what his face said.

I've lived in or near Cycad Center all my life; in fact, since long before it was Cycad Center. I moved to Wyoming when I was six months old. Obviously I had no conscious effect on all that. I was born in White Plains, New York, but all I know about the place that is my hometown by a mere technicality is that it was the first American city to institute busing for the purpose of school integration.

As I say, we moved, my parents and I. We settled on a cattle ranch at the foot of the Sybille Canyon, nearly thirty miles from the nearest town. We had no electricity, no running water, no power implements. We used kerosene lanterns after dark, drew our own water from a well with a hand-pump, trudged across the backyard to the outhouse, and had a team of huge horses to pull the mower and hay rake. This was not at the turn of the nineteenth century. This was right after World War II.

My parents and I would always be strangers here. The ranch on which we lived was the Jones Ranch, and that's how it would remain for all the years we were there. Our name was not Jones. My mother kept a little of her New York accent. My father and I had none. My father was a tinkerer, an inventor who had been trained as an engineer during the Great Depression when he went to the University of Chicago for a term, would drop out to work on an ore boat on Lake Superior, then go back to school and so on. He never got his degree. He ended up a rancher because his wife's father offered investment money to buy a ranch in Wyoming. My grandfather, though a New York lawyer, had always loved Zane Grey novels. He wanted to live on a western ranch. He got that wish. He also died out here, but happy.

Wyoming was a not altogether hospitable land. It was bad enough that we were strangers. I remember the Shamrock Station up on the blacktop about two miles from our house. There were two outdoor spigots folks used for drinking water the hot months of the summer. One was unmarked. The other had a sign hung from it that said simply, "Mexicans." I never forgot that.

When I was still in grade school, our ranch went under and my family had to move into town where my dad got a job with the State Highway Department. He found himself doing an engineer's job at less pay since he didn't have his degree. All he had to offer was ability. And expertise. That came in handy when the town began its transmutation in the eighties.

By that time, I had my law degree and was in general practice in my hometown. I had my own home outside of town, a wife, and two little daughters. I also had two brothers, one of whom was still here, working for the local school system. The other brother wanted to be an artist. He went away to New York and now we only hear from him every other year or so. I don't know what-all he's doing.

Life was comfortable, but I guess a little boring, when the change came. The change was because of the energy boom that first exalted, then devastated the West. At first nothing much impacted (we quickly learned to use those new terms) the sleepy little town of Goshen. Then a private consortium built the huge, multi-gigawatt,

106

coal-fired generating plant over in Stubblefield, fifty or sixty miles to the west. After three years of construction, the plant went online and a dozen huge steam plumes rose up toward heaven. But only so far. The prevailing winds bent those plumes of cooling vapor down toward the earth. They made contact with the ground again right here in Goshen.

That's the long of it. The short is that the climate changed. This had been arid plains. It quickly became a vest-pocket climate that you couldn't hardly tell from the way all this countryside had been during the Cretaceous. And so that's when people had the big idea. The town needed money badly. I guess someone here had been up to that dinosaur theme park outside Calgary. If the Canucks could do it, why couldn't we, and better?

We did. Nestled in this basin at the end of a gently sloping valley, the town got some state and federal help, along with selling more bonds than you might believe to the locals. We all bought into our mutual future.

Paleo State Park was born. I don't remember why it ended up called that. Probably because Cretaceous State Park was too hard to spell. At any rate, we did everything from pass municipal ordinances saying people here could no longer cultivate flowering plants, to getting some laid-off Disney people to build us some dinosaurs. At first we just had replicas that stood in place and roared a little when tourists approached. But then, as the money started to generate and we could roll things over, we could afford more elaborate attractions. It didn't take all that long before we started putting in the programmed robosaurs that roamed the whole town. The town was the park and the park was the town, and we all made out like bandits.

That's when the Japanese fellow came to town representing moneyed interests back home who were interested in buying in, expanding, and upgrading what we had.

I don't know. Mr. Nakashima might have had a good shot until that disastrous Friday night when the stego ruined his expensive suit and gave him the scare of a lifetime.

But Saturday morning was worse.

You might have thought somebody had used a paint sprayer to decorate the inside of the motel room with blood.

The room was 101 at the Prairie Wheel and the blood was Mr. Nakashima's. There wasn't a whole lot left of the rest of his body. Doc Fancher was there, of course, along with a crime crew Karl Denham had requested from the State Patrol. They'd driven up from Cheyenne and were standing around with cameras and print brushes and all the rest of their paraphernalia. The room was so godawful, though, that most didn't stay inside long. We all had to go out every few minutes to get some air. Some just kept right on going to retch over the railing into the parking lot.

What we could tell of Mr. Nakashima was in the form of long, ragged strips, sort of like chicken when you shred it off the bone. I wasn't positive, but it looked like he was still wearing the ripped suit jacket he'd had on the night before. The fabric looked right, at least that which wasn't soaked in blood.

"He got back okay with Lil," said Karl. The chief looked around the room and shook his head. "She let him out at the office. He said he could get back to his room just fine. I guess he did."

"Looks like they were waiting for him when he opened the door," said Doc Fancher.

"They?" said Karl.

"Lots of tracks in the blood. I figure three, maybe four."

I knew what the doc was talking about. I could recognize the tracks too. The killers looked to be bipedal and two-toed. I knew what the evidence seemed to indicate. Obviously you weren't going to get a gang of tyrannosaurus rexes into a motel room to ambush a Japanese business emissary.

I took a breath through the handkerchief over my mouth. It was a hot morning. I loved the pack of deinonychus the town had recently installed in the park. A dozen six-foot-tall carnosaurs with their distinctive sicklelike claws on the back of each foot lent the sometimes too-placid park a sense of danger we all knew the tourists would love. Obviously the robo-carnivores were programmed to do nothing more dangerous than to circle tourist groups and look menacing.

"Something went wrong," said Doc Fancher quietly. He knew what I was thinking.

Had it ever.

* * *

I stuck around the Prairie Wheel for a while, or at least as long as my stomach would allow, and then went back to my office. I wasn't there behind my desk for five minutes before the crazy man barged past the receptionist.

"Well, Ben," he said, without so much as a civil 'good morning,' "we got big trouble."

"I know."

He looked confused for a moment. "Oh, the Jap fellow? Not that. I mean *real* problems."

I twiddled with the pen set the Chamber had given me upon my first reelection. "I think Mr. Nakashima encountered some *real* problems."

The crazy man shrugged. "Those people believe in reincarnation." He grinned. "He'll make out. If not now, then next time around."

Dick, my secretary, stuck his head into the doorway. "Can I get you some coffee, Mr. Goreham?"

The crazy man, whose name was H. D. Goreham, said, "Tea. Earl Grey. Hot."

"You got it."

"So," I said. "Trouble."

"I just got a fax from Washington saying the NEA's turned down my request."

I attempted to steeple my fingers sympathetically. "So no steam bison, at least not this biennium."

He looked at me irritably. "The bastards are a bunch of reptile chauvinists."

"Sorry," I said. "Cold blood is our bread and butter, or something like that."

He got up from his chair and began to pace. "I'm pursuing other routes."

"Good luck." Something in my voice, some nuance of doubt must have betrayed me.

"Don't patronize me, boy." He glared at me as though I were wearing a button bearing the word MAMMAL with a scarlet circle and slash across it. Then his expression changed as though the sun had come out from behind a storm front. "I've got something to show you."

"I'm kind of busy today," I said.

"The head—I spent all last night attaching it."

"Well, that's great, but—"

"Please?" His voice turned plaintive. *"Please?"*

I thought about it. I'd already talked to Great Sundance Insurance, and I knew the call in to the Cloverly Corporation would take a while to generate an answer—after all, they'd want to talk to their own legal department first.

His eyes, the same shade of dark brown as mine, looked like they might even tear up. "Okay," I said, "just a quick look. Guess I could use a break."

We left. I walked past Dick standing disconsolately with a cup of Earl Grey in hand and reminded him to collect return numbers with any messages.

"You want this in a take-out?" he said to the crazy man.

H. D. Goreham nodded gratefully and Bob decanted the tea into a styrofoam cup.

His workshop was only four blocks away from the town hall. The crazy man used some underutilized space in the Highway Department shops. We went in the back where I blinked, trying to adjust to the darkness.

The crazy man flipped the switch for the overheads and two banks of fluorescents buzzed on.

I had to admit it: the bison was magnificent. As tall at the shoulder as the top of my head—and I'm not short—the replica of the great prehistoric beast humped dramatically out of the workshop gloom. The crazy man hadn't bothered yet to comb out the shaggy synthetic hair around its neck, so I could see the joints where the head assembly had been riveted in place.

"I can fire him up for you," Goreham said hopefully.

I shook my head. "Thanks, but I really can't stay. I'll take a raincheck."

The crazy man walked over to the bison's flank, then stared up at the shiny, lifeless eyes. At first he seemed to be petting the huge beast, but then I realized he was stroking the creature's shiny chromed steam vents.

I said sincerely, "He's absolutely magnificent, Dad."

My father beamed.

On the way back to the office, I ran into Arnie Palenque. He was walking his bike across the intersection of Prehistoric Highway and Roy Chapman Andrews Way. The corner used to be First and Oak, but things, of course, changed.

"Morning, sir," said Arnie. He was always a polite boy for all the years I'd known him growing up. His family lived in what used to be called Little Juarez, a poor clump of about eight frame houses located literally right across the Burlington Northern tracks. Now the area pretty much just gets called the East Side of town. Nearly everybody who lives there is Mexican.

"Morning, Arnie," I said. "I've got to tell you, that play of yours last night was one hellacious achievement." I didn't want to admit I'd missed most of the final act.

"Sorry you had to leave early," said Arnie. He grinned, but the expression wasn't nasty.

I smiled apologetically. "Business."

"That rogue stego?"

I stared at Arnie, a little startled. "How much do you know about all that?"

The boy—young man, rather—shrugged. "Things get around this town pretty fast." His grin widened. "Besides, my girlfriend had an appointment before school with Doc Fancher."

"Ah," I said. "The drums speak. So, you have any theories?"

"Way I figure it," said Arnie, "the stego could have been just a software glitch. But the deino pack—" He lost the grin. "That's scary." He seemed to hesitate.

"*What*, Arnie?"

"Well, if I were writing a play, I think probably Mr. Nakashima's death would turn out to be murder most foul."

I nodded. "That's the way I figure it too."

For a while we both watched the traffic go by. Most of the tourists didn't seem to know yet what had happened in room 101 of the Prairie Wheel. That would change. By nightfall, I guessed, we'd have more morbid curiosity-seekers than there'd be motel space to hold them. Not a few would try for room 101, or at least the rooms next door.

"There'd have to be a motive," I said.

"Maybe someone doesn't want our town to grow anymore. This might do it."

"Who'd want that?" I said. "We're all making money."

"But at what cost to our souls?"

"That's pretty grown-up thinking," I said.

Arnie met my look steadily. "I'm going to graduate soon. I'm obliged to participate in your American dream."

"That's true," I said. "You've got scholarships and awards up the wazoo. Ain't it hell?"

We both laughed. Arnie said, "Yeah, well, I'm going to be a software engineer."

I was puzzled. "I thought you were going to be a whatchacallit, a neo-Shakespearean playwright."

"Can't I do both?" said Arnie. "This is America."

The light turned green our way again, and we finally crossed. A bus loaded with German tourists—the windows were open and they were gabbling a blue streak in harsh syllables—rumbled past. The way they were all talking and pointing, I had the feeling they weren't just amazed and enthralled purely by Dinny, the giant apatosaurus dipping and drinking out of the fake-rock fountain in the middle of town.

A bus full of African students followed close after and passed us.

"So what do you think, Mr. Goreham," said Arnie, "you suppose that someday racism will be as dead as the dinosaur?"

I thought a moment. "The dinosaurs seem to have needed a kick in the rear from Nemesis, that death-star comet thingamajig."

Arnie smiled easily, without guile, I thought. "Exactly," he said.

Maybe ninety seconds in my office, and I was called out by the sound of automatic weapons fire in the street. I should have known better than to pursue a normal workday.

As I cleared the door of City Hall, I heard Karl Denham yell, "Hold your fire, hold your fire, all of you."

I looked cautiously around. The scene could have been out of *High Noon* or *Shane* or some other old western. The police chief stood about ten paces to my left, right square in the middle of Prehistoric Highway. His legs were a little apart, his right hand rested on the butt of his sidearm. I could see that the safety strap was unsnapped.

Karl glanced at me. "Stay back, Ben!"

I looked to the right. Maybe thirty feet down the blacktop was an adult stego. It was one of the new-generation Bakkers; mossy green undercarriage, body a burnt orange, deepening to umber along the ridge plates. From tiny head to pointed tail, thick body in between, the stegosaurus was close to twenty feet long. It pawed the pavement with its right front leg. Then it thumped the highway with its spiked tail.

"What the hell are you going to do?" I called to Karl.

"Keep this thing cornered," said the chief. "Got a call into a robo-paleo gal named Shelton. She's here on vacation. Figure she can give us an opinion on this bastard."

"This here the rogue?"

"Beats me," said Karl. "I think so. Kids who called me said it's been acting kind of weird."

I squinted and thought I saw foam oozing from the stego's jaws.

Then it opened its mouth and bellowed.

Karl started to pull his automatic from its holster.

Good thing, because then the reptile charged. The stego sure looked clumsy, but it didn't take long at all to work up a full head of steam. Karl had his pistol out now and was firing from a two-handed stance. His target didn't slow down.

The air was suddenly full of sound and lead. I saw four officers firing from the cover of parked cars. Two were blasting away with the Remington pumps we'd gotten with Title 32 funds. The others raked the stegosaurus with fire from assault rifles set on full automatic.

To be honest, the dino got nearly to Karl before it keeled over nose first into the asphalt. His officers kept up their fire for a while, just in case, I suppose. The carcass jumped and shivered with the impacts.

"Okay, hold your fire," Karl finally shouted. He gingerly approached the felled dino and nudged its snout with one boot. The stegosaurus didn't quiver. The chief replaced his pistol in its holster. "Time for a little electronic autopsy."

The patrolmen reloaded their weapons. It really hadn't been much like *High Noon* after all. More like *The Wild Bunch.*

*   *   *

That was all before noon.

I was going to have a quiet lunch at the Dew Drop Inn, back in the private dining room that ordinarily was kept for Kiwanis and Lions Club lunches. No group had the room today, I knew, so I figured it was a chance for some peace and quiet so I could do some thinking.

But then my loony dad showed up and kidnapped me for the second time in as many hours.

"I fixed some sandwiches," he said. "Bologna, your favorite."

"It's not my favorite," I said helplessly.

"You're a politician, it might as well be your favorite."

"But—"

He reminded me what day it was. I knew too, but I'd tried to forget it. I glanced at the calendar, though I didn't have to. It was the anniversary.

"All right," I said, "but I need to pick up some flowers."

"Got 'em."

"For everybody?" I said.

"Enough." He impatiently led me out of the room.

The stones were mossy in the town cemetery. If you didn't know where to go and what you were looking for, it might be easier to feel the letters with your fingers than to try and read them.

I knew where to go. We both did.

My father and I sat on the fern-shaded grass and stared at the three graves while we ate our sandwiches. He had lied; he'd fixed me a tuna salad on rye, the way he knew I liked it—a little dill, some chervil; good guy, my dad.

Down the row, some little plant-eaters scurried away from the shade toward warmer stones. Or maybe they were real lizards. It was hard to tell from this distance.

"You haven't been here for a while," said my father.

I guess I felt a little guilty. I just nodded.

"It's damned important not to forget."

I rotated a bound clutch of lily stems between my palms. "I don't forget."

"Yes," said the crazy man, "but they got to know."

"They're beyond knowing now," I said.

"I'm not so sure about that anymore. After all, the dinosaurs came back."

"That's ludicrous," I said. "They're replicas, damn clever, but fake."

"Artificial reptile intelligence." My father took the lilies from me and laid them on my wife's grave.

"Bull," I said. "That's plain crazy."

"I'm not so sure." He sat back down beside me. "You can remember all this and not end up a cripple because of it." More time passed. "Yes, you can, Benjamin."

Finally I said something that was very painful to me. "I'll get around to healing, Dad."

His grip on my wrist was surprisingly strong for one I thought of as an old man. "Heal up before I'm dead, Ben. I truly need that."

I bit my lip like a kid and looked away from those intense brown eyes. "I'm working on it."

He took his hand away from my lower arm and clapped me on the shoulder. "I believe you."

We finished our sandwiches in silence, contemplating those three silent graves: my wife, his grandchildren, all of them dead about as stupidly, cruelly, and unnecessarily as death can be.

Chip failure. That never used to be included in any coroner's report. Lack of adequate quality control standards. What bullshit euphemisms for a technological era. I could feel my blood pressure rising, muscles tensing, head starting to ring at the temple. I felt cooling tears rising to my eyes.

"Ben," said my father. I looked at him.

He inclined his head. "The fence."

I stared over there. We sat about twenty yards inside the perimeter of the cemetery. The grounds were surrounded by a five-foot-high stone wall.

Six carnivores stared back at us from the other side. The heads were miniatures of tyranno skulls, synthetic reptile skin colored in various shades and patterns of green and ocher. Young adult deinos, just tall enough to peer over the cemetery wall. Looking at them was like contemplating a nest of gaily painted Easter eggs with teeth.

"Hope they're not here for a picnic, too," my father said.

We stayed where we were. No sudden moves. The robosaurs too remained where they stood.

The stare-down continued for about a minute.

Then, as one, the pack of deinonychus whistled and grunted like eighteen-wheelers releasing airbrakes, wheeled, and bounded away and out of sight.

"Maybe we should get back to town," said my father.

We walked carefully, watchfully, as we returned to the Cherokee. Not a predator in view. But I still didn't look back at the graves as we departed.

I turned on the radio and we listened to Kizzin Kuzzin Charlie Burkle. KIZN is the town's lone station. It's staffed mainly by part-timers who can't pronounce most proper names from outside the county or any word with more than two syllables. As for the music, if you don't like country, dinner's over. But the station's the one piece of communication that tends to get into everybody's home and truck cab.

"So just to remind you folks again," said Kuzzin Charlie, "Chief Karl Denham of the Cycad Center Police Department, along with the sheriff's department and the State Patrol, want you to all know there's one of them APBs out for this gang of deinonychus critters." He put the accent wrong, on the "nych" rather than the "non," but the tone in his voice got the message across. Kuzzin Charlie went on. "Chief Denham says there's a dozen of these killers, all about six feet tall, nine feet long, stand on two feet, have a long stiff tail and jaws full of teeth. You catch sight of these lizards, you call the police right quick." He gave the number. "Just remember they're dangerous. They're suspected in this morning's killing of Tokyo"—he pronounced it with three syllables—"businessman L. T. Nagashuma." Kuzzin Charlie got the name all bollixed up. I hope nobody from the Chamber of Commerce was listening.

I said to my father, "I'll tell them where half the fugitives are."

"*Were*," he said. "They're fast and smart."

"Only as smart as their programs."

My father smiled wanly. "They're smart."

Back at my office—again—after dropping off my dad, I found Karl Denham waiting for me with a tall, well-put-together woman dressed in faded jeans and a clean sweatshirt that said Tyrrell Museum on it. After she opened her mouth and started talking about dinos, I realized she was a real smart cookie too.

"Ben, this here's Miz Shelton from the University of Texas. She's the paleo lady I believe I told you about earlier."

Miz Shelton stuck out her hand. I took it. Her grip was firm. "Glad to meet you, Mr. Goreham." She had a pronounced Texas accent.

"Ben," I said.

She smiled.

"So now let's sit down and find out what you discovered," said Karl to Miz Shelton.

She lost her smile. "Gentlemen, I really do appreciate the situation you've got here in Cycad Center. No question about that. You've apparently got a pack of robotic carnosaurs acting irrationally—then there's the stegosaurus too—but what you really need are some qualified engineers who've trained on these ARI systems."

"Miz Shelton," said Karl, "the Cloverly Corporation makes these predators, and they're flying in some of their people as soon as they can. But those experts aren't here yet, and you are. I'm sorry you're on vacation and all, but I figured you might be able to give us a lead."

She spread her hands slightly. "I'm a little more used to digging plesiosaur fossils out of the Shoal Creek down in Austin than I am analyzing reptile automatons—"

Karl said, "You've worked with museum displays, those animated ones. You said that earlier. We're looking for *anything* here." There was what sounded a little like pleading in his voice. I'd never heard that from him before.

"It's been a long time since either reptile anatomy or basic electronic engineering," said Miz Shelton. I realized then that she must have already been put to dismantling the stego. I tried to ignore my lawyer's concern that this might have voided our service contract with Cloverly. "I didn't find very much that seemed unaccountable," Miz Shelton continued. "There was one anomaly."

"The foam," said Karl.

She nodded. "It's not really foam, not in the salivary sense. Don't forget, we're dealing with a machine. It was highly acidic"—she wryly held up a blistered thumb—"and it was apparently a suspension for an agglomeration of what appeared to me to be bits of microcircuitry. Most of the chip remains had already been dissolved when I examined the samples. I tried to neutralize what was left, but—" She shrugged.

"So what was all that stuff you found?" said Karl.

The paleontologist from Texas spoke slowly and carefully. "I'm guessing it was some piece of machinery alien to the original creature. Perhaps a behavior-modifying device with a self-destruct capability." She smiled slightly, but apparently without humor. "Or maybe your stegosaurus just had a software glitch."

I couldn't smile back.

From across town, we all heard a ragged volley of gunfire. One of Karl's officers burst into my office. "Chief, we just cornered some of those bastards over by the Quik-Mart." He glanced at Miz Shelton and said, "Sorry, ma'am."

She smiled again, more generously this time. "Well, maybe you gentlemen had better go and shoot those bastards quick, before they kill someone."

"Thanks. Dick'll get you lunch or anything you want," I called back over my shoulder. We hit the doorway running.

I didn't notice until the street that Miz Shelton was following us, and keeping up.

I admit it. I had a drink with Miz Shelton that night down at the Globe Hotel Lounge. She wore a denim skirt and white blouse with some lace around the collar and looked nice. This wasn't any kind of romantic rendezvous, though she was a very attractive woman. I needed to talk to her about what folks were already calling the Quik-Mart Massacre.

There had been six of the *Deinonychus antirrhopus*. After the last twenty-four hours, I had no problem either spelling or pronouncing the name. I knew that the name meant "terrible claw," and referred to the large sicklelike claw on each hind foot. Back about 120 million years ago, right near the bottom of the Lower Cretaceous, the deinos used to hunt in packs and were probably the terror of their environment. I don't know what would be the equivalent today; maybe gangs of young skinheads rampaging with knives through a mall.

"Their hands could rotate on the wrist," said Miz Shelton. "You know they could do that?"

I admitted I didn't.

"If there had been doors with knobs back then, they could have opened them." Miz Shelton laughed and her eyes shone in the light from the neon Bud sign. "Only known dinosaur who could do that. Obscure fact of the day."

"Must be how they got into Nakashima's room," I muttered.

"Not unless they had a passkey too," said Miz Shelton. "Or Mr. Nakashima left his door unlocked."

"Doubtful. So I guess it's back to figuring out who was on the inside."

Miz Shelton sipped her beer. "You mean who altered their programming?"

I nodded. "Motive and opportunity. That's what Karl Denham's working on. It's what Arnie Palenque mentioned. Me, I'm hoping to make the big, intuitive jump." I realized I was a little tipsy. I'd already outpaced my companion by three beers to one, plus I'd started with rum and Coke before she got here.

More than once, Dad had been on my back about drinking. God knew, I agreed with him. But living in this town tended to breed such temptation. Dinosaurs or not, there really wasn't a whole hell of a lot to do outside of work. Especially for somebody who was single again after years of marriage, a wife, and two kids.

"I'm acquainted with Karl," said Miz Shelton. "So who's Arnie Palenque?"

"I'm Arnie Palenque."

We both looked up. I don't know about Miz Shelton, but I sure as shit was startled. There he stood, just as handsome as life. I glanced back at my companion. "Good kid," I said. "Smart as a whip, and talented too."

"Brilliant, troubled, and unwelcome in this, his native land."

"I never said either of those two last things," I answered. "And what the hell are you doing here in the bar?"

"I'm with my parents," said Arnie. I looked over and saw Mr.

119

and Mrs. Palenque at a table by the wall. They both smiled at me. I smiled back. "A congratulatory iced tea after the cast party. The gate tonight wasn't everything we could have hoped."

"I think that's understandable," I said. "Folks see stuff in their backyards that might have passed for location filming of *1,000,000 Years B.C. II*, and the Bard suffers."

The pack of deinonychosaurs trapped behind the Quik-Mart hadn't managed to disembowel anyone, but it wasn't for want of trying. There were officers in County Memorial tonight who could testify to that. The final score had been *Homo sapiens* 6, reptiles zip.

"If Shakespeare were alive today, he would be *writing* films like that."

I swigged half my Bud. "Yeah, probably, sequels and all."

Which was what *we* were facing. An unpleasant sequel. Six dead—or maybe dismantled was a more accurate description— deinos was just the half of it. The original pack had numbered an even dozen. Somewhere in the county, half a dozen more of the toothy predators were scampering around. A sheriff's party had checked out the cemetery, tracked the group my dad and I had seen, and lost them in Brushy Creek.

"I'm forgetting my manners," said Arnie. He exchanged a handshake with Miz Shelton, who introduced herself while I was still getting the words together. He flashed another brilliant grin and excused himself to return to his parents.

"Quite a young man," said Miz Shelton.

"Good parents," I commented. "His father was a doctor before coming up here."

"Was? What is he now?"

"Laborer. Or course," I hastily added, "if he'd just come up these days, he could probably test out and get an American license. It was all a long time ago. He'll never catch up now."

Miz Shelton looked a mite somber. "That's sad."

I shook my head. "It's life in a small town."

"What about your life?" said Miz Shelton. "You're married?"

I held up my left hand and inspected the band. "Not anymore." I was feeling the alcohol. "They're all dead." She looked at me questioningly. "My wife and two daughters. They all died." She was still looking at me and saying nothing. "I don't talk about it much." Miz Shelton reached over and touched my hand. "Hardly ever."

"If it bothers you—"

"Machines killed them," I said. After a moment, I added, "Sort of like with Mr. Nakashima. It was a face-to-face thing. A brain died."

Miz Shelton looked confused.

"They said later it was like an electronic aneurysm, you know, a cerebral hemorrhage for gadgets." I paused, remembering. "It was in the cortex of a factory robot in Osaka. My family and I were touring the plant back when the town was shopping for a new generation of beasties. There were—There was—" I lost track of what I was saying because the tapes were playing in front of my eyes.

I saw the three of them—Marianne, Jennifer, and Donnie— staring entranced at the spiderlike chromed machine as it delicately, firmly, inexorably assembled torso after torso of Snow White's dwarves. Multiply jointed, three-fingered hands spun around at the ends of steel wrists.

Then— I heard the whoop of the alarm klaxon first. I was standing a few yards behind Marianne and the kids, talking to the plant supervisor. What I saw was the robot convulsing like a spider on a hotplate, the arms lashing out and drawing in anything within grasp. That included my wife and daughters.

I was told later they were crushed to death almost instantly. The blood flew everywhere. The robot continued to spasm, then jerked to a stop as technicians rushed to the control boards across the large white room.

My family . . . their bodies no longer even twitched. The screaming kept on, and I realized it was mine. I was beating the machine with my fists, my knuckles bloody and breaking.

The workers gently, but so very firmly, dragged me away from the dead robot. They couldn't stop my yelling and carrying on.

I must have said *something* of that, because both Miz Shelton's hands were tight around mine. "I'm so very sorry," she kept saying. "I read about that. I didn't know it was you and your family."

I took my right hand away from hers and lifted the beer glass to my lips. At least I mostly kept away from the hard stuff. Maybe it was time for a change.

Miz Shelton skooched her chair around the table beside mine and put her arm around my shoulders. She didn't say anything for a while, and it was good just to feel the touch and the heat of her body there.

"At least you've still got your father. That must help, doesn't it?"

I laughed, and it probably didn't sound all that healthy. "Well, I really haven't told you all that much about my dad, have I?" She shook her head. "Around here, the politer folks call him the crazy man." I chuckled ruefully. "And it's true. He's crazy as a bedbug. A brilliant man, but he spends all his time, now that he's retired from the State, using borrowed space to build his giant steam-powered bison. Hell of a dream, but he's making it work, even if nobody else around here thinks he can do it. Or *should*."

"Should?" said Miz Shelton.

"The town's making it big on outsize reptiles," I replied. "They erected this bizarre image of a tourist mecca that's set on things like forbidding people to grow flowering plants because none were around back in the Cretaceous. They look dimly on the idea of adaptive little mammals scurrying around in the dark and eating the dinosaurs' young." I almost started to giggle. "Just metaphor, I assure you. Anyhow, they don't think much of *big* mammals either. They don't like my dad because he's just too nuts for them, and they hate the whole idea of his dream bison."

Miz Shelton shook her head violently. "That's insane."

"My dad or the town?"

I saw what looked like tears in her eyes. "You know what I mean."

"Yeah," I said. "I reckon I do." I leaned down into the hollow of her neck and head.

I really don't know where it would have gone from there. Maybe nowhere. But we never had a chance to find out because some guy I didn't know in a Pendleton shirt and blue hunter's cap burst through the door and yelled that Chief Denham needed any man with a weapon to come hunt some cornered killer lizards. "And women too, if they got a gun!"

It was a mob.

Or it was the greatest demonstration of civic-minded citizenry I'd ever seen in Cycad Center. Judging from the guns and torches,

122

and even the occasional pitchfork raised night-skyward in a cal-loused hand, I finally had to pick the former definition.

These were my neighbors and they were out to kill something. Six somethings. They didn't care that a far-traveler from Asia had been ripped apart by a bunch of sickle-clawed monsters. But they did care that their town was in jeopardy. I tossed my now empty Bud bottle aside and heard it break on brick. Never to be reassembled whole again. Shattered glass. Christ, I was suddenly maudlin. Buck up, guy.

I turned my head. Miz Shelton was there, expression grimly set. She said something, but it was lost in the noise of men shouting and pickups revving. She yelled it.

"Tourists!"

She was right. They shouldn't be here. The night was lousy with fat people in Hawaiian shirts, camcorders clutched tightly to their bodies. There were skinny people too—polyester polo shirts and Japanese SLRs slung around their necks.

I thought about liability claims. Shit. It was too late. All too late.

This was like wading a mountain river. Miz Shelton and I were in too deep, too far toward the middle of the stream. The crowd swept us along. We just tried to keep up; not to go down, not to drown in hot, hysterical flesh armed with 30.06 deer rifles and .357 Magnums.

The mob flowed off Prehistoric Highway—Main Street—and onto Avenue Before Time—Pine.

A slight breeze lifted the tall ferns lining the street. The filtered streetlights generated long, angular, eerie shadows. I realized the wind lifting the fronds must be generated by all of us—the crowd.

One of the little bipedal plant-eaters, about the size of a housecat, scampered out from a clump of cycads and tried to cross in front of us. Someone swung the stock of his 12-gauge like a Louisville slugger and the little dino came apart like a model kit. The body— headless now—scrambled upright and spun in a real close orbit like a decapitated chicken with one foot nailed to the floor. The man who'd clubbed it reversed his weapon and pulled the trigger.

The plant-eater disintegrated, splintered circuits and broken servo-mechanisms flying every which way.

Miz Shelton sagged against my shoulder for a second and I reached to steady her. I couldn't hear what her lips were saying, but I sure as hell could read them: "Bastards."

What my ears could make out were the shots up ahead. I saw muzzle flashes in the darkness on the next block. The bottom dropped out of my gut. I knew exactly where we were going.

"There!" A voice bayed above the crowd-rumble.

There was the Highway Department Shop building.

Oh, Christ! I grabbed Miz Shelton's hand and pulled her after me. If my dad were inside there—

My neighbors were popping away from behind a perimeter of safety sawhorses the police had set up about twenty yards from the shop's big double doors. The reflective stripes shone in the winking light from the lamps clamped to the crossbars.

The shooting was ragged. One shot would trigger a cluster, and guys would empty their weapons. Then the gunmen would stop to reload. It didn't look like it was the cops who were doing most of the firing.

"Okay, hold it!" That was Karl Denham's voice speaking through a bullhorn. "Cease fire! And that means *you*," he added in an apparent aside to Harley Prague, the local Enco bulk dealer who was standing a few feet away and sighting down the barrel of a .410. Harley looked disappointed, but he desisted. Then he said something to the two Collins boys—they worked for him at the station— and the pair vanished back in the crowd.

"Cease fire," said Karl. "Stop the shooting. *Now!*" Since there was no other leader giving orders, the crowd pretty much complied.

Harley yelled, "Chief, let my boys use a couple jerry cans of unleaded on those critters—that'll flush 'em out to where we can bag 'em good."

"Hold on there," came a voice.

Miz Shelton pounded on my arm. She pointed. "Look! It's your father."

My dad looked old and tired, but he stood straight as he fought his way up to the front of the crowd. Our neighbors quieted somewhat, but the tone of what they were saying got nasty.

"What's the crazy man want?"

"He *works* in there, don't he?"

"Maybe he's been screwing around with those killer lizards."

"Harley *oughta* burn him too. Wouldn't take hardly any more gas."

Miz Shelton's fingers tightened on my arm and I could feel her nails as I started forward.

"There'll be no more talk of that," said Karl. "This is a police department operation. It'll remain that."

I was close enough to hear them now, even if they didn't use the bullhorn. I felt real sober. All the buzz and fuzziness were gone.

"I reckon they're in there, all right," said my father. "But so's my bison."

"I'm right sorry about that, H. D.," said Karl, "but I guess what it's boiling down to is that the public's welfare and safety outweigh one man's art."

"Damn straight," chimed in Harley.

Karl hesitated. "I really *do* think it's art, H. D."

"Can't let you do it, then," said my father. He took a small silver automatic from his right front pants pocket.

"Oh, shit," said Harley.

Karl said, "Put that down right now, H. D."

My dad shook his head. He didn't point the pistol at Harley or Karl or anyone else. "I'll go in and do the job myself." He turned toward the Shop Building.

I didn't even think about it. I dove forward and flattened Dad like a John Deere tractor running over a bush. The automatic went skittering across the asphalt lot and somebody must have picked it up.

Christ! What if I'd broken every rib in his chest? I scrambled off him. My dad turned over on his back, looked up at me and groaned. "You stupid bastard," he said, "I had the right way to do it."

I shook my head and offered him a hand, which he disdained. "You may be right about the rest of it," I said, "but I'm no bastard."

My dad slowly got to his feet. "You will be after I disown you."

Then there was heat in my face, and light, and I realized it wasn't from strong feeling. Someone had torched the Highway Department building. I squinted as the flames licked up both sides of the shop area. Two figures were running toward us. Looked like the Collins boys.

"*Somebody* had to do something." There was considerable self-satisfaction in Harley's voice. "Couldn't just wait around all night. More folks might have gotten hurt."

I saw the stricken look on my dad's face. I swung back to punch Harley in his goddamned smug mouth, but Karl caught my hand.

"Enough of the Clint Eastwood shit," he said.

"My bison," I heard Dad moan softly.

"Oh, my god," said Miz Shelton. "Look!"

We all heard the rumble as the big double doors of the Highway Department shop ground open. The first thing I saw was the harsh glare and the moving shadows inside. The fire was within as well as without.

Then it registered what else I was seeing. The six *Deinonychus antirrhopus* were evenly spaced across the front of the shop area. They stood as unmoving as stone, each staring impassively back at us, each with forelegs crossed across its chest. It was like looking at a picture of lined-up statues guarding an Egyptian temple.

And then their master appeared.

I guess I'd suspected, but really hadn't wanted to believe. But who else was smart enough, and who else wanted to hurt the town so badly?

Arnie Palenque stood out in front of the line of carnosaurs like a general at the head of his troops.

"What's that little beaner think he's doing?" said Harley.

If Arnie had a speech, it was lost in the roar of both the mob and the fire. I know he did shout something, but I couldn't make it out. Then he pointed some gadget that looked like a cable remote at the deinos.

One after another, from the left to the right, their heads exploded. Bright fountains of silver and gold and crimson sparks went up like Fourth of July fireworks displays.

Then the deinonychosaurs burned fiercely, like the torches in the mob.

From where he stood close to me, my father said, "Listen!"

I heard it too. It was a hissing, like a breath from the father of all snakes. Like brakes being bled on some giant eighteen-wheel dragon.

"The little bastard!" cried my father. "He's fired up my bison!" He started forward and I tripped him. Didn't mean to, but when I reached to grab his collar, our feet got tangled up.

Looking across the parking lot and into the open doors of the shop building was like peering through a peephole into hell. There was flame almost everywhere in there now.

Arnie Palenque finally made his move. I saw him bow ironically to us all. Then he turned, ran a great broken-field course through the line of burning dinosaurs, used a workbench as a vaulting horse, and landed astride the back of the great steam bison.

The creature came to life. Now I could see the steam venting from the chrome pipes as the mechanical muscles bunched and released beneath the shaggy coat.

The bison automaton moved forward, slowly at first, smoothly, gaining momentum. I could feel the vibration of the hooves coming down on first the concrete, then the asphalt.

One watcher fired. Then another. And another. Arnie crouched low along the bison's massive neck, using the horns as a shield. He was a dozen feet above the ground. The bison must have weighed tons. I felt that through my soles.

As the mechanical creature cleared the burning building, the flames licked its coat. For a crazy moment, I prayed that my father had used a fire-retardant fiber for the thick hair.

No such luck. The flames caught, first exploding the frayed outer ends of the bison's coat. As a teenage boy, I had once helped the volunteer fire department tackle a forest fire. The crown fire—with the blaze leaping from treetop to treetop—had been terrifying. This now was the same.

Then the flames dug inward toward the bison's thicker fur, and black smoke flooded back in the creature's wake.

Out of time, out of sync with the cretaceous world of Cycad Center, my father's steam bison puffed and chugged and loped heavily toward us.

"Get out of the way!" Karl screamed into his bullhorn as people, indeed, scattered like chickens finding a coyote in the henhouse.

I tried to grab both Miz Shelton and my dad and yank them out of harm's way.

"Dear god," said Miz Shelton, and it was like a prayer.

Arnie had caught fire too. His black, curly hair blazed up like a burning bush as the steam bison cleared the police line. Wooden safety horses splintered and scattered everywhere. As the bison thundered past, close enough to singe my own hair, I didn't hear Arnie say anything at all. He didn't scream or cry out, just hung on grimly.

There were plenty of screams from our neighbors, though.

I saw Harley and the older of the Collins boys trampled right under the bison's steel hooves. Sparks leapt up from the pavement, meeting and swirling with the sparks drifting down from the creature's flaming hide.

The spooky thing was the ghostly wailing from the bison. It sounded like ten thousand lost souls trying to get home. My dad told me later that had been the safety vents, letting all the excess steam go, so the bison wouldn't explode and take half the town with it.

The great steam bison thundered and wailed down to the end of the block, then lurched and turned into Prehistoric Highway. It headed downtown.

Karl and Dad and Miz Shelton and I and a whole bunch of the others rushed after it, but the bison had a full head of steam now, and it was motoring for all it was worth.

When it was all over and done, it seemed to me that it had been like watching a game of cosmic billiards, with a flaming meteor making the damnedest complex bank shot you ever saw.

The burning bison caromed from one side of the street to the other, smashing glass and leaving bits of fire behind it. Businesses started to burn.

We lost Bauer's Flowers, the Bridger Bar, the Coast to Coast store, the Globe Hotel, even the old Ramona Theatre. Half the downtown of Cycad Center went up.

News crews had come to town to report on Mr. Nakashima's death. They got most of the conflagration on tape.

Screaming now like a banshee—Dad said Arnie must have opened up the throttles completely—the steam bison thundered out of downtown and collided with Harley's Enco Super Service station. Talk about irony. The pumps tumbled like bowling pins.

The fireball was awesome.

When the VFD got the hoses going and cooled things off, there wasn't much left of the great steam bison of Cycad Center. And they never found *anything* they rightly could identify as Arnie Palenque.

Karl Denham spent the rest of the night with Doc Fancher and all the emergency personnel, getting things under control.

Miz Shelton, Dad, and I quietly left, strolled our way through the forests of frozen dinosaurs—the microwave control tower for the lesser creatures had gone down when the bison grazed City Hall—toward the edge of town. I couldn't remember where I'd parked the Cherokee. All of us wanted some cool, clear air without smoke, and some quiet time with no screams.

We found Vimbo's Truckstop still open, and settled in for a long bout of talk and black coffee.

Time has proceeded.

Not even a geological blink, but for me, endless emptied bottles and overslept alarms. Fourteen months, maybe? Fifteen.

The town's come back, more determinedly cycadean than ever. New robosaurs prowl the glades: newer safeguards are touted to the vistors. Naturally the tourist trade has only increased.

Arnie Palenque's mother and father uprooted and moved their family to parts unknown. His little brothers and sisters are frighteningly brilliant, and his parents want them to have a better life, even if it's in the inland valleys of California. At least that's my guess.

Miz Shelton still writes me from Texas. Right after all the flak from the *Deinonychus antirrhopus* episode had died down, her university received a huge grant from overseas to develop a museum designed to demonstrate paleontology's application to contemporary humanity. She was appointed curator. Needless to say, she's been busy. She keeps asking me to come visit, but there've always been reasons not to. I'm not stupid. I realize I'm spending less and less time at the cemetery, and when I do think of Marianne and the girls, there's a kind of cool, healing distance there. But it all takes time.

Grief takes its own sweet, dark time to die. And so does rage.

Maybe after the next pot-possession trial or petty-theft hearing, I'll just say the hell with it, buy a ticket for Austin, drive to Cheyenne, and catch a plane. Hello, Anne Louise Shelton.

My dad quotes T. S. Eliot to me and says my life is measured out in swizzlesticks—but ever fewer, he admits, and that's good for both of us. I figure I can trust his perceptions.

It's other things I wonder about. Ever get curious about how many of the jigsaw puzzle pieces that show a picture of reality are really in your possession?

Why did Arnie pick the Highway Department shop to hide the pack of deinonychosaurs?

Why was he so familiar with the workings of Dad's steam bison?

Was his programming ability good enough to build the devices that twisted the hardwired natures of the rogue dinos?

I've asked Dad these questions more than once. He smiles and won't answer me directly. He usually parries my question and goes back to working on his new project.

It's the new project that's been giving me some pretty strange dreams.

From downtown, you can see the scaffolding rising out west of Cycad Center, right at the head of the gentle valley that funnels down to the basin where the town is built. These days you can see the cliffs being erected. They show up nicely, silhouetted against those spectacular western sunsets we're so proud of.

One of these months they'll be ready, those cliffs where the pterosaurs will nest and perch and launch from as they soar on the thermals of our little world. The cliffs are designated as a memorial.

I have to admit I was surprised when I found out that Mr. Nakashima was the son of the CEO of Dai-su Dinoland. The only child of the corporate founder.

I was more surprised when Dai-su announced the outright cash gift earmarked for the artificial cliff site and the flying reptile habitat. The citizens of Cycad Center were ecstatic.

But I was *most* surprised when Dai-su stipulated that my father would design the cliffs and act as project manager during their construction.

A last hurrah? I wondered. The traditional Japanese respect for the venerable artisan? Nothing about this seemed to make sense. After all, my father was crazy.

But the cliffs are rising rapidly, sharp, angular peaks cutting bladelike into the sky. I visit Dad at the construction site perhaps twice a week. I asked him about all the internal piping that's going into those cliffs.

"Heating," he said. "Keep them cold-blooded reptiles warm during our Wyoming winters."

Fine. After all, the cliffs are to have a ribbon-cutting opening in another month, at the end of February. But those cold-blooded reptiles? They're only robots.

And why are the alleged heating units rated for liquid nitrogen? Hell, I can read the labels stenciled on the machinery.

So I don't sleep well. I have the dream, and maybe I'll fly to Texas for Valentine's Day and stay.

The dream.

It's the end of February and those hard-edged cliffs, as solid and durable as modern technology can fabricate them, loom against the gray winter sky. The people of Cycad Center are ready, there in their warm, moist little nest.

It's time to slash that satin ribbon. It's my father's crowning glory, his ultimate moment. The designer and builder of the great steam bison steps up to the control lever. The familiar crowd murmurs. They mocked and scorned him before. Now they're grudgingly quiet.

Perhaps the mists will part in the Wyoming wind. The onlookers will see the glittering cliffs and gasp.

No winged reptiles perched high. None.

Just the end of a world.

And my father will plunge the control lever forward, like a knight plunging his sword into the heart of a dragon. The machinery will start up—irrevocably, I fear.

Because through the mist, we will see the towering, frozen, cliffs of ice as they begin to rumble down toward us all. Cold-bloodedness will die, my father will triumph, and only the adaptive mammals will survive.

And we will know, finally, how the dinosaurs perished.

Kit Reed
CALLING HOURS

Sometimes change is not affected by
time, but rather by viewpoint. Our
hometowns muddle along, warm and safe
as always until, one day, we open our
eyes a bit wider and see someting that
may always have been there but we never
"saw" before. This holds true for Kit
Reed in "Calling Hours."

Kit Reed has experienced a great deal
of change in her life. Although born in
Connecticut, she moved to St. Petersburg, Florida, at the age of nine, a
change that was dramatic for her. "I got
marooned in St. Petersburg when I was
nine years old," she writes.

I emerged in the summer before the
tenth grade and moved back for a year
and a half after college to work for one
of the best independent newspapers in
the country, the St. Petersburg *Times*.
But imagine going out to play and finding out that most of the houses are shut
tight and most of the neighbors are old.
Imagine walking past the Princess Mar-

tha Hotel on the way to do a story at the courthouse, running the gauntlet of aging gents in rocking chairs.

The scene has changed; the town has changed; my feelings for the town have changed; I spend a certain amount of time looking forward to seeing lifelong friends and walking on dream beaches under 360-degree skies. And I know that in spite of efforts to the contrary, hey, I too am going to get old. There is, however, this lingering sense of bizarre juxtapositions, of landscape and local lore and legend and fact. There was in fact a woman named Beulah, whose husband served Cokes to guests in a widely celebrated burial palazzo on the South Side. He may even have played the piano for them, but fiction is supposed to court, not beggar, belief.

Kit Reed is considered one of today's foremost writers of short fiction. Her work resists categorization; she has written science fiction, horror, realistic fiction, and novels for both adults and young adults, exploring a variety of themes. The one unifying factor of her work is that it is all topnotch reading—and "Calling Hours," a chilling and mesmerizing tale, fits *very* well into this "category."

CALLING HOURS
Kit Reed

ON SATURDAYS when they'd used up the malls and wrung the last giggle out of the afternoon movie, when it was too late to start anything new but too early to lie to everybody and sneak away with the one person you most needed to get next to, the fearsome five piled in Vinnie's car. Restless, crazy for night, they bombed around the South Side until the afternoon was dead at last and it was time to begin the night.

It was a nothing time of day, Lacy thought, and the South Side was noplace. Right for now.

They got off on the contrast. In Vinnie's red car they were all racket and color; with the tube tops and lobster shirts and the fringed vests and the plastic wraparounds with the DayGlo frames and the orange boom box, they were a parade. When they moved, they jangled—the earrings! *Bring some life into this graveyard.*

In the dead of summer the South Side looked like a city that had been nuked but not damaged, empty and intact. On the streets leading downtown and along the waterfront there was life even in deep August; in Florida you always ran into people fishing, no matter how hot it got, boaters heading for the bay; there were shoppers, cops cooping in air-conditioned cruisers, lounging but on the alert for you. But on the South Side there was nobody. The heat had blown them all away; the long, flat streets looked blasted and empty, like the surface of the moon. Nothing moved.

You could do anything.

But, today. Today they could not. Get. Going. Instead they revolved in the Tyrone parking lot like the undead: Jane hanging on to Archie—*dibs*—Lacy torn between Fred and Vinnie, dark, restless Vinnie and good Fred with the big hands and the brilliant grin. Vinnie was hung up on this magazine clipping he had; should they, shouldn't they? Fred tried to see. "So. What?"

Vinnie jerked it away. "Show you when we get there."

Saturday. Lacy was into it. Her eyes made promises to Vinnie that her body was not necessarily going to keep. He whirled, studying her; she pushed the look a little harder. "Let's go."

Vinnie looked at her for a long minute. "Right."

But it was Fred who came around and shoveled her into the car with those big, warm hands. Okay, Lacy thought, accidentally leaning into Fred in all the best places; okay, so it was not going to be Vinnie after all. For a minute there, Fred leaned back, warm body, *oh, Fred,* but then he just shut her in back with Jane and Archie and climbed in front. "Okay, let's go for it."

Saturday, right? In no-man's-land. Time for a new adventure in the territory; they had Vinnie at the wheel, Fred riding post; they were drinking: Ripple, wine coolers, whatever went down. They were ready for: whatever. Lacy's mind ran ahead to the night.

They rolled into the still South Side with the boom box blasting, heading—where? Weird as he was today, focused on something they didn't know about, Vinnie kept to the ritual. In all this sandy flatness they were heading for the one unflat place, one solitary ripple in the landscape.

Halfway down Third Street, Vinnie roared into the big one: Thrill Hill, which was no thrill, but which they felt compelled to take from many different angles: oh, no-o-oh . . . Eeek: whatever: it was important to act terrified, and if Lacy flung her arms in the air on the rise and Fred was moved to twist in his seat and grab them, saying—no, *going*—"Easy, babe," well fine.

Tonight, *oh Fred* . . . Tonight was ahead.

For now she was high on humming along in the car with Jane and the guys, these guys; if God or medical science came down and said she had to be fixed in one position for the rest of her life Lacy would be perfectly happy with this one. For the rest of her life let it be like this: Saturday, the fearsome five cresting Thrill Hill like a demo-car in a chase movie, Ga-*dum*, Lacy caught in midair, forever jouncing, with the boom box playing and her Fred *this close* and everything between them still in the future.

But even Thrill Hill gets old, and Vinnie knew to quit while they were still into it, everybody, like, "Once more," going, "Hey, wait!" "Oh, man." "Oh, Vinnie."

Lacy saw what he was doing. He was saving it up for next time. Next time . . . Futures; *only the future works*, Lacy thought, hung up on possibilities. "Future. Go for it!"

In front, Fred was too intent on what was coming to hear, and next to her, Jane was too engaged with Archie, rubbing, murmuring—no fair—too early in the day for these moves in the game. And Vinnie? He'd just hung a left into a gate that led to a road unwinding through live oaks draped with practically the last Spanish moss left anywhere.

"So. What?" Fred said.

"South Side cemetery," Vinnie said.

"What is this," Fred said, "a high school horror movie?"

"Ooops," Lacy said. "Cliché."

"You know me better. It's not what you think."

It was not like anything they knew. Most folks in this dead, sandy place looked to be sunk or planted or stashed in urns, but here on an avenue that looped next to the cemetery fence, there was this aboveground—grave? It was this, like, stucco house, or was it, temple, this upscale graveyard condo with Parthenon columns, perfect miniature, with a fountain in front and a neon glimmer coming from inside; amazing; all this for somebody who had no choice because she was dead. It snagged Lacy: *no choice*. Stone letters over the door spelled out her name. MURIEL.

"Okay, guys, this is it."

"Oh, wow."

Somewhat drunk but not disorderly, only crazy enough to blight the landscape, to lay waste and pillage just a little bit, the five piled out. Unshelled, they were itchy, already beginning to sweat.

Fred said, "This is *it*?"

Vinnie handed him the clipping. "Guy built this for his wife."

"Oh, man." *Garish*. Lacy stopped cold, bemused. Heard herself saying, without knowing where the thought came from, "I wonder what she did that made him so mad?"

136

"No, no, you don't get it." Vinnie's look was dark, intent. "He *loved* her."

There were plastic flowers in plastic urns next to the door; the garish doormat had fake daisies stuck in rubber grass; *garish*. Strange new word flickering through her head. From where? *Garish*. Poor dead woman, whoever she was, put away in the middle of all this high tack. Lacy wondered what burial dress he'd chosen: ugly, Lacy bet, Muriel's least favorite. "That's what you think," Lacy said.

That was recorded music playing inside, the funny, retro big-band sound that took this town's old folks back where they came from every afternoon, and the difference? This music scratched and crackled, lifted direct off some old-timey platter with a worn-out needle.

"Wait. This guy." Fred looked up from the clipping. "This was a long time ago."

Still hates me. What?

Vinnie shrugged. "Well, he's in there. They're both in there."

Wrong: the old man was standing in the doorway, watching them. In spite of the heat he had on a summer suit and a straw hat, two-tone shoes and a natty figured tie; he was dead bald and old, *old*, with spotty, shaking hands and yellowing false teeth, and next to Lacy, warm Fred muttered, "I'm never going to get like that."

"Futures," Lacy murmured to Fred, glad to be *this* close to him. "I guess the future is longer than you think"; heard, from somewhere, *God, yes.*

And Vinnie? Proud, going, "Did I tell you, or what?" while

Jane and Archie looked up from what they were doing: "Wuow, let's get out of here,"

but the old man was saying, "I'm so glad you've come,"

and only Lacy, who heard, clearly, *watch out*, had the automatic grace to say the right thing to excuse them all: "Just looking, thank you."

"And Muriel is glad you've come."

Vinnie couldn't go in but he couldn't leave either. "Don't know."

"Let's go." While Vinnie lingered, jittering, Fred tugged Lacy's hand. "Come *on*."

Warmed by his touch, Lacy found herself pulled in the opposite

137

direction by something she did not so much hear as know: *Oh, please.*

Fred was saying, "Babe?"

"Come in, Muriel is lonely," the old man said; he was ancient, teetering.

"I'm sorry," Lacy said; they should be out of here.

Vinnie said, "Better split."

Fred tugged. "Horrible to be that old."

"Shh, Fred." Lacy could not stop trying to see inside.

"My Muriel." Spit webbed the corners of the old man's mouth. "You're too young to understand . . ."

At her back Fred muttered, "I'm going to off myself before I get that bad."

End this.

Frightened, Lacy said softly, "Guys . . ."

Then the old man looked right through Fred as if he had heard every word and took all the implications and said, "We are all beyond choices. Now do as I tell you and come in."

Vinnie stopped; Fred stopped; Lacy stopped; even Jane let go of Archie and paid attention; it was weird.

At least inside it was cooler.

Garish.

"Sit down," the old man said, glaring so fiercely that they had to. In this cramped place the old man changed. Standing in the doorway he was nothing, pathetic; in here, he was the power. "Have Cokes. My treat."

Weird! He popped cans out of a machine. Right next to Muriel's sarcophagus, underneath this blue neon sign in script that spelled her name and to the left of the garish oil portrait on velvet, there stood a Coke machine.

"Later, you can sign the guest book." It was maroon plush encrusted with shells and it stood on a little gilt stand on top of the sarcophagus. Above it, Muriel looked out from her portrait with an embarrassed little smile: *terrible likeness.* Drawn by the portrait, Lacy was disturbed. Muriel's face was sweet but the colors of the dress and the background, the maroonish auburn the artist had used for her hair, all looked as if they had been put on to make her look bad.

To her own surprise, Lacy said, "It doesn't do her justice."

The old man snapped forward, studying her. "It's a perfect likeness."

But Vinnie was elbowing her: So is this something, or what? And the others, who had come in reluctantly, seemed to think it was a hoot. Even Fred grinned; he was into it. Only Lacy slouched, depressed. Poor Muriel!

"Your names will go down with some really famous visitors," the old man said. "Claude Pepper came in his time, and the people from *Life* magazine, and one of those Irish tenors. I could go on, but here, you don't have your Cokes . . ."

He had Lacy and the others in a half-circle of folding chairs set on a Persian rug. They were arranged like an audience around the pink granite box that contained Muriel.

"As you can see," he said, "Muriel liked everything nice."

Around her, the others were beginning to snicker; what a trip! Maybe, Lacy thought, they hadn't focused on the sarcophagus, Muriel lying under there in a dress she hated, probably, poor lady! Probably the only thing she wanted in the world was a quiet burial in some deserted part of the graveyard with no husband and no visitors so she could get some rest. He's getting even for something.

Lacy jumped. The old man was staring right into her. "I got together all the little woman's favorite things . . ."

She scoped the decorations: plaster masks, one smiling, one crying, dozens of dead plants in ceramic planters, paintings so tacky that they made her want to weep. Nobody would want to be remembered this way, yet here Muriel was, and here he was. Vinnie caught her expression and winked.

". . . and I keep packages of her favorite food."

"You must really have loved her," Vinnie said.

". . . and I try to play her favorite music," the old man said, but he sounded tired; his voice was beginning to fade.

Crammed in the corner to the left of Muriel was a record player, and once he'd popped the tops of five Cokes and handed them around, the old man took his place in front of the Victrola in a bamboo chair that got in his way every time he had to change a record, which he did now.

"In her time," he said, "Muriel was a noted soprano."

Fred was snorting, almost out of control.

"I know she'd want you to hear her sing."

No.

He put on Muriel's record and then sat down hard, as if spent. She didn't sound all that bad, warbling, what was it, "The Indian Love Call," in a gummy voice that oozed around in the crevices like something you put on pancakes, and as she listened Lacy was certain Muriel knew she was not a good singer and grieved to hear this sick rendition underscored, all right, by the way they laughed. It was terrible, fascinating, sad, although around her the others giggled and snorted into their Cokes and Vinnie began to put polite questions, starting with, "What gave you the idea?"

"Everybody wants to be remembered," the old man said.

And then because she was bummed, Lacy— Mistake! Lacy let it tumble out. "But, like this?"

The old man dragged his eyes across her face like claws. "I know what's best for my darling," he said in a tight voice, and in the next second gave it all away to Lacy, at least. "I have her where I want her now."

Dear God!

But the others didn't even see. "Oh wow," Vinnie said, "how great."

"I just have to keep it going," he said.

Even Fred was taken in, Fred, who was spooked by old age and put off futures by this ancient, ancient guy. "You must have really loved her," he said and Lacy could see the confusion of thoughts ripping around inside him. "To do all this."

The old man said, "It's my life."

Lacy jolted up, heard it clearly: warning, *warning*, but Vinnie said, "Shh, babe, the man is talking," and Fred put a warm hand on hers and pulled her down.

"Amazing," Vinnie was saying. "This place. You should be famous."

"We were." The old man's eyes filmed. "We were famous in our time, but now . . ." He faltered, apparently near the end of his strength.

Lacy snapped forward. Was he sick?

Fred said, "We'll tell the newspapers."

If he died, somebody would close the tomb and end the vigil.

Yes.

Vinnie said, "We can get other kids to come."

No.

Jane picked up the enthusiasm. "TV, the works."

If he died . . .

The old man said to Lacy, without speaking, *Not dead yet.*

She looked around at the others. Did they hear? Did they know? God, no. They were getting into it: "Pilgrims should come."

He pulled himself together. "You understand."

The misery!

Lacy's voice was sharp, "Oh, please."

". . . I have to keep this going, for her."

Deep inside the box, Lacy knew, the old lady sighed. She was dying here, stifling, terrified, and yet the other four were lolling in their chairs scarfing up Cokes and the terrible cookies the old man had produced, he could have been luring them, or drugging them or seducing them or worse and yet they loved it. Outside, the orange Florida sun was going down; it was late! Lacy was restless, anxious, terrified; it was late and here were Vinnie and the others, happy to hang out here forever; Lacy could not get moving, could not get them moving, thought, Oh-oh, captive audience, but she was wrong.

"Closing time," the old man said suddenly, and just as suddenly got up and scowled at the fearsome five until they stood.

Stalling, Vinnie said, "Say what?"

"Eight o'clock. The end of calling hours."

Vinnie and the others were moving slowly, reluctant to let go, but Lacy found herself squirming under the old man's yellow stare. His eyes bored in, snagging her somewhere deep, *No!* Panicked, she broke free. She pushed past the others, who were making their manners, and bolted, running hard for the car.

Fred was the first to follow. "Babe," he said when he reached her: Fred, just who she wanted, but how did he find her?

Helpless, gasping, rattling with fright. "I can't . . ."

"What's the matter, babe?"

"It's all so *old*," she said, thinking, my God, forget futures! Let me not have to go too many years past now.

"True love," Fred said. "It's kind of neat."

"It's creepy, that pink marble box, and that old, old guy!"

"It's not creepy," Fred said.

"It's a trap."

"He loves her." *No.* He left the rest unspoken but his arms slid around Lacy and he hugged her, opening all the doors inside her as he said, "Lacy?"

Oh, Fred.

"If we have to get old, I want to do something just as good as that for you."

"Don't," she cried, frightened. "No more futures!"

"Dipshit, I'm trying to say I think I love you!"

"Oh, Fred!" She leaned her forehead against him, taking in the warmth, the promises about tonight, tomorrow, a lot of tomorrows and then, as the others came along, Lacy backed off, tickling the palm of his big hand with her index finger, a promise.

He took the message. "Babe!"

"Yes," she said, but to her astonishment and grief she blurted, "If I can!"

They were all jabbering as Vinnie roared out of the cemetery with the boom box going and all flags flying, heading for Central Avenue and the land of the living; Archie was piping "When I'm calling you-ooo-ooo . . . ," while Vinnie numbered the objects in the bizarre little tomb item for item and everybody laughed. They were way into it: the adventure of the year, while inside Lacy something boiled.

—Tomorrow they'd come back with gangs of people to see Muriel during calling hours, what a hoot! Lace?

But Lacy was turned in on herself, trying to see what.

—Cokes for all, and that horrible portrait, and all that ugly stuff! They'd keep it going until it got old.

What she had to do.

On Snell Isle Vinnie let Jane off and Archie off; he rolled into the older Northeast section and at Lacy's corner he looked at Fred and said, "So?" and Fred looked at Lacy, saying, "So?"

"Oh, Fred." So there it was: the future was just ahead, and with her heart tugging out of her chest and trying to throw itself at Fred, Lacy found herself stopped cold, foiled. Dragging her fingers across Fred's outstretched hand, torn in two by regret, she got out of the car, saying, "I can't tonight."

"Lacy!"

"I want to, but I can't."

He tugged at her. "Why not?"

Agonized, she tore free. "I can't even say!"

She was aware of the car lingering for several minutes, Fred halfway up her front sidewalk, hoping, but she ran around back and stood inside the kitchen door trembling with grief until he gave up on her and got back in the car with Vinnie and they scratched off.

By the time her parents came back from Tampa with the family station wagon, Lacy had fixed on it: what she had to do. It was strange, she thought, her degree of prescience, or was it only what her psych teacher called accuracy of role-taking? She knew that poor dead lady hated everything her husband had collected to put around her; she hated calling hours, she hated the rug, and the portrait? Muriel was mortified, and the old man knew. For whatever reasons, the dead Muriel and her husband were locked in some unholy vendetta; the old man was on top for now, and his revenge?

His revenge had gone on for much too long.

Lacy was sober, clever, much too smart to do anything dumb. She was going to do what she could for poor Muriel and hope it was enough.

She was headed back there to clean out the place. With the old man gone for the night she would prize open the door to Muriel's tomb and take out everything in the place that embarrassed or offended the dead lady—the blue neon, the terrible portrait, the scratchy recordings of poor Muriel in bad voice, the horrible ornaments and the ghastly guest book encrusted with shells. She had to take everything ugly out of that horrible place and dump the lot in Tampa Bay. If she could get away with enough stuff she might release the trapped Muriel, was certain the vengeful old man was using all these hideous objects to ensnare his wife's soul. *The humiliation.*

Intent on it, she backed the family station wagon as close to the entrance to Muriel's tomb as she could manage and started on the lock. First she'd liberate the portrait and the ugly Persian rug; then she'd seize the guest book encrusted with shells. She would like to go further, crack open the sarcophagus and rescue Muriel, wake her up and carry her off in the car, the big getaway that, what, who knows? Might guarantee them both perpetual freedom, but working away there in the moonlight, Lacy knew her limits. She'd have to remove the malevolent objects and hope that did the job.

For whatever reasons, she had to do this before she could be free to love Fred. Owed it to—who, Muriel? Herself?

The lock yielded so easily that she should have been suspicious, but by this time she was so fixed on what she wanted to do for the trapped Muriel that she did not hear or note her warning, *Watch out.*

Which is how in her own way Lacy found herself not ending but perpetuating this monstrous vigil as she blundered inside and in seconds and without any sense of transition became what she beheld.

She saw the vengeful old man sitting there in the bamboo chair with his hands locked on the head of a gold-headed cane, with his eyes fixed on her in concentration so pure that she could not know for certain until too late whether he was living or in transition or already dead. Horrified, beholding, she found herself drawn in, sucked into that withering flesh, pulled inside the barely covered skull, sixteen-year-old Lacy, who had been pretty, if ordinary, was not so much extinguished as

—somehow—

subsumed.

In the next second she was trapped inside, looking out.

What Lacy saw: her beautiful young body deserted, crumpled like an abandoned coat; the surroundings, garish ornaments, sarcophagus, guest book, the lot. Her own hands, liver-spotted and contorted, resting on the head of her cane, her bony knees in the seersucker, shanks that had fallen away to nothing; instead of freeing Muriel she had in this split second of return *become* this:

The old man in his perpetual vengeance, chuckling: "New life."

The vigil. "It's important for this to continue."

His revenge. "I will never forgive her for despising me."

Could hear the words rattling around in the ugly, overdecorated and claustrophobic tomb but could no longer hear Muriel because the dead wife was the despised one now, trapped just as Lacy was but powerless, fixed forever in the silence of the dead.

Stood up. "Good. Calling hours just as usual tomorrow. Maybe those kids will come again."

Ian Watson
THE TALK OF THE TOWN

Ian Watson grew up in the northeast of
England, studied at Oxford, and now
calls Daventry, England, the setting of
this story, home. He lives in a house
charmingly yet ironically called "Daisy
Cottage"—ironically considering the
sometimes dark prose he creates there.

"The Talk of the Town" also deals
with change, as does Kit Reed's tale, but
in this story, home is changed by a sudden new awareness of the familiar
"sounds of home." "The Talk of the
Town" is the story of Daventry's "voice"
and, as Ian writes *after* doing this story,

> "I've been astonished to discover that
> the town of Daventry *does* have a voice.
> I switched on the radio, and heard the
> words, "Daventry Calling, Daventry
> Calling." This turned out to be part of
> a poem, which some listener requested,
> by the now neglected poet Alfred
> Noyes, written to celebrate the start of
> transmissions in 1935 from the first
> long-range radio station, at Daventry.

Intrigued, I ordered the *Collected Poems* of Alfred Noyes from the library . . . only to discover no such poem in the whole book. Noyes mustn't have thought much of his "Daventry Calling" poem.

Poor Daventry . . . it must have thought it was going to speak to the world for a long time. And all that passed away.

Thanks to Ian Watson, however, it hasn't passed away. In "The Talk of the Town," Daventry once again speaks and we come to learn that home is sometimes a place that we—and we alone—can understand.

THE TALK OF THE TOWN
Ian Watson

COULD MY UNIQUE EXPERIENCE have some connection with the radio masts on Borough Hill?

There are, oh, a dozen of those. At night they become anorexic Christmas trees lit up to warn off low-flying planes. The transmitters are high-powered. Now and then drivers of posh fuel-injection cars complain that their engines cut out on the main road that runs below Borough Hill, though the radio engineers deny responsibility.

Borough Hill is also where the magic mushrooms grow. Wire fences weave a wide cordon around the radio station, but the barrier's insecure. A teenager can squirm underneath the wire where a badger has scooped a pit or where rabbits have sapped the soil. Several adventurers did so, to gather the hallucinogenic mushrooms. When one of these bold spirits, my friend Tim Hewitt, was rushed to hospital and died of poisoning, the local rag—known to everyone, including itself, as "The Gusher"—mounted a crusade. As a result bales of barbed wire, ribboned with the wool of itchy sheep, now reinforce the perimeter.

That was in the year when two of the town councillors ran off to a love-nest by the seaside a hundred and fifty miles away. A few months later Mr. Jarvis and Mrs. Leacock straggled back separately to face forgiveness and embarrassment. Their romantic escapade had failed.

Tim died before he could supply me with a handful of *Amanita muscaria* to blow my mind right out of town. Yet somehow when

147

my hometown begins to talk to me I imagine that some conjunction of those mushrooms and those radio masts may be responsible; as though, through the roots of their guy-wires and stays, the tall steel trees are sucking up essence of rotting *Amanita* and are broadcasting a delirium into my skull.

My parents, Matt and Pat, adore country and western music, which I suppose is their own style of escape. After a day as local bus driver and supermarket checkout lady respectively, Matt and Pat will dress up as sequined cowboy and cowgirl. He'll strum away loudly at the electronic guitar while she will warble stuff about divorce and truckers, drunks and waitresses. Every fortnight or so they perform in one or other of the town pubs, to a fair amount of applause.

Personally I find their activities dead embarrassing, but I can't help noticing how many American songs seem to mythologize by name a whole string of towns and cities which really possess a very short history compared with your average British town or city. How many songs mythologize British towns, however?

> Daventry, oh Daventry,
> I can see your radio station;
> And it fills me with elation.
> I blow my nose
> And twiddle all my toes . . .

Mrs. Taylor, one of the history teachers at my old school, said that our town took its name from the time of the Vikings and referred to Danish invaders. This origin led to the christening of the Daneholme housing estate which backs on to the country park—a semiwooded reservoir where fisherman angle, where shags and geese touch down to delight the bird-watchers with their binoculars, where dogs shit on the paths.

I found an old book in the town library which says that the name stems from "Dafa's Tree," Dafa being the name of some ancient Briton. Perhaps because this isn't the usual explanation I prefer it. I visualize Dafa as a hairy, smelly rough-tough clad in an ill-cured sheepskin.

Did Dafa own the tree in question? Was there only one tree in the vicinity? That hardly seems likely. So far as I know, the whole land used to be cloaked in virgin forest, of oak and ash and sweet chestnut, ever since the glaciers retreated thirteen thousand years ago.

Maybe Dafa used to sacrifice people to his special tree. Maybe he was a great local chief, and when he was buried, his kin had planted an acorn on his chest. Those were the days.

In the era of the stagecoach the town became an important stopover, as the ramshackled old hotel at the top of Sheaf Street still bears witness. Joseph Priestley, discoverer of oxygen, went to school in that street. (Did everyone hold their breath until Priestley arrived?)

History has sagged and rotted since. I don't think the Luftwaffe actually bombed the town, aiming ineptly for the radio masts. The center simply has the appearance of a bomb site.

I have walked around it a million times.

Before it speaks to me.

The voice comes from around my head—from a few inches away—rather than from within.

"Greetings, Owen!" It's a deep, mellow, benign voice.

In Bowen Square shoppers' cars crawl around under a gray January sky, headlights lit at noon, hunting for parking spaces. Members of the Jesus Army are blocking part of the pavement, jigging and singing about the love of their invisible lord.

These people form a powerful little economic empire locally, what with their organic farms, their grocery shops, their builders' merchant yards and general building business. A few dark rumors circulate as to how kids in their various communes can't watch television and are beaten for transgressions; even how the naked corpse of a runaway was found frozen in wintry fields near New Creation Farm. The head of the army pointed out that a lot of its members are former drug addicts and runaways who have been rehabilitated in Christ. Jesus people take the army theme seriously, wearing paramilitary uniforms at their rallies. However, these singers today look somewhat more hippy. Dowdy hippy.

> "Hey-ho, wherever you may be,
> "I am the lord of the dance," said he,
> "And I'll lead you all, wherever you may be—"

"Greetings, Owen!"

Can this be the voice of the lord of the Jesus Army? Am I on the brink of a conversation, as if those singers have sneezed in my face and I instantly caught cold?

"Who are you?" I utter the words deep in my throat, moving my lips as little as possible.

"I'm Daventry, Owen. What can I do for you?"

"You're . . . Daventry?"

"The very same. Let me prove it. Ask me a favor."

"Okay. Make the sun shine on me."

"Certainly, Owen. Give me a few minutes."

I walk on through the Foundry Place arcade—housing yet another greeting card shop, yet another travel agent. In Sheaf Street I halt by the window where the jolly automaton cobbler forever thumps a hammer up and down upon a last. A cutting wind funnels up the sloping street of mostly sandstone shops, cafés, and whatnot. Mist hides the dip through which the bypass road runs, and masks the Headlands housing estate that rises beyond.

On such a day of puzzling visibility I often imagine that Sheaf Street plunges down to a seafront and that the haze in the dip is ocean. It isn't, of course, and it doesn't. Maybe Mr. Jarvis and Mrs. Leacock were infected by a similar illusion and fled away to locate the source of their fancy. Before trickling back home like condensation down a plate-glass window.

Just then, the gray overcast parts. A shaft of golden light floods the upper stories of the street. The reflection from a wondow dazzles me.

"There you are, Owen: sunshine."

"Thanks, Daventry."

"My pleasure." Such a deep, measured, noble voice; though at the same time ingenuous, guileless.

The freak sunlight lasts until I pass the pet shop, outside of which stand bins of dog biscuits. I loathe dogs. Messy animals, by turns slavish and vicious. So far as I'm concerned there are only two categories of dog: Rottweilers, and bonsai Rottweilers. Roaming loose despite a notice to the contrary fixed to a lamppost, one of the latter variety is busy dropping its dirty load on a paving slab. Risking an attack on my ankles, I direct a kick at its ribs.

"Thank you, Owen."

"Maybe it isn't such great shakes being a town? Dog dirt, car exhausts, litter, people letting parts of you go derelict, your roads breaking out into acne with the frost . . ."

"I am content."

Since leaving school three years ago I tried to be a clerk in the brand-new district council offices, but that didn't last. The tedium, and low pay. So basically I'm unemployed.

Have a few friends, though no girlfriend. I guess I'm shy in that area. I read a lot; pick up long words the way tramps pick up cigar butts. Walk around town a lot. That doesn't take long. My favorite spot is the graveyard behind the parish church. Steel meshes protect the lower windows of the locked edifice on account of kids chucking stones. Long grass and brambles hide most of the graves, though one clear space, marked by no headstone, looks as though a Rottweiler has buried a bone to which it must obsessively return. A homemade signboard planted in the overturned soil reads: *Leave Our Baby's Grave Alone*.

Pathetic, really.

I thought the whole town was pathetic. In my mind I privately renamed it Desultory.

Until it spoke to me.

Can I have been hurting its feelings? Am I uniquely sensitive to it?

Can it work other wonders similar to that sudden flood of sunlight?

Does anyone else know? Does anyone else notice?

I walk round town now with a different step and with other eyes. Each brick is a cell in its body. Each building is an organ.

Masts, mushrooms . . . I reject any such notions. As well as the notion of madness, of course, since I don't feel at all mad.

Daventry only speaks to me while I'm in physical contact with its horny skin of pavements or tarmac. When I lie in bed at home, strain as I might there's silence.

"Do you hear me, Daventry?"

Not a whisper.

Nor does the town address me when I'm inside shops or coffee bars or the post office. Maybe this is discretion on the town's part—not wishing to expose me, or our relationship, should I mumble too noisily. Maybe Daventry can't communicate when other people are close by, cooped up next to me. Like a doleful hound left at a doorway, Daventry stays outside, waiting. Well now, a loony would mutter to an imaginary acquaintance anywhere without exception, wouldn't he? If, on the other hand, I'm suffering from some phobia connected with walking the streets—a phobia which is causing the voice—surely I should find Daventry's words scary and oppressive, driving me indoors? Whereas I don't.

"Do you talk to other people?" I ask in the High Street another day as I'm passing the frozen food center.

"Only to you currently, Owen."

"Why me?"

"Because you can hear me."

"Can other *places* hear you? Are you friends with the villages hereabouts?"

"A cow can't be friendly with a squeaky mouse."

"How about with other towns your size?"

"Those cows live in far-flung fields."

"Roads link you."

"Yes, roads . . ." Daventry sounds scornful—as well a town might, when the last thing it can do is pull up its roots and shuffle somewhere else.

"I guess you must know the answer to this: are you named after Dafa, or the Danes?"

"I have a secret name of my own, Owen. It's Rambalundabalgi," confides Daventry.

"What language is that?"

"My very own."

"Who else speaks it?"

"Only me. I need a constant language which doesn't change down the centuries."

"So do you talk to yourself in it?"

"Hambadoolapoo, homboloin, impolooli," says Daventry.

It dawns on me that I'm not nuts. It's my hometown that is cuckoo, batty as a coot. Not in any spectacular, psychotic fashion, I hasten to add. More in a quiet, depressive style.

Disconcerting! Still, I'm not scared. I wonder what I can get it to do for me.

"Rambabalgi, I need some—"

"Rambalundabalgi, please."

"Sorry. Ramba-lunda-balgi, I need some money."

"Try the cash dispenser at the bank," suggests Daventry.

"I don't have money in any bank."

"Nevertheless."

"And I don't have a plastic card to stick in the slot."

"Hoodsbonda poloobola."

When I reach the niche in the bank wall, the little screen lights up invitingly of its own accord with its menu of options. Glancing to left and right—and seeing no one in the offing—I press the CASH button.

"Now key twenty pounds," advises Daventry. "Ambobooda doo-looli."

I do as it says. The machine clicks and whirrs and churns within as if actually printing the money, and a single crisp banknote emerges. I scarper up the street.

"Why not fifty quid?" I ask my benefactor. "Why not a hundred?"

"Twenty is adequate for your present needs, Owen."

I go into the Plume of Feathers and buy a lager, leaving me about nineteen quid.

So there are miracles—but I'm going to be rationed. Daventry mustn't want me to become too independent.

"How about providing a dishy-looking girlfriend for me?" I ask Rambalundabalgi a few days later, hoping that this request won't make my town jealous.

The town hums and haws. But it has already persuaded its good citizens to stand on one leg for a while, to please me. That trick didn't pose too much of a problem. For a good fifteen seconds the little marketplace resembled a colony of drab flamingos in overcoats and anoraks when a score of people hoisted a leg to rub an itch or for whatever other motive. A few noticed the supposed coincidence and giggled or looked embarrassed.

"Aw, come on, town of mine. Do your stuff."

"We shall see. Amoorche chamoori."

"That's the spirit."

I bump into Cynthia Danvers outside of the Help the Aged charity shop. She clings to me to avoid falling over. Since we're in a clinch it seems only reasonable for us to kiss briefly, and laugh.

"Why, Owen," she exclaims, "I haven't seen you for ages." Actually, she has; on other occasions she simply hasn't been paying any attention. "What a slippery pavement!"

Slim blond Cynthia works part-time in a hair styling salon these days . . .

Walking toward my home together, arm in arm, it seems as if a treasure hunt is in progress. A chap in overalls is walking slowly along our street with what appears to be a metal detector, which emits the occasional whistle. Old women's faces peer from behind curtains.

I hail him. "Found gold yet, have we?"

"Suspected gas leak," says the fellow. "I can't find anything."

"Is there going to be an explosion?" Anxiously Cynthia squeezes my arm.

Oh yes, I think to myself, there'll be an explosion, though not of gas.

"That'll be the smell from the paint factory," I reassure her. "It comes when the wind's from the west. Depending on what they're making." I must get Rambalundabalgi to do something permanent about the smell . . .

The man with the gas detector packs up and drives off in a van. As soon as I let Cynthia into our empty house and embrace her, her attitude to me shifts like the wind. She wrinkles up her pert nose.

"Stop pawing me, Owen," she says. "I only came for a cup of coffee."

"Amoorcha chamoori," I chant.

"*What?*"

Alas, I'm overlooking the fact that Daventry's writ apparently doesn't extend within my home. Or any other building, either? Cynthia's enchantment hasn't lasted.

"Name of a new rock group," I tell her with a shrug.

"Weirdo." Her tone doesn't convey much enthusiasm.

I make us some coffee and we chat in a vague way, although

once she leaves—as soon as she's outside the door—she agrees brightly to take a stroll around the country park with me the evening after.

In the middle of January, yes. As she walks off she glances back, mildly puzzled.

Standing in the garden I tell Rambalundabalgi, "I need a tent and a sleeping bag. Cancel that! I need a *van* with a good heater and a sleeping bag." We can take a drive to a pub beforehand to oil the wheels of love. Though not to a country pub, or I'll be outside of Rambalundabalgi's sphere of influence. Oh God, not even to a pub . . . I need a bottle of red vino for us to share in the van.

"But Owen, you haven't passed your driving test."

"You'll see to it that I'm not caught, won't you?"

"Choobaloo hompobeli."

Seemingly human nature imposes other limits. One leg in the air, it transpires, but not both legs. "I'm not going *all* the way," Cynthia protests in the back of the van which I borrowed from the New Street car park, having found the keys left in the ignition. Yes, from right opposite the fuzz shop itself, within a stone's throw of the police station.

"In fact," and she giggles tipsily, "I don't know why I'm doing this much!" An owl hoots from the nearby trees. "Isn't this good enough?" The van's engine throbs softly, running the heater. My own engine throbs, causing, after a while, an urgent desire to pee. When I climb back aboard, Cynthia's sitting in the passenger seat waiting for me to drive her home.

After doing so, I repark the van without problems other than scraping one wing against a concrete bollard; and I prowl the streets frustratedly.

"Rambalundabalgi!" I cry. "Is it really much use at all knowing you?"

"Ah, but you're the actor in my dream, Owen. I need an actor, don't you see?"

"What do you mean?"

"Chamoori choobaloo, my young friend! Can everything that you desire come true in dreams? Ah no. How often does prohibition step in between the desire and its fulfillment! The anchors of guilt, conscience, and repression drag the actor back from the brink of the orgy. As indeed must be the case! Would you see this street fill with tropical fishes from the tanks in yonder pet shop? Shoals of rainbow fish swimming about freely in midair as if over a coral reef? Would you see all those Rottweilers burst into flames spontaneously or explode, splattering the shop windows with red graffiti? Would you have the moon shine warmly, heating the dark of the night, and the sun gleam coldly so that daylight hours are the best time to snuggle in bed? Would you see the people strolling about merrily in their underwear, drunk with freedom and imagination, singing arias?"

"Why not? Why not?"

"Do you propose a revolution? An invasion by caprice?"

"Yes, *Desultory*," I say insultingly.

"Then you must learn my language and lose your own."

"I will!"

Rambalundabalgi teaches me so quickly. Hompobeli. Hambadoolapoo. Homboloin.

And those things come to pass. Fish swim through the air. Dogs explode. The moon warms me. People of all ages spill into the streets in their nighties and pyjamas to dance around the stone cross by the marketplace which burns like a candle.

For a while I still understand the words of the *other* people— those ghosts in overcoats, anoraks, leather jackets, police uniforms—though I can't answer them except in Rambalundabalgi's lingo. Those ghosts are fading, old words are fading . . .

Hoodabonda?

Shoochoo moochobal; aaap hooloo peeph foochali. Sooramangi? Sha! Choobaloo. Ambolongapangi.

"Rambalundabalgi?"

"Chamoori, Owen. Chamoori."

Jane Yolen
GREAT GRAY

Now, here is an unexpected tale—a won-
derfully chilling little story from Jane
Yolen. Jane is more noted for her poetry,
humorous fiction, fantasy, folktales and
picture books for children than for grue-
some horror. Her writing spans all genres
and age groups and has received the recognition it justly deserves. In addition to
the numerous awards her juvenile literature has received, her 1989 fantasy novel,
Sister Light, Sister Dark, was nominated
for a Nebula Award.

   Owls were the subject—but in a *very*
different way—of her Caldecott Award-
winning picture book, *Owl Moon*, illus-
trated by John Schoenherr. When asked
for a story about her hometown, Jane said
that she had wanted to do something
more with owls for quite a while. She
wanted to tell a story revolving around a
curious incident that happened in her
town, Hatfield, Massachusetts, a number
of years ago. A large number of Great
Gray owls suddenly appeared. "People
came out to see them," she said. "But it

looked as if they were worshiping the owls." In "Great Gray," Jane uses that event and we come to realize that sometimes the most seemingly insignificant happening can turn our old, familiar hometowns topsy-turvy into strange and eerie unknown places. If owls come to roost in *your* hometown, you too may look at them very differently after reading this story . . .

GREAT GRAY

Jane Yolen

THE COLD SPIKE of winter wind struck Donnal full in the face as he pedaled down River Road toward the marsh. He reveled in the cold just as he reveled in the ache of his hands in the wool gloves and the pull of muscle along the inside of his right thigh.

At the edge of the marsh, he got off the bike, tucking it against the sumac, and crossed the road to the big field. He was lucky this time. One of the Great Grays, the larger of the two, was perched on a tree. Donnal lifted the field glasses to his eyes and watched as the bird, undisturbed by his movement, regarded the field with its big yellow eyes.

Donnal didn't know a great deal about birds, but the newspapers had been full of the *invasion*, as it was called. Evidently Great Gray owls were Arctic birds that only every hundred years found their way in large numbers to towns as far south as Hatfield. He shivered, as if a Massachusetts town on the edge of the Berkshires was south. The red-back vole population in the north had crashed and the young Great Grays had fled their own hunger and the talons of the older birds. And here they were, daytime owls, fattening themselves on the mice and voles common even in winter in Hatfield.

Donnal smiled, and watched the bird as it took off, spreading its six-foot wings and sailing silently over the field. He knew there were other Great Grays in the Valley—two in Amherst, one in the Northampton Meadows, three reported in Holyoke, and some twenty others between Hatfield and Boston. But he felt that the two in Hatfield were his alone. So far no one else had discovered them. He had been biking out twice a day for over a week to watch them, a short three miles along the meandering road.

A vegetarian himself, even before he'd joined the Metallica commune in Turner's Falls, Donnal had developed an unnatural desire to watch animals feeding, as if that satisfied any of his dormant carniverous instincts. He'd even owned a boa at one time, purchasing white mice for it at regular intervals. It was one of the reasons he'd been asked to leave the commune. The other, hardly worth mentioning, had more to do with a certain sexual ambivalence having to do with children. Donnal never thought about *those* things anymore. But watching the owls feeding made him aware of how much superior he was to the hunger of mere beasts.

"It makes me understand what is meant by a little lower than the angels," he'd remarked to his massage teacher that morning, thinking about angels with great gray wings.

This time the owl suddenly plummeted down, pouncing on something which it carried in its talons as it flew back to the tree. Watching through the field glasses, Donnal saw it had a mouse. He shivered deliciously as the owl plucked at the mouse's neck, snapping the tiny spinal column. Even though he was much too far away to hear anything, Donnal fancied a tiny dying shriek and the satisfying *snick* as the beak crunched through bone. He held his breath in three great gasps as the owl swallowed the mouse whole. The last thing Donnal saw was the mouse's tail stuck for a moment out of the beak like a piece of gray velvet spaghetti.

Afterward, when the owl flew off, Donnal left the edge of the field and picked his way across the crisp snow to the tree. Just as he hoped, the pellet was on the ground by the roots.

Squatting, the back of his neck prickling with excitement, Donnal took off his gloves and picked up the pellet. For a minute he just held it in his right hand, wondering at how light and how dry the whole thing felt. Then he picked it apart. The mouse's skull was still intact, surrounded by bits of fur. Reaching into the pocket of his parka, Donnal brought out the silk scarf he'd bought a week ago at the Mercantile just for this purpose. The scarf was blood red with little flecks of dark blue. He wrapped the skull carefully in the silk and slipped the packet into his pocket, then turned a moment to survey the field again. Neither of the owls was in sight.

Patting the pocket thoughtfully, he drew his gloves back on and strode back toward his bike. The wind had risen and snow was beginning to fall. He let the wind push him along as he rode, almost effortlessly, back to the center of town.

Donnal had a room in a converted barn about a quarter of a mile south of the center. The room was within easy walking to his massage classes and only about an hour's bike ride into Northampton, even closer to the grocery store. His room was dark and low and had a damp, musty smell as if it still held the memory of cows and hay in its beams. Three other families shared the main part of the barn, ex-hippies like Donnal, but none of them from the commune. He had found the place by biking through each of the small Valley towns, their names like some sort of English poem: Hadley, Whately, Sunderland, Deerfield, Heath, Goshen, Rowe. Hatfield, on the flat, was outlined by the Connecticut River on its eastern flank. There had been acres of potatoes, their white flowers waving in the breeze, when he first cycled through. He took it as an omen and when he found that the center had everything he would need— a pizza parlor, a bank, a convenience store, and a video store— had made up his mind to stay. There was a notice about the room for rent tacked up in the convenience store. He went right over and was accepted at once.

Stashing his bike in one of the old stalls, Donnal went up the rickety backstairs to his room. His boots lined up side by side by the door, he took the red scarf carefully out of his pocket. Cradling it in two hands, he walked over to the mantel which he'd built from a long piece of wood he'd found in the back, sanding and polishing the wood by hand all summer long.

He bowed his head a moment, remembering the owl flying on its silent wings over the field, pouncing on the mouse, picking at the animal's neck until it died, then swallowing it whole. Then he smiled and unwrapped the skull.

He placed it on the mantel and stepped back, silently counting. There were seventeen little skulls there now. Twelve were mice, four were voles. One, he was sure, was a weasel's.

Lost in contemplation, he didn't hear the door open, the quick intake of breath. Only when he had finished his hundredth repetition of the mantra and turned did Donnal realize that little Jason was staring at the mantel.

"You . . ." Donnal began, the old rhythm of his heart spreading a heat down his back. "You are not supposed to come in without knocking, Jay. Without being . . ." He took a deep breath and willed the heat away. "Invited."

Jason nodded silently, his eyes still on the skulls.

"Did you hear me?" Donnal forced his voice to be soft but he couldn't help noticing that Jason's hair was as velvety as mouse skin. Donnal jammed his hands into his pockets. "Did you?"

Jason looked at him then, his dark eyes wide, vaguely unfocused. He nodded but did not speak. He never spoke.

"Go back to your apartment," Donnal said, walking the boy to the door. He motioned with his head, not daring to remove his hands from his pockets. "Now."

Jason disappeared through the door and Donnal shut it carefully with one shoulder, then leaned against it. After a moment, he drew his hands out of his pockets. They were trembling and moist.

He stared across the room at the skulls. They seemed to glow, but it was only a trick of the light, nothing more.

Donnal lay down on his futon and thought about nothing but the owls until he fell asleep. It was dinnertime when he finally woke. As he ate he thought—and not for the first time—how hard winter was on vegetarians.

"But owls don't have that problem," he whispered aloud.

His teeth crunched through the celery with the same sort of *snick-snack* he thought he remembered hearing when the owl had bitten into the mouse's neck.

The next morning was one of those crisp, bright, clear winter mornings with the sun reflecting off the snowy fields with such an intensity that Donnal's eyes watered as he rode along River Road. By the water treatment building, he stopped and watched a cardinal flicking through the bare ligaments of sumac. His disability check was due and he guessed he might have a client or two as soon as he passed his exams at the Institute. He had good hands for massage and the extra money would come in handy. He giggled at the little joke: *hands . . . handy.* Extra money would mean he could buy the special tapes he'd been wanting. He'd use them for the accompan-

162

iment for massages and for his own meditations. Maybe even have cards made up: *Donnal McIvery, Licensed Massage Therapist*, the card would say. *Professional Massage. By Appointment Only*

He was so busy thinking about the card, he didn't notice the car parked by the roadside until he was upon it. And it took him a minute before he realized there were three people—two men and a woman—standing on the other side of the car, staring at the far trees with binoculars.

Donnal felt hot then cold with anger. They were looking at *his* birds, *his* owls. He could see that both of the Great Grays were sitting in the eastern field, one on a dead tree down in the swampy area of the marsh and one in its favorite perch on a swamp maple. He controlled his anger and cleared his throat. Only the woman turned.

"Do you want a look?" she asked with a kind of quavering eagerness in her voice, starting to take the field glasses from around her neck.

Unable to answer, his anger still too strong, Donnal shook his head and, reaching into his pocket, took his own field glasses out. The red scarf came with it and fell to the ground. His cheeks flushed as red as the scarf as he bent to retrieve it. He knew there was no way the woman could guess what he used the scarf for, but still he felt she knew. He crumpled it tightly into a little ball and stuffed it back in his pocket. It was useless now, desecrated. He would have to use some of his disability check to buy another. He might have to miss a lesson because of it; because of *her*. Hatred for the woman flared up and it was all he could do to breathe deeply enough to force the feeling down, to calm himself. But his hands were shaking too much to raise the glasses to his eyes. When at last he could, the owls had flown, the people had gotten back into the car and driven away. Since the scarf was useless to him, he didn't even check for pellets, but got back on his bike and rode home.

Little Jason was playing outside when he got there and followed Donnal up to his room. He thought about warning the boy away again, but when he reached into his pocket and pulled out the scarf, having for the moment forgotten that the scarf's magic was lost to him, he was overcome with the red heat. He could feel great gray wings growing from his shoulders, bursting through his parka, sprouting quill, feather, vane. His mouth tasted blood. He heard the *snick-snack* of little neck bones being broken. Such a satisfying sound. When the heat abated, and his eyes cleared, he saw that the boy lay on the floor, the red scarf around his neck, pulled tight.

For a moment Donnal didn't understand. Why was Jason lying there; why was the scarf set into his neck in just that way? Then when it came to him that his own strong hands had done it, he felt a strange satisfaction and he breathed as slowly as when he said his mantras. He laid the child out carefully on his bed and walked out of the room, closing the door behind.

He cashed the check at the local bank, then pedaled into Northampton. The Mercantile had several silk scarves, but only one red one. It was a dark red, like old blood. He bought it and folded it carefully into a little packet, then tucked it reverently into his pocket.

When he rode past the barn where he lived, he saw that there were several police cars parked in the driveway and so he didn't stop. Bending over the handlebars, he pushed with all his might, as if he could feel the stares of townsfolk.

The center was filled with cars, and two high school seniors, down from Smith Academy to buy candy, watched as he flew past. The wind at his back urged him on as he pedaled past the Main Street houses, around the meandering turns, past the treatment plant and the old barns marked with the passage of high school grafitti.

He was not surprised to see two vans by the roadside, one with out-of-state plates; he knew why they were there. Leaning his bike against one of the vans, he headed toward the swamp, his feet making crisp tracks on the crusty snow.

There were about fifteen people standing in a semicircle around the dead tree. The largest of the Great Grays sat in the crotch of the tree, staring at the circle of watchers with its yellow eyes. Slowly its head turned from left to right, eyes blinked, then another quarter turn.

The people were silent, though every once in a while one would move forward and kneel before the great bird, then as silently move back to place.

Donnal was exultant. These were not birders with field glasses

164

and cameras. These were worshipers. Just as he was. He reached into his pocket and drew out the kerchief. Then slowly, not even feeling the cold, he took off his boots and socks, his jacket and trousers, his underpants and shirt. No one noticed him but the owl, whose yellow eyes only blinked but showed no fear.

He spoke his mantra silently and stepped closer, the scarf between his hands, moving through the circle to the foot of the tree. There he knelt, spreading the cloth to catch the pellet when it fell and baring his neck to the Great Gray's slashing beak.

Robert Silverberg
THE LAST SURVIVING VETERAN OF THE WAR OF SAN FRANCISCO

From the sheer number of his achieve-
ments and awards, one might expect
Robert Silverberg to be an aged, white-
haired octogenarian rather than the dis-
tinguished-looking, youthful man he is.
Robert Silverberg has had an exceptional
career in the science fiction and fantasy
field. His work has netted him numerous
awards and distinctions including the
Hugo Award, Nebula Award, and the
Prix Apollo. Most recently, his "Enter a
Soldier. Later: Enter Another" was nominated for a Nebula and received a Hugo
Award in 1990.

A concern with the inability to communicate effectively pops up often in
Bob's novels and stories and it emerges
again in this tale, but in a unique and
enthralling way. As the title indicates,
this story is set in San Francisco, Bob's
adopted hometown; like his wife, Karen
Haber, he is originally from the East
Coast. When asked why he chose that
locale, he wrote, "It's where I live. It's a
pretty place and I enjoy living here very

166

much except during moments of seismic instability." In this story of San Francisco's future, the changes Bob envisions are not dark changes as seen in other stories in this anthology but, rather, they glorify San Francisco. Not only is the city lovely but, in the here and now of this tale, San Francisco has also become the "capital of the Empire."

THE LAST SURVIVING VETERAN OF THE WAR OF SAN FRANCISCO

Robert Silverberg

THE CITY ON THE OTHER SIDE of the bay was putting on its best show that morning: bright, shimmering, glorious in the clear December sunlight. Lovely old San Francisco. The capital of the Empire, now and always. Carlotta, busily readying her great-great-multi-great uncle for his first trip over there in forty-three years, paused for a moment, looking up to take in the view from the picture window of the Berkeley War Veterans Center where he was the only remaining resident. She could see the hills, newly green after the season's first rains, rising far in the distance, and the venerable twentieth-century white towers of the downtown buildings closer in, and the lacy, sparkling roadbed of the New Bay Bridge, running parallel to the majestic stumps of the old one.

"Isn't it beautiful?" she said, turning him in his swivelseat so he could have a look at it too.

"What?"

"The city. San Francisco. You see it out there, don't you? Right there across the bay?" She touched the Visuals node that jutted like a tiny titanium mushroom from his left temple, giving it a quarter turn. Maybe the sharpness was off a little. Sometimes the old man fiddled with his nodes while he slept. "We're going over there in a little while."

"All the way to the city, are we?"

"*You* know. For the ceremony. The anniversary of the end of the war. They're going to give you a medal. Don't tell me you've forgotten already."

The timeless face, leathery but supple, stretched and twisted like taffy, rearranging its sallow sagging folds into what was probably meant as a smile. "You say the war's over? I'm a civilian again?"

"You bet you are, Uncle."

The wrinkled eyelids made three or four quick traversals of the hazel-colored fiberglass bundles that were his optical inputs. He leaned forward in that alert-looking way he affected sometimes, while the information percolated through the spongy layers of his mind.

"When did all that happen?" he asked finally.

"The war's been over for a hundred years, Uncle James. A hundred years today."

He emitted what might have been a whistling sound. "No shit! A hundred years?" She could see him rotating the number in his head, playing with it, evaluating its magnitude. Muscle-stalks moved slowly around in the crepey convolutions of his cheeks. "Imagine that. A hundred years. That's one goddamn long time." He was silent again. Then he said, after a moment, "Who won?"

"We did, Uncle."

"We did? You sure?"

"We're still a free country, aren't we? Nobody tells the Empire of San Francisco what to do, do they? We're the most powerful country in Northern California, isn't that so?"

He digested that for a moment. His eyes clouded over. Then he nodded. "Yeah. Yeah, of course we won. I knew that. Really I did." He sounded a little doubtful. He generally did, about everything. Well, he had a right. He was one hundred forty-three years old, give or take a few months, and most of him was machinery now, practically everything except the soggy old gray brain sitting behind his optical inputs. His wrists were silicone elastomer, his femurs were polyurethane and cobalt-chromium, his eardrums were teflon and platinum, his metacarpal joints were silicone with titanium grommets. His elbows had plastic bushings; his abdominal walls were dacron. And so on, on and on and on. Why anyone wanted to keep seniors alive that long was more than Carlotta could figure out. Or why the seniors wanted to be kept. But she was only nineteen. She allowed for the possibility that she might take a different view of things when she got to be as old as he was.

"We're just about ready to go, now," she told him. "Let's do the checkout, all right?" Obediently he held out his arm. Pushing back the thin sleeve, she opened his instrument panel and began keying in the life-support readouts that ran like a row of bright metal tacks from his wrist to elbow. "Respiratory—Circulatory—Metabolic—Katabolic—there, that's a good reading—Audio Appercept—Optical Appercept—Biochip Automaintain—Aminos—Hemoglobin—Enzyme Release—Glucose Level—"

There were two dozen of them, some of them pretty trivial. It was always a temptation to skip a few. But Carlotta diligently ran down the whole list, tapping in a query and getting a Green from each little readout plate before going on to the next.

It wasn't just that she'd feel bad if the old man died on her during this excursion, but once he died the whole Veterans Center would shut down, and new jobs weren't that easy to come by. So she checked him out from top to bottom. It took close to ten minutes. The newer model senior-rehab equipment had just a single readout, which gave you a Go or a No Go, and if you got the No Go you could immediately request data on specific organic or pseudo-organic malfunctions. But Uncle James was one of the early models and there was no money in the rehab budget for updating citizens left over from the previous century.

At last she slid the panel shut.

"You think I'll live?" he asked her, suddenly feisty.

"For another five hundred years, minimum. Come on. Let's go to San Francisco."

Quickly, deftly, she finished the job of making him ready to leave the building. She disconnected the long intravenous line from the wall and put him on portable. She disabled his chair control override so that she alone could guide the movements of his vehicle via the remote implant in her palm. She locked the restraining bars in place across his chest to keep him from attempting some sudden berserk excursion on foot out there. More than ever now, the old man was the prisoner of his own life-support system.

Just as she finished the job Carlotta felt a strange inner twisting and jolting, as though an earthquake had struck, and had the unexpected sickening sensation of seeing herself in his place, old and withered and shrunken and mostly artificial, feeble and helpless in the grip of a life-support. Her long slender legs had turned into pretzels, her golden hair was thin, colorless straw, her smooth oval face was a mass of dry valleys and crevasses. Her eyebrows were gone, her chin jutted like some old witch's. The only recognizable aspect of her was her clear blue eyes, and those, still bright, still quick and sharp, glared out of her ruined face carrying such a charge of hatred and fury that they burned through the air in front of her like twin lasers, leaving trails of white smoke.

She shuddered and desperately drove the image from her mind. Not me, she thought. Not ever, not like that. I won't let it.

She pressed down hard on her palm implant and sent the old man's chair rolling toward the door, which opened at his approach. And out they went into the hallway.

Carlotta had been working as a nurse at the Center for a year and a half, ever since she'd left high school. It wasn't the kind of work she had hoped for—she had imagined doing something with singing in it, or music, at any rate, or maybe acting, at least—but the aptitudes just hadn't been there, and these days you took what you could get. When she had first come to the Center there had still been seven veterans living there, and a staff of twelve to look after them, but one by one the old guys had undergone random system malfunctions, probabilistic events that became statistically unavoidable the deeper you got into your second century, and now only Uncle James was left, the last survivor of the army that fought in the War of San Francisco. The staff was down to four: Dr. McClintock, the director, and the three nurses, each working an eight-hour shift. The only reason they had kept Carlotta on this long was that Uncle James was her distant relative. But everybody understood that when Uncle James finally went they'd all lose their jobs. Naturally Uncle James got tremendous care. When the invitation had come for him to attend the Armistice Centennial celebration, the other two nurses had been dead set against his going; he was too precious to risk, they said, he was their meal ticket, let him stay home and do the ceremony by solido replica. Carlotta had been leaning in that direction herself. But Dr. McClintock had overruled them all. "He's in fine health. What kind of reflection would it be on the care we're giving him if we say he's too frail to travel even as far as San Francisco?"

That morning, when Carlotta showed up for work, there was a

note from Sanchez, the night nurse, waiting for her in the staff room. *God help you if anything happens to your uncle in the city today,* Sanchez had written.

Fuck you, Carlotta thought angrily. Sanchez could go screw herself. Did Sanchez think Carlotta was any more eager to lose her job than she was? But it was time for Sanchez to start facing reality. Some time soon—five years from now, five minutes, who could say?—Uncle James was going to have his random system malfunction, and that would be that. You could keep people alive close on a century and a half nowadays, sometimes a little longer, but you couldn't make them last forever. Not even Uncle James. And when he went, it would be tough titty for the Veterans Center and its devoted staff of four.

"Hot weather today," Uncle James said, as they emerged from the building.

"Very nice for December, yes."

"Hot. Not just nice. Hot. It must be a hundred degrees."

"A hundred's impossible, Uncle. It doesn't get that hot even in Death Valley. A hundred and a whole world would melt."

"Bullshit. It was a hundred degrees the day the war started. Everybody remembers that. The fourteenth of October, and it was hot as blazes, a hundred degrees smack on the nose at three in the afternoon. That was when those Nazi Stukas started coming over the horizon like bats out of hell, three in the afternoon."

"Nazis?" she said. "What Nazis?"

"The invading force. Hitler's Wehrmacht."

"That was a different war, Uncle. A long time before even you were born."

"Don't be so smart. Were you there? I was. Like eagles, they were, those planes. Merciless. They strafed us for hours in that filthy heat. Blam! Blam! Chk-chk-chk-chk-chk! Blam!" He glowered up at her. "And it's a hundred degrees right now, too. If you don't think so, you're wrong. I know what a hundred degrees feel like."

The temperature that morning, Carlotta guessed, was about 18, maybe 20. Very nice for December, yes. A temperature of 100 was a lunatic notion. But then she realized that the degrees he was talking about must be the old kind, the Fahrenheit kind. They ran a lot higher than modern degrees. One hundred degrees on the old scale might be 40 or 45 real degrees, she figured. Something like that. If he thought it was that hot today, he might be having some appercept trouble, or maybe even a boilover in the metabolism line. She leaned over and checked the master chair readout. Everything looked okay. He must just be excited about getting to go to the city, she told herself.

The car that the Armistice Centennial people had sent was waiting out front. It had a hinged gate and a wheelchair ramp, so she could roll him right into it. The driver looked like an android, though he probably wasn't. Uncle James sat quietly, murmuring to himself, as the car pulled away from the curb and headed down the hill toward the freeway.

"We in the city yet?" he asked, after a time.

"We're just reaching the bridge, Uncle."

"The bridge is broken. That was the first thing they bombed in the war."

"There's a new bridge now," Carlotta said. The new bridge was older than she was, but she didn't see much purpose in telling him that. She swung him around to face the window and pointed it out to him, a delicate, flexible ribbon of airy suspension cable swaying in the breeze. It was like a bridge of glass. The shattered pylons of the old bridge that rose from the bay alongside it seemed as ponderous as dinosaur thighs.

"Some bridge," he muttered. "Looks like a piece of rope."

"It'll get us there," she told him.

According to the Center records, he had been taken to San Francisco for his hundredth birthday, but hadn't been there since. He hadn't been much of anywhere since, it seemed: a daily noontime spin around the Center's courtyard, an occasional excursion to the zoo, once in a while a picnic in Tilden Park. And the rest of the time sitting in his chair, doing nothing, living on and on. If you called that living, Carlotta thought. Old James had outlived his son by more than a century—he had been killed at the age of something like twenty-two in the War of San Francisco, during the raid by the Free State of Mendocino. He had outlived his grandson, too, a victim of an unexplained sniper attack while visiting Monterey. A hell of a thing, to outlive your own grandson. James's closest relative was his great-granddaughter, who lived in Los Angeles and hadn't come north in decades. And then me, Carlotta thought.

She felt sorry for the old man. And yet he had managed to have one big thing in his life: the war. That was something. His moment of glory, which he had been dining out on for the past hundred years.

Her life had had nothing in it at all, so far, except the uneventful getting from age zero to age nineteen, and that was how it looked to remain. The world was pretty empty, locally, these days. You couldn't expect much when you lived in a country thirty miles across, that you could drive from one end of to the other in an hour, if you could drive. At least Uncle James had had a war. But even wars had been scarce commodities the past hundred years, and everyone expected that it was going to stay that way.

They were on the bridge now, meshed with its transport cable, whizzing westward at a hundred kilometers per hour. Carlotta pointed out landmarks to the old man on the way, in case he had forgotten them. "There's Alcatraz Island, do you see? And that's Mount Tamalpais, away across on the Marin County side. And back over there, behind us, you can see the whole East Bay, Oakland, Berkeley, El Cerrito—"

He seemed interested. He responded with a jumble of military history, hazy memories intermixed with scrambled details out of the wrong wars. "The Mendocino people came in right through there, where the San Rafael bridge used to be, maybe two hundred of them. We fixed their wagons. And then the Japs, General Togo and Admiral Mitsubishi, but we drove them back, we nuked their asses right out of here. Then a week afterward there was a raid by San Jose, came up through Oakland, we stopped them by the Almeda Tunnel—no, it was the bridge—the bridge, right, we held them, they were cursing at us in gook and when we went in to clear them out we found that Charlie had planted Bouncing Betties everywhere, you know, antipersonnel mines . . ."

She didn't know what he was talking about, but that was all right. Most of the time she didn't know what he was talking about, nor, she suspected, did he. It didn't matter. He rambled on and on. The bridge crossing took ten minutes—there was hardly any traffic—and then they were gliding down the ramp into the city.

Carlotta felt a little wave of excitement stirring within her. Approaching the city could do that to you. It was so lovely, shining there in the bright sunlight with the waters of the bay glittering all around it. It was a place of such infinite promise and mystery. Let me have an adventure while I'm over there, she prayed. Let me meet someone. Let something really unusual happen, okay?

She hadn't been in the city herself in six or eight months. You tended not to, without some special reason. If only she could park the old man for a couple of hours, and go off to have some fun, see the clubs, maybe check out the new styles, meet someone lively. Well, that wasn't going to happen. She had to stick close by Uncle James. But at least she was here, on this perfect day, blue sky, warm breezes blowing. The city was where everything that was of any interest in Northern California went on. It was the capital of the Empire of San Francisco, and the Empire was the center of the action. Everything else was small time, even if the small-time places wanted to give themselves fancy names, the Republic of Monterey, the Free State of Mendocino, the Royal Domain of San Jose.

Once upon a time, of course, all the little empires and kingdoms and republics had been part of the State of California, and California had been part of the United States of America. But that had been long, long ago, when Uncle James himself had been young, before all the big and little wars had split things into fragments. And all the king's horses and all the king's men weren't going to put anything together again, not now, not for a long, long time.

"San Francisco," Carlotta said. "Here we are, Uncle!"

They came off the bridge at the downtown off-ramp. There were bright banners everywhere, the imperial colors, green and gold. Crowds were in the streets, waving little flags. Carlotta heard the sound of a brass band somewhere far away. The driver was taking them up the Embarcadero, now, around toward the plaza at Market Street, where the emperor was going to preside over the ceremony in person. Because theirs was just about the only car in the vicinity, the spectators had figured out that someone important must be riding in it, and they were cheering and waving.

"Wave back, Uncle! They're cheering you. Here. Here, let me help you."

She touched her finger to his motor control and his right arm came stiffly up, fingers clenched. A little fine-tuning and she had the fingers open, the palm turned outward, the arm moving back and forth in a nice sprightly wave.

"Smile at them," she told him. "Be nice. You're a hero."

"A hero, yes. Purple Heart. Distinguished Service Cross. *Croix de Guerre.* You ought to see my medals sometimes. I've got a box full of them." He was leaning forward, peering out the car window, smiling as hard as he could. His arm jerked convulsively; he was trying to move it himself. Good for him. She let him override her control, and he waved with surprising energy, stiffly, a jerky wave, almost robotic, but at least he was doing it under his own power.

They had a big platform made out of polished redwood up at the plaza, with a crowd of VIPs already there. As the car approached, everyone made room for it, and when it halted just in front of the platform Carlotta hopped out and guided Uncle James' chair down the car's wheelchair ramp and into the open.

"Ned Townes," a fat sandy-haired man with a thick brown mustache told her, pushing his face into hers. "The emperor's adjutant. Splendid of you to come. What a grand old soldier he is!" He gave Uncle James a sidelong glance. "Is he capable of hearing anything I say, do you think?" He leaned down next to Uncle James's ear and in a booming voice he bellowed, "Welcome to San Francisco, General Crawford! On behalf of His Imperial Majesty Norton the Fourteenth, welcome to—"

Uncle James shot him a withering scowl. "You don't have to shout like that, boy," he said. "I can fucking well hear better than you can."

Townes reddened, but he managed a laugh. "Of course. Of course. Foolish of me."

Carlotta said, "Is the emperor here yet?"

"In a little while. We're running a bit late, you understand. If you and the general will take seats over there until we're ready to call him up to receive his medal—well, of course, he's seated already, but you know what I—"

"Aren't we going to sit on the platform?" Carlotta asked.

"I'm afraid that's reserved for city officials and dignitaries."

She didn't move. "Uncle James is a dignitary. We came all the way from Berkeley for this, and if you're going to shunt him into some corner for hours and hours while you—"

"Please," Townes said.

"He's a hundred forty-three years old, do you realize that?"

"Please," he said. "Bear with me." He looked about ready to cry. "The emperor himself will personally decorate him. But until then, I have to ask you—"

He seemed so desperate that Carlotta gave in. She and Uncle James went into a roped-off area just below and to the left of the platform. Uncle James didn't seem to mind. He sat quietly, lost in dreams of God knows what moment of antique heriosm, while Carlotta, standing behind his chair, kept one eye on his systems reports and took in the sights of downtown San Francisco with the other—the huge tapering buildings, the radiant blue sky, the unusual trees, the shining bridge stretching off to the east.

Uncle James said suddenly, "What are all these foreigners doing here?"

"Foreigners? What foreigners?"

"Look around you, girl."

She thought at first that he meant people from the neighboring republics and kingdoms, San Jose, Santa Cruz, Monterey, Mendocino. It wouldn't be surprising that they'd be here, considering that was a celebration intended to commemorate the signing of the Armistice that had ended the war of everybody against everybody and guaranteed the independence of all the various Northern California nations. But how could Uncle James tell a Santa Cruzian or a Montereyan from a San Franciscan? They didn't look any different down there. They didn't dress any different.

Then she realized that he meant actual and literal foreigners, tourists, visitors from the countries beyond the seas. And indeed there were plenty of them all around the plaza, a lot of exotic people carrying cameras and such, Japanese, Indians, Latin Americans, Africans. They were wearing exotic clothing, most of them, and most of them had exotic faces. The old man was staring at them as though he had never seen tourists before.

"San Francisco is always full of visitors from far away, Uncle. There's nothing new about that."

"So many of them. Gawking at us like that. They dress like gooks, girl. Didn't we fight that war to keep San Francisco for the San Franciscans? That's what I thought. A pure nation of pure people. Look at them all. *Look* at them!"

"It's the most beautiful city in the world," Carlotta said. "People have been coming from all over to see it for hundreds of years. You know that. There's nothing wrong with—"

He was raging, though. "Yellow people! Black people! Brown people! Why not green people too? Why not purple people? Their faces! Their eyes! And the clothes they wear! Who let them in? What are they all *doing* here?"

"Uncle," she said, reaching down surreptitiously to give his adrenaline damper a little downtwist.

"Leave that thing alone, girl!"

"I don't want you getting all worked up."

"Look at them," he said again, quietly.

They seemed to have noticed, now, that the celebrated last surviving veteran of the War of San Francisco was right down here among them at street level. They came crowding in suddenly from all sides of the plaza, five or ten of them at first, then a couple of dozen at least, maybe more, an eager horde, crossing into the roped-in area, pushing, jostling, pointing, grinning, waving at the old man as though he were some zoo creature. At such close range Carlotta understood why Uncle James had begun to get so upset by them. These people looked really *strange*. The Bay Area was full of people whose ancestors had been born in distant countries, but time had blurred their genes and they simply looked like people. These were different: the authentic, original, foreign item, mysterious, alien. She found herself engulfed in a sea of disturbingly unusual faces, odd-shaped noses, gleaming intense eyes, unfamiliar facial expressions. And everybody jabbering in different languages, everybody shouting questions she couldn't comprehend. It was like a frantic carnival scene, some wild festivity in some remote tropical land. The ones closest in rubbed their hands curiously along the wheels of Uncle James's chair, touched his sleeves, even reached out to finger his pendulous rubbery cheeks. Cameras were everywhere, clicking and buzzing, a swarm of goggle-eyed lenses, video, holo, solido, every kind she had ever heard of and some she wasn't able to identify at all. Microphones sprouted like toadstools in a rain forest. Everyone wanted a piece of Uncle James.

Carlotta waved her hands furiously at them, making an angry shooing gesture.

"Get back! Get *back!* He's a very old man! You'll scare him! He'll have a stroke! Give him air! Give him air!"

Parade marshals helped her push them away. They retreated reluctantly but good-humoredly, continuing to jabber in unknown languages and snapping pictures of Uncle James every step of the way. After a few moments of continued confusion they were all outside the ropes again. Carlotta looked back to see how the old man had withstood the onslaught.

He seemed okay. He was sitting forward alertly in his chair, beady-eyed, obviously angry, shaking his fist, shouting curses at them.

But somehow one of the foreigners had avoided the marshals and was still within the enclosure, standing right next to Uncle James and trying to say something to him. He was tall and stately, a portly man of great presence and authority, and maybe he had contrived to persuade them that he was one of the parade dignitaries. But obviously he was a foreigner: some sort of Latin American, from the looks of him, with a soft, pudgy olive-toned face and glossy black hair. Both his skin and his hair were very sleek, as though he oiled them daily. He was expensively dressed in a way that no local could afford: gray cashmere trousers and a finely cut camel hair jacket, and there was an emerald the size of an eyeball in a ring on his plump hand.

Carlotta went over.

"Your pardon," he said at once. "This is the celebrated veteran of the famous war, who will be honored here today?"

"He's General James Crawford, yes."

"Obrigado. A grand pleasure to make his acquaintance."

"Listen, you aren't supposed to be—"

"One moment, only a moment. You will permit me? I am Humberto Maria de Magalhaes, of Minas Gerais, which is in Brazil. I am visiting here, a trade delegation. Your city is so splendid, I love it so much. I revere this city. Its beauty, its long tormented history."

She looked around for the marshals, but they had moved on.

"You really aren't supposed to be—"

"Yes. Yes. With your permission. If I could speak with the general, after the ceremony? He indicated an elaborate recorder, easily a ten-thousand-dollar job. "The study of history, it is my passion. Your history, the tragic tale of your country, its greatness, its downfall. To speak with the general, to hear from his lips the reminiscences of his days of battle, the actual descriptions of the warfare—

179

it would be ecstasy for me. Ecstasy. Do you understand my words?"

"His Imperial Highness Norton the Fourteenth!" cried a man with an enormous voice. Carlotta looked around. A ground-effect palanquin bedecked with gaudy banners was floating solemnly up the street toward the plaza.

"You've got to go now," Carlotta said. "Look, the emperor's arriving. We can't talk about this now."

"But later, perhaps?"

"Well—"

"It is for the sacred purpose of scholarship only. Half an hour to speak with this great man—"

"All welcome His Imperial Highness!" the immense voice called.

"Later," the Brazilian said urgently. "Please!"

He slipped under the rope and was gone.

Carlotta shrugged. If the Brazilian only knew that nothing Uncle James said made sense, he wouldn't be so eager. She put the man out of her mind and turned to stare at the emperor, atop his palanquin. She had never seen him live before. The emperor was a surprisingly small man, very frail, about fifty, with pale skin and tiny hands, which he held extended to the crowd in a kind of imperial blessing. The palanquin, drifting a little way above the pavement, came forward to the reviewing stand and halted like an obedient elephant. Members of the imperial guard helped him out, and up the stairs of the platform to the position of honor.

Someone began a long droning speech of welcome. The mayor of San Francisco, Carlotta supposed. It went on and on, something about this grand occasion, this triumphant day of the commemoration of the hundred-year peace, on and on and on, yawn and yawn and yawn. The foreigners' cameras and recorders whirred diligently. Uncle James seemed to be sleeping. Carlotta's attention wandered. Now and then a cheer rose from the assembled citizens, but she had no idea why. Perhaps it was just as well that she and Uncle James weren't up on the reviewing stand with the bigwigs. She'd have to pretend to be listening then.

She could see the sleek Brazilian in the crowd. His eyes never left Uncle James. He was staring at the old man as though he were a mound of emeralds. Then he noticed Carlotta watching him, and he flicked his gaze toward her, letting his eyes rest on her in a warm insinuating way, and smiled a sleek smile that gave her shivers. It was as if he were buying her with that smile.

What did he want, really? Just to *talk*?

Uncle James was awake again. Instead of looking at the emperor, who had begun to speak in response to the mayor's oration, he was peering at the rows of foreign tourists, gaping at them as though they came not merely from other continents but from other planets. In a way, Carlotta thought, they did. Who could get to Japan or Brazil or Nigeria from here? They come to us; we don't go to them. It used to be different, she knew. Hundreds of years ago, before everything fell apart, when America had been all one country of incomprehensible size that stretched from ocean to ocean, its citizens had gone everywhere in the world. But now there were thousands of little principalities where America had been, and no one went anywhere much. That was how it had been for the last hundred and fifty years or thereabouts, and it wasn't likely to be any different for a long time to come.

"A century ago," the emperor was saying, "the fate of this entire area was at stake. Every man's hand was raised against his neighbor. Cities that long had lived in peace had gone to war against their fellow cities. But then, on this day, exactly one hundred years ago, the climactic battle of the War of San Francisco was fought. This city and its valiant allies in the East Bay and Marin stood firm against the invaders from the outlying lands. And on that day of triumph, when the peace and security of the Empire of San Francisco was made certain forever—"

"Start moving the old man up to the top of the platform," Ned Townes whispered. "He's going to get his medal now."

Uncle James was asleep again. Carlotta gave him a little adrenaline jolt.

"It's time, Uncle," she whispered.

They had a ramp around back. She touched her palm control and the wheelchair began to glide up it. The big moment at last, she told herself.

The whole thing was over before she knew it, though. The emperor smiled, shook Uncle James's hand the way he would shake a turkey's claw, said a few words, this gallant survivor, this embodiment of history, this remnant of our glorious past, and put a sash around his neck. At the end of the sash there was a mud-colored medal the size of a cookie, which seemed to have a portrait of the emperor on it. That was it. Carlotta found herself wheeling Uncle James down the ramp a moment later. Evidently the old man wasn't expected to say anything in reply. They couldn't even stay on the platform.

For this they had traveled all the way from Berkeley?

"Will you find us our driver?" she said to Ned Townes. "We might as well go back home now."

Townes looked shocked. "Oh, no! You can't do that. There are further ceremonies, and then a banquet at the palace this afternoon for all the celebrities."

"Uncle James doesn't eat banquet food. And he's getting very tired."

"Even so. It would be terrible if you left now." Townes tugged at his jowls. "Look, stay another hour, at least. You can't just grab the medal and disappear. That's the *emperor* up there, young lady."

"I don't give a damn if he's—"

But Townes was gone. The emperor was awarding another medal, this time to a wide-shouldered woman who already was wearing an assortment of decorations that had a glittery Southern California look about them.

"Permit me," a deep confident voice said.

It was the Brazilian again. Leaning over the rope, tapping her on the shoulder. Carlotta had forgotten all about him.

He said, "Is it possible to discuss, now, an opportunity for me to record the great general's reminiscences, perhaps?"

"Look, we don't have time for that. I just want to get my uncle out of here and back across the bay."

The Brazilian looked distressed. "But before you leave—half an hour—fifteen minutes—"

She glanced down at the emerald ring. A gleam came into her eyes. "There's a fee, you know. For his time. We can't just let him talk to people for free."

"A fee? Payment, you mean?"

"Absolutely."

"Yes. Yes, of course. Why should there not be a fee? It is no problem. We will discuss it." He offered her an engraved card, holding it close in front of her face as if he wasn't sure she knew how to read and holding it close might help. "This is my name. As I told you, Humberto Maria de Magalhaes. I am at the Imperial Hotel. You know that hotel? You will come to me when this is over? With the general? You agree?"

"Sorry, sir," a marshal said. "This area is for official guests only."

"Of course. Understood." The Brazilian began to back away, nodding, bowing, smiling brilliantly. To Carlotta he said, "I will see you later? Yes? I am very grateful. Obrigado! Obrigado!" He disappeared into the crowd of foreign visitors. Behind her, on the reviewing stand, the emperor was giving a medal to a man in a uniform of the San Jose air force.

It was almost noon now. People were coming out of the nearby office buildings, drifting over to see what was going on. Some of them were carrying sandwiches. Carlotta began to feel fiercely hungry. Townes had talked about a banquet that afternoon, but the afternoon seemed a long way away. Uncle James got fed by intravenous line, but she needed real food, and soon. Emperor or no emperor, she had to get out of here, and Townes could go whistle. Maybe the thing to do was find the Brazilian, strike a deal with him, let him take her to his hotel and buy her lunch. And then he could interview Uncle James all he wanted, so long as the old man's strength held out.

All right, she thought. Let's get moving.

But where had the Brazilian gone?

She didn't see him anywhere. Leaving Uncle James to look after himself for a moment, she slipped under the rope and went over to the place where the foreign visitors were clustered. No, no sign of him. People began to jabber at her and take her picture. She brushed her hand through the air as though they were a cloud of gnats. Producing the Brazilian's card, she said, to no one in particular, "Have you seen Humberto—Humberto Jose de Magal—Magal—" It was a struggle to pronounce his name. She did her best.

He must have gone, though. Perhaps he was on his way to his hotel, to wait for them.

She rushed back to Uncle James. Some people had crept into the roped-off area and were pushing microphones into his face again. Angrily Carlotta hit her palm control, backing up his wheelchair and pulling it toward her right through the flimsy rope. At a brisk

pace she headed across the street to the parking area where she
hoped their driver was waiting. Ned Townes, red-faced, materialized
from somewhere and furiously wigwagged at her, but she smiled and
waved and nodded and kept on going. He shouted something to
her, but didn't pursue.

The driver, miraculously, still was there.

"Imperial Hotel," she said, when Uncle James had been loaded
aboard.

"Where?"

"Imperial Hotel. It's downtown somewhere."

"I'm supposed to take you back to the East Bay when this is
over."

"First we have to go to the Imperial. There's a reception there
for my great-uncle."

The driver, sullen, androidal, looked right through her and said,
"I don't know about no reception. I don't know no Hotel Imperial.
You're supposed to go to the East Bay."

"First we stop at the Imperial," she said. "They're expecting us.
It's very important. I'll show you how to get there," she told him
grandly.

To her amazement he yielded, swinging the car around in a
petulant U-turn and shooting off toward Market Street. Carlotta
studied the signs on the buildings, hoping to find a marquee that
proclaimed one of them to be the Imperial, but there were no hotels
here at all, only office buildings. They turned right, turned left
again, started up a steep hill.

"This is Chinatown," the driver said. "That where you hotel is?"

"Turn left," she said.

That took them down toward Market Street again, and across
it. At a stoplight she rolled down the window and called out. "Does
anyone know where the Imperial Hotel is?" Blank faces stared at
her. She might just as well have been speaking Greek or Arabic.
The driver, on his own, turned onto Mission Street, took a left a
few blocks later, turned left again soon after. Carlotta looked around
desperately. This was a district of battered old warehouses. She
caught sight of a sign directing traffic to the Bay Bridge, and for a
moment decided that it was best to forget about the Brazilian and
head for home, when unexpectedly a billboard loomed up before
them, a glaring six-color solido advertising, of all things, the Im-

perial Hotel. They were right around the corner from it, apparently.

"That what you want, lady?" the driver asked.

The Imperial was all glass and concrete, with what looked like giant mirrors at its summit, high overhead. It must have been two or three hundred years old, from the look of its architecture. They hadn't built buildings like that in San Francisco for a long time. Carlotta got Uncle James out of the car, told the driver to wait across the street, and signaled to a doorman to help them go inside.

"I'm here to see this man," she announced, producing Magalhaes's card. "We have an appointment. Tell him that General James Crawford is waiting for him in the lobby."

The doorman seemed unimpressed.

"Wait here," he said.

Carlotta waited a long time. Uncle James muttered restlessly. Some hotel official appeared, studied the Brazilian's card, studied her, murmured something under his breath, went back inside. What did they think she was, a prostitute? Showing up for a job with an old man in a life-support chair to keep her company? Another long time went by. A different hotel person came out.

"May I have your name," he said, not amiably.

"My name doesn't matter. This is General James Crawford, the famous war hero. Can you see the imperial medal around his neck? We've just been at the armistice celebration, and now we're here to see the delegate from Brazil, Mr. Humberto Maria—"

"Yes, but I need to know your name."

"My name doesn't matter. Just tell him that General James Crawford—"

"But your name—"

"Carlotta," she said. "Oh, go to hell, all of you." She pressed the palm control and started to turn Uncle James around. There was no sense enduring all this grief. Just then, though, an enormous black limousine glided up to the curb and Humberto Maria de Magalhaes himself emerged.

He took in the scene outside the hotel and sized up the situation at once.

"So you have come after all! How good! How very good!"

The hotel man said, "Senor Magalhaes, this woman claims—"

"Yes. Yes. Is all right. I am expecting. Please, let us go inside. Please. Please. Such a great honor, General Crawford!" He extended his arms in a gesture so splendid that it would have been worthy of the emperor himself. "Come," he said. He led them into the building.

The lobby of the Imperial was a great glittering cavern, all glass and lights. Carlotta felt dizzy. The Brazilian was in complete command, shepherding them to some sort of secluded alcove, where waiters in brocaded livery came hustling to bring champagne, little snacks on porcelain trays, a glistening bowl brimming with fruit. Magalhaes pulled a recorder from his pocket, a holido scanner, and two or three other devices, and set them on the table before them.

"Now, if you please, General Crawford—"

"The fee," Carlotta said.

"Ah. Yes. Yes, of course." Magalhaes seemed untroubled by that. He pulled some crumpled old dirty bills from his wallet, imperial money, green and gold. "Will this be enough, do you think?"

She stared. It was more than she made in six months.

But some demon took hold of her and she said, recklessly, "Another five hundred should do it."

"Of course," the Brazilian said. "No problem!" He put another bill on the edge of the table and aimed his lens at the old man. "I am so eager to record his memories, I can hardly tell you. Now, if you would ask the general to discuss the day of the famous battle, first—"

Carlotta bent close to the old man's audio intake and said, "Uncle, this man wants you to talk about your war experiences. He's going to record a sort of memoir of you. Just say whatever you can remember, all right? He'll be taking your picture, and this machine will record your words."

"The war," Uncle James said. And immediately lapsed into silence.

The Brazilian watched, big-eyed, holding his breath as if he feared it would interfere with the flow of the old man's words. But there were no words. Carlotta, who had tactfully left the Brazilian's money on the table, thinking it would look a little better not to pocket it until after the interview, began to wish now that she had taken it right away.

The silence became very long indeed.

She reached down and gave the old man a little spurt of heptocholinase through the IV line. That seemed to do it.

186

"—the invasion," Uncle James said, as if he had been speaking silently for some time and only now was bothering to come up to the audible level. And then words came pouring out of him as she had never heard them come before, a steady bubbling, nonstop spew. It was like the breaking of a dam. "We were dug into the trenches, you understand, and the Boche infantry came sneaking up at us from the east, under cover of mustard gas—oh, that was awful, the gas—but we called in an air strike right away, we hit them hard with napalm and antipersonnel shrapnel, and then we came ashore with our landing craft, hit them at Anzio and Normandy both. That was the beginning of it. Our entire strategy, you understand, was built around a terminal nuclear hit at Bull Run, but first we knew we had to close the Dardanelles and knock out their command center back of Cam Ranh Bay. Once we had that, we'd only need to worry about the Prussian cavalry and the possibility of a Saracen suicide charge, but that wasn't a real big risk, we figured, all the Rebels were pretty well demoralized already and it didn't make sense that they'd have the balls to come back at us after all we'd thrown at them, so—"

"What is he saying, please?" the Brazilian asked softly. "He speaks so quickly. I am not quite understanding him, I think."

"He does sound a little confused," said Carlotta.

"Well, we drove the Turks completely out of the Gulf of Corinth, and were heading on toward Lepanto with sixty-four galleys, full steam ahead. Then came a message from Marlborough, get our asses over to Blenheim fast as we knew how, the French were trying to break through—or was it the Poles—well, hell, it was a mess, the winter was coming on, that lunatic Hitler actually thought he could take out Russia with a fall offensive and damned if he didn't get within eighty miles of Moscow before the Russkies could stop him, and then—then—" Uncle James looked up. There was a stunned expression on his face. All his indicators were flashing in the caution zone. His cheeks were flushed and he was breathing hard.

Carlotta let her hand rest lightly on the little stack of banknotes. "He's very overexcited," she explained to Magalhaes. "This has been a big day for him. He hasn't been in San Francisco for forty-three years, you know. And to see the emperor, to get the medal and all—"

"Wait," Uncle James said. He stretched a hand toward the Brazilian. "There's something that I need to say."

There was an unfamiliar note in his voice suddenly, a forcefulness, a strange clarity. The cloudiness was gone from it, the husky senile wooliness. It sounded now like the voice of someone else entirely, someone a hundred years younger than Uncle James.

The Brazilian nodded vigorously. "Yes, tell us everything, General! Everything."

Uncle James smiled. There was an eerie look on his face.

"I wasn't a general, for one thing. I was a programmer. I never fought an actual battle. I certainly never killed anybody. Not anybody. It's all a lie, that I was any kind of hero. It was just an error in the computer records and I never said anything about it to anybody, and now it's so long ago that nobody remembers what was what. Nobody but me. And most of the time I don't even remember it myself."

Uh-oh, Carlotta thought.

As secretively as she could manage it, she slid the bills from the table into her purse. The Brazilian didn't appear to notice.

Uncle James said, "It was only a two-bit war, anyway. A lot of miserable skirmishes between a bunch of jerkwater towns gone wild with envy of what they each thought the other one had, and in fact nobody had anything at all. That was what ended the war, when we all figured out that there was nothing anywhere, that we were wiped out from top to bottom." He laughed. "And there I sat in the command center at the university the whole time, writing software. That was how I spent the war. A hundred goddamn years ago."

The Brazilian said, "His voice is so clear, suddenly."

"He's terribly tired," said Carlotta. "He doesn't know what he's saying. I should have just taken him right home. The interview's over. It's too much of a strain on him."

"Could we not have him continue a small while longer? But perhaps we should allow him to rest for a little," the Brazilian suggested.

"Rest," Uncle James said. "That's all I fucking want. But they don't ever let you rest, do they? You fight the Crusades, you fight the Peloponnesian, you fight the Civil, you get so tired, you get so fucking tired. All those wars. I fought 'em all. Every one of them at once. You run the simulations and you've got the Nazis over here and Hannibal over there and the crowd from Monterey trying to bust in up the center, and Hastings, and Tours, and San Jose—Grant and Lee—Charlemagne—Napoleon—Eisenhower—General Patton—"

His voice was still weirdly lucid and strong.

But it was terrible to sit here listening to him babbling crazy nonsense like this. Enough is enough, Carlotta decided. She reached down quickly and hit Main Cerebral and put him to sleep. Between one moment and the next he shut down completely.

The Brazilian gasped. "What has happened? He has not died, has he?"

"No, he's all right. Just sleeping. He was too tired for this. I'm sorry, Mr. Magal—Magal—" Carlotta rose. The money was safely stowed away. "He's badly in need of rest, just as you heard him say. I'm going to take him home. Perhaps we can do this interview some other time. I don't know when. I have your card. I'll call you, all right?"

She flexed her palm and sent the chair moving out into the main lobby of the hotel, and toward the door.

The driver, thank God, was still sitting there. Carlotta beckoned to him.

They were halfway across the bay before she brought the old man back to consciousness. He sat up rigidly in the chair, looked around, peered for a moment at the scenery, the afternoon light on the East Bay hills ahead of them, the puffy clouds that had come drifting down from somewhere.

"Pretty," he said. His voice had its old muddled quality again. "What a goddamn pretty place! Are we on the bridge? We were in the city, were we?"

"Yes," she told him. "For the anniversary of the armistice. We had ourselves a time, too. The emperor himself hung that medal around your neck."

"The emperor, yes. A fine figure of a man. Norton the Ninth."

"Fourteenth, I think."

"Yes. Yes, right. Norton the Fourteenth," the old man said vaguely. "I meant to say Fourteenth." He fingered the medal idly and seemed to disappear for a moment into some abyss of thought where he was completely alone. She heard him murmuring to himself, a faint indistinct flow of unintelligible sound. Then suddenly he said, reverting once more to that tone of the same strength and lucidity that he had been able to muster for just a moment at the Imperial Hotel, "What happened to that slick-looking rich foreigner? He was right there. Where did he go?"

"You were telling him about General Patton at Bull Run, and you got overexcited, and you weren't making any sense, Uncle. I had to shut you down for a little time."

"General Patton? Bull Run?"

"It was that time you nuked the Rebels," Carlotta said. "It's not important if you don't remember, Uncle. It was all so long ago. How could anyone expect you to remember?" She patted him gently on the shoulder. "Anyway, we had ourselves a time in the city today, didn't we? That's all that matters. You got yourself a medal, and we had ourselves a time."

He chuckled and nodded, and said something in a voice too soft to understand, and slipped off easily into sleep.

The car sped onward, eastward across the bridge, back toward Berkeley.

Connie Willis
CIBOLA

Connie Willis lives in Colorado with her husband and daughter, Cordelia—and what seems like an entire roomful of writing awards. In 1989, she won her fourth Nebula Award for her novelette "At the Rialto" which was also nominated for a Hugo Award, as was her novella "Time-Out."

Connie often moves through time to explore history in her stories, as she does in her most recent novel, *Doomsday Book* which deals with the plague. In "Cibola," she similarly calls upon the past to create a story that makes us question our notions of reality and time.

"Cibola" is set in Denver, where Connie grew up, of which she writes,

> Most people who grew up in a big city have a love-hate relationship with it. Denver has some of the worst traffic and the worst weather in the known world (both especially bad whenever the Broncos play on "Monday Night Football"), but it also has wonderful Christmas

lights, a golden capital dome, and a great view of the Rockies.

Most of the time I like Denver (not at five o'clock north-bound on the Valley Highway), I'm amused by it nearly all the time (especially during Bronco season), and some of the time, depending on the weather and the road conditions, I love it.

The other "different expressions of home" in this collection have portrayed home as a refuge or as a guide, changing or unchanged, sanctuary or trap. Home has been a place to escape from or return to, understand or defend. Yet no matter what the view of home, in each story there is a current running beneath, a stream of affection for place that flows deep or lies just under the surface of the tale. In "Cibola," this undercurrent does at last "come home," rising to the surface. Here we see clearly that, no matter how it has changed in reality or in our dreams, there is a dazzling beauty to our homes, our hometowns, that often we fail to recognize until someone shows it to us. Here, that someone is Connie Willis and she portrays that beauty in a witty, entrancing—and even magnificent—way.

ℭIBOLA

Connie Willis

"CARLA, you grew up in Denver," Jake said. "Here's an assignment that might interest you."

This is his standard opening line. It means he is about to dump another "local interest" piece on me.

"Come on, Jake," I said. "No more nutty Bronco fans who've spray-painted their kids orange and blue, okay? Give me a real story. Please?"

"Bronco season's over, and the NFL draft was last week," he said. "This isn't a local interest."

"You're right there," I said. "These stories you keep giving me are of no interest, local or otherwise. I did the time machine piece for you. And the psychic dentist. Give me a break. Let me cover something that doesn't involve nuttos."

"It's for the 'Our Living Western Heritage' series." He handed me a slip of paper. "You can interview her this morning and then cover the skyscraper moratorium hearings this afternoon."

This was plainly a bribe, since the hearings were front page stuff right now, and "historical interests" could be almost as bad as locals—senile old women in nursing homes rambling on about the good old days. But at least they didn't crawl in their washing machines and tell you to push RINSE so they could travel into the future. And they didn't try to perform psychic oral surgery on you.

"All right," I said, and took the slip of paper. "Rosa Turcorillo," it read and gave an address out on Santa Fe. "What's her phone number?"

"She doesn't have a phone," Jake said. "You'll have to go out there." He started across the city room to his office. "The hearings are at one o'clock."

"What is she, one of Denver's first Chicano settlers?" I called after him.

He waited till he was just outside his office to answer me. "She says she's the great-granddaughter of Coronado," he said, and beat a hasty retreat into his office. "She says she knows where the Seven Cities of Cibola are."

I spent forty-five minutes researching Coronado and copying articles and then drove out to see his great-granddaughter. She lived out on south Santa Fe past Hampden, so I took I-25 and then was sorry. The morning rush hour was still crawling along at about ten miles an hour pumping carbon monoxide into the air. I read the whole article stopped behind a semi between Speer and Sixth Avenue.

Coronado trekked through the Southwest looking for the legendary Seven Cities of Gold in the 1540s, which poked a big hole in Rosa's story, since any great-granddaughter of his would have to be at least three hundred years old.

There wasn't any mystery about the Seven Cities of Cibola either. Coronado found them, near Gallup, New Mexico, and conquered them but they were nothing but mud-hut villages. Having been burned once, he promptly took off after another promise of gold in Quivira in Kansas someplace where there wasn't any gold either. He hadn't been in Colorado at all.

I pulled onto Santa Fe, cursing Jack for sending me on another wild-goose chase, and headed south. Denver is famous for traffic, air pollution, and neighborhoods that have seen better days. Santa Fe isn't one of those neighborhoods. It's been a decaying line of rusting railroad tracks, crummy bars, old motels, and waterbed stores for as long as I can remember, and I, as Jake continually reminds me, grew up in Denver.

Coronado's great-granddaughter lived clear south past Hampden, in a trailer park with a sign saying OLDE WEST MOTEL over a neon bison, and Rosa Turcorillo's old Airstream looked like it had been there since the days when the buffalo roamed. It was tiny, the kind of trailer I would call "Turcorillo's modest mobile home" in the article, no more than fifteen feet long and eight wide.

Rosa was nearly that wide herself. When she answered my knock, she barely fit in the door. She was wearing a voluminous turquoise housecoat, and had long black braids.

"What do you want?" she said, holding the metal door so she could slam it in case I was the police or a repo man.

"I'm Carla Johnson from the *Denver Record*," I said. "I'd like to interview you about Coronado." I fished in my bag for my press card. "We're doing a series on 'Our Living Western Heritage.' " I finally found the press card and handed it to her. "We're interviewing people who are part of our past."

She stared at the press card disinterestedly. This was not the way it was supposed to work. Nuttos usually drag you in the house and start babbling before you finish telling them who you are. She should already be halfway through her account of how she'd traced her ancestry back to Coronado by means of the I Ching.

"I would have telephoned first, but you didn't have a phone." I said.

She handed the card to me and started to shut the door.

"If this isn't a good time, I can come back," I babbled. "And we don't have to do the interview here if you'd rather not. We can go to the *Record* office or to a restaurant."

She opened the door and flashed a smile that had half of Cibola's missing gold in it. "I ain't dressed," she said. "It'll take me a couple of minutes. Come on in."

I climbed the metal steps and went inside. Rosa pointed at a flowered couch, told me to sit down and disappeared into the rear of the trailer.

I was glad I had suggested going out. The place was no messier than my desk, but it was only about six feet long and had the couch, a dinette set, and a recliner. There was no way it would hold me and Coronado's granddaughter, too.

The place may have had a surplus of furniture but it didn't have any of the usual crazy stuff, no pyramids, no astrological charts, no crystals. A deck of cards was laid out like the tarot on the dinette table, but when I leaned across to look at them, it was a half-finished game of solitaire. I put the red eight on the black nine.

Rosa came out, wearing orange polyester pants and a yellow print blouse and carrying a large black leather purse. I stood up and started to say, "Where would you like to go? Is there someplace close?" but I only got it half out.

"The Eldorado Cafe," she said and started out the door, moving pretty fast for somebody three hundred years old and three hundred pounds.

"I don't know where the Eldorado Cafe is," I said, unlocking the car door for her. "You'll have to tell me where it is."

"Turn right," she said. "They have good cinnamon rolls."

I wondered if it was the offer of the food or just the chance to go someplace that had made her consent to the interview. Whichever,. I might as well get it over with. "So Coronado was your great-grandfather?" I said.

She looked at me as if I were out of my mind. "No. Who told you that?"

Jake, I thought, who I plan to tear limb from limb when I get back to the *Record*. "You aren't Coronado's great-granddaughter?"

She folded her arms over her stomach. "I am the descendant of El Turco."

El Turco. It sounded like something out of *Zorro*. "So it's this El Turco who's your great-grandfather?"

"Great-*great*. El Turco was Pawnee. Coronado captured him at Cicuye and put a collar around his neck so he could not run away. Turn right."

We were already halfway through the intersection. I jerked the steering wheel to the right and nearly skidded into a pickup.

Rosa seemed unperturbed. "Coronado wanted El Turco to guide him to Cibola," she said.

I wanted to ask if he had, but I didn't want to prevent Rosa from giving me directions. I drove slowly through the next intersection, alert to sudden instructions, but there weren't any. I drove on down the block.

"And did El Turco guide Coronado to Cibola?"

"Sure. You should have turned left back there," she said.

She apparently hadn't inherited her great-great-grandfather's scouting ability. I went around the block and turned left, and was overjoyed to see the Eldorado Cafe down the street. I pulled into the parking lot and we got out.

"They make their own cinnamon rolls," she said, looking at me hopefully as we went in. "With frosting."

We sat down in a booth. "Have anything you want," I said. "This is on the *Record*."

She ordered a cinnamon roll and a large Coke. I ordered coffee and began fishing in my bag for my tape recorder.

"You lived here in Denver a long time?" she asked.

"All my life. I grew up here."

She smiled her gold-toothed smile at me. "You like Denver?"

"Sure," I said. I found the pocket-sized recorder and laid it on the table. "Smog, oil refineries, traffic. What's not to like?"

"I like it, too," she said.

The waitress set a cinnamon roll the size of Mile High Stadium in front of her and poured my coffee.

"You know what Coronado fed El Turco?" The waitress brought her large Coke. "Probably one tortilla a day. And he didn't have no shoes. Coronado made him walk all that way to Colorado and no shoes."

I switched the tape recorder on. "You say Coronado came to Colorado," I said, "but what I've read says he traveled through New Mexico and Oklahoma and up into Kansas, but not Colorado."

"He was in Colorado." She jabbed her finger into the table. "He was *here*."

I wondered if she meant here in Colorado or here in the Eldorado Cafe.

"When was that? On his way to Quivira?"

"Quivira?" she said, looking blank. "I don't know nothing about Quivira."

"Quivira was a place where there was supposed to be gold," I said. "He went there after he found the Seven Cities of Cibola."

"He didn't find them," she said, chewing on a mouthful of cinnamon roll. "That's why he killed El Turco."

"Coronado killed El Turco?"

"Yes. After he led him to Cibola."

This was even worse than talking to the psychic dentist.

"Coronado said El Turco made the whole thing up," Rosa said. "He said El Turco was going to lead Coronado into an ambush and kill him. He said the Seven Cities didn't exist."

"But they did?"

"Of course. El Turco led him to the place."

"But I thought you said Coronado didn't find them."

"He didn't."

I was hopelessly confused by now. "Why not?"

"Because they weren't there."

I was going to run Jake through his paper shredder an inch at a time. I had wasted a whole morning on this and I was not even going to be able to get a story out of it.

"You mean they were some sort of mirage?" I asked.

Rosa considered this through several bites of cinnamon roll. "No. A mirage is something that isn't there. These were there."

"But invisible?"

"No."

"Hidden."

"No."

"But Coronado couldn't see them?"

She shook her head. With her forefinger, she picked up a few stray pieces of frosting left on her plate and stuck them in her mouth. "How could he when they weren't there."

The tape clicked off, and I didn't even bother to turn it over. I looked at my watch. If I took her back now I could make it to the hearings early and maybe interview some of the developers. I picked up the check and went over to the cash register.

"Do you want to see them?"

"What do you mean? See the Seven Cities of Cibola?"

"Yeah. I'll take you to them."

"You mean go to New Mexico?"

"No. I told you, Coronado came to Colorado."

"When?"

"When he was looking for the Seven Cities of Cibola."

"No, I mean when can *I* see them? Right now?"

"No," she said, with the "How dumb can anyone be?" look. She reached for a copy of the *Rocky Mountain News* that was lying on the counter and looked inside the back page. "Tomorrow morning. Six o'clock."

One of my favorite things about Denver is that it's spread all over the place and takes you forever to get anywhere. The mountains finally put a stop to things twenty miles to the west, but in all three other directions it can sprawl all the way to the state line and apparently is trying to. Being a reporter here isn't so much a question of driving journalistic ambition as of driving, period.

The skyscraper moratorium hearings were out on Colorado Boulevard across from the Hotel Giorgio, one of the skyscrapers under discussion. It took me forty-five minutes to get there from the Olde West Motel trailer park.

I was half an hour late, which meant the hearings had already gotten completely off the subject. "What about reflecting glass?" someone in the audience was saying. "I think it should be outlawed in skyscrapers. I was nearly blinded the other day on the way to work."

"Yeah," a middle-aged woman said. "If we're going to have skyscrapers, they should look like skyscrapers." She waved vaguely at the Hotel Giorgio, which looks like a giant black milk carton.

"And not like that United Bank building downtown!" someone else said. "It looks like a damned cash register!"

From there it was a short illogical jump to the impossibility of parking downtown, Denver's becoming too decentralized, and whether the new airport should be built or not. By five-thirty they were back on reflecting glass.

"Why don't they put glass you can see through in their skyscrapers?" an old man who looked a lot like the time machine inventor said. "I'll tell you why not. Because those big business executives are doing things they should be ashamed of, and they don't want us to see them."

I left at seven and went back to the *Record* to try to piece my notes together into some kind of story. Jake was there.

"How'd your interview with Coronado's granddaughter go?" he asked.

"The Seven Cities of Cibola are here in Denver only Coronado couldn't see them because they're not there." I looked around. "Is there a copy of the *News* someplace?"

"*Here?* In the *Record* building!?" he said, clutching his chest in mock horror. "That bad, huh? You're going to go work for the *News?*" But he fished a copy out of the mess on somebody's desk and handed it to me. I opened it to the back page.

There was no "Best Times for Viewing Lost Cities of Gold"

column. There were pictures and dates of the phases of the moon, road conditions, and "What's in the Stars: by Stella." My horoscope of the day read: "Any assignment you accept today will turn out differently than you expect." The rest of the page was devoted to the weather, which was supposed to be sunny and warm tomorrow.

The facing page had the crossword puzzle, "Today in History," and squibs about Princess Di and a Bronco fan who'd planted his garden in the shape of a Bronco quarterback. I was surprised Jake hadn't assigned me that story.

I went down to Research and looked up El Turco. He was an Indian slave, probably Pawnee, who had scouted for Coronado, but that was his nickname, not his name. The Spanish had called him "The Turk" because of his peculiar hair. He had been captured at Cicuye, *after* Coronado's foray into Cibola, and had promised to lead them to Quivira, tempting them with stories of golden streets and great stone palaces. When the stories didn't pan out, Coronado had had him executed. I could understand why.

Jake cornered me on my way home. "Look, don't quit," he said. "Tell you what, forget Coronado. There's a guy out in Lakewood who's planted his garden in the shape of John Elway's face. Daffodils for hair, blue hyacinths for eyes."

"Can't," I said, sidling past him. "I've got a date to see the Seven Cities of Gold."

Another delightful aspect of the Beautiful Mile-High City is that in the middle of April, after you've planted your favorite Bronco, you can get fifteen inches of snow. It had started getting cloudy by the time I left the paper, but fool that I was, I thought it was an afternoon thunderstorm. The News's forecast had, after all, been for warm and sunny. When I woke up at four-thirty there was a foot and a half of snow on the ground and more tumbling down.

"Why are you going back if she's such a nut?" Jake had asked me when I told him I couldn't take the Elway garden. "You don't seriously think she's on to something, do you?" and I had had a hard time explaining to him why I was planning to get up at an ungodly hour and trek all the way out to Santa Fe again.

She was *not* El Turco's great-great-granddaughter. Two greats still left her at two hundred and fifty plus, and her history was as garbled as her math, but when I had gotten impatient she had said,

"Do you want to see them?" and when I had asked her when, she had consulted the News's crossword puzzle and said, "Tomorrow morning."

I had gotten offers of proof before. The time machine inventor had proposed that I climb in his washing machine and be sent forward to "a glorious future, a time when everyone is rich," and the psychic dentist had offered to pull my wisdom teeth. But there's always a catch to these offers.

"Your teeth will have been extracted in another plane of reality," the dentist had said. "X-rays taken in this plane will show them as still being there," and the time machine guy had checked his soak cycle and the stars at the last minute and decided there wouldn't be another temporal agitation until August of 2158.

Rosa hadn't put any restrictions at all on her offer. "You want to see them?" she said, and there was no mention of reality planes or stellar-laundry connections, no mention of any catch. Which doesn't mean there won't be one, I thought, getting out the mittens and scarf I had just put away for the season and going out to scrape the windshield off. When I got there she would no doubt say the snow made it impossible to see the Cities or I could only see them if I believed in UFOs. Or maybe she'd point off somewhere in the general direction of Denver's brown cloud and say, "What do you mean, you can't see them?"

I-25 was a mess, cars off the road everywhere and snow driving into my headlights so I could barely see. I got behind a snowplow and stayed there, and it was nearly six o'clock by the time I made it to the trailer. Rosa took a good five minutes to come to the door, and when she finally got there she wasn't dressed. She stared blearily at me, her hair out of its braids and hanging tangled around her face.

"Remember me? Carla Johnson? You promised to show me the Seven Cities?"

"Cities?" she said blankly.

"The Seven Cities of Cibola."

"Oh, yeah," she said, and motioned for me to come inside. "There aren't seven. El Turco was a dumb Pawnee. He don't know how to count."

"How many are there?" I asked, thinking, this is the catch. There aren't seven and they aren't gold.

201

"Depends," she said. "More than seven. You still wanta go see them?"

"Yes."

She went into the bedroom and came out after a few minutes with her hair braided, the pants and blouse of the day before and an enormous red car coat and we took off toward Cibola. We went south again, past more waterbed stores and rusting railroad tracks, and out to Belleview.

It was beginning to get fairly light out, though it was impossible to tell if the sun was up or not. It was still snowing hard.

She had me turn onto Belleview, giving me at least ten yards' warning, and we headed east toward the Tech Center. Those people at the hearing who'd complained about Denver becoming too decentralized had a point. The Tech Center looked like another downtown as we headed toward it.

A multicolored downtown, garish even through the veil of snow. The Metropoint Building was pinkish-lavender, the one next to it was midnight blue, while the Hyatt Regency had gone in for turquoise and bronze, and there was an assortment of silver, seagreen, and taupe. There was an assortment of shapes, too: deranged trapezoids, overweight butterflies, giant beer cans. They were clearly moratorium material, each of them with its full complement of reflecting glass, and presumably, executives with something to hide.

Rosa had me turn left onto Yosemite, and we headed north again. The snowplows hadn't made it out here yet, and it was heavy going. I leaned forward and peered through the windshield, and so did Rosa.

"Do you think we'll be able to see them?" I asked.

"Can't tell yet," she said. "Turn right."

I turned into a snow-filled street. "I've been reading about your great-grandfather."

"Great-*great*," she said.

"He confessed he'd lied about the cities, that there really wasn't any gold."

She shrugged. "He was scared. He thought Coronado was going to kill him."

"Coronado *did* kill him," I said. "He said El Turco was leading his army into a trap."

She shrugged again and wiped a space clear on the windshield to look through.

"If the Seven Cities existed, why didn't El Turco take Coronado to them? It would have saved his life."

"They weren't there." She leaned back.

"You mean they're not there all the time?" I said.

"You know the Grand Canyon?" she asked. "My great-great-grandfather discovered the Grand Canyon. He told Coronado he seen it. Nobody saw the Grand Canyon again for three hundred years. Just because nobody seen it don't mean it wasn't there. You was supposed to turn right back there at the light."

I could see why Coronado had strangled El Turco. If I hadn't been afraid I'd get stuck in the snow, I'd have stopped and throttled her right then. I turned around, slipping and sliding, and went back to the light.

"Left at the next corner and go down the block a little ways," she said, pointing. "Pull in there."

"There" was the parking lot of a doughnut shop. It had a giant neon doughnut in the middle of its steamed-up windows. I knew how Coronado felt when he rode into the huddle of mud huts that was supposed to have been the City of Gold.

"This is Cibola?" I said.

"No way," she said, heaving herself out of the car. "They're not there today."

"You *said* they were always there," I said.

"They are." She shut the car door, dislodging a clump of snow. "Just not all the time. I think they're in one of those time-things."

"Time-things? You mean a time warp?" I asked, trying to remember what the washing-machine guy had called it. "A temporal agitation?"

"How would I know? I'm not a scientist. They have good doughnuts here. Cream-filled."

The doughnuts were actually pretty good, and by the time we started home the snow had stopped and was already turning to slush, and I no longer wanted to strangle her on the spot. I figured in another hour the sun would be out, and John Elway's hyacinth blue eyes would be poking through again. By the time we turned onto Hampden, I felt calm enough to ask when she thought the Seven Cities might put in another appearance.

She had bought a *Rocky Mountain News* and a box of cream-filled doughnuts to take home. She opened the box and contemplated them. "More than seven," she said. "You like to write?"

"What?" I said, wondering if Coronado had had this much trouble communicating with El Turco.

"That's why you're a reporter, because you like to write?"

"No," I said. "The writing's a real pain. When will this time-warp thing happen again?"

She bit into a doughnut. "That's Cinderella City," she said, gesturing to the mall on our right with it. "You ever been there?"

I nodded.

"I went there once. They got marble floors and this big fountain. They got lots of stores. You can buy just about anything you want there. Clothes, jewels, shoes."

If she wanted to do a little shopping now that she'd had breakfast, she could forget it. And she could forget about changing the subject. "When can we go see the Seven Cities again? Tomorrow?"

She licked cream filling off her fingers and turned the *News* over. "Not tomorrow," she said. "El Turco would have liked Cinderella City. He didn't have no shoes. He had to walk all the way to Colorado in his bare feet. Even in the snow."

I imagined my hands closing around her plump neck. "When are the Seven Cities going to be there again?" I demanded. "And don't tell me they're always there."

She consulted the celebrity squibs. "Not tomorrow," she said. "Day after tomorrow. Five o'clock. You must like people, then. That's why you wanted to be a reporter? To meet all kinds of people?"

"No," I said. "Believe it or not, I wanted to travel."

She grinned her golden smile at me. "Like Coronado," she said.

I spent the next two days interviewing developers, environmentalists, and council members, and pondering why Coronado had continued to follow El Turco, even after it was clear he was a pathological liar.

I had stopped at the first 7-Eleven I could find after letting Rosa and her doughnuts off and bought a copy of the *News*. I read the entire back section, including the comics. For all I knew, she was using "Doonesbury" for an oracle. Or "Nancy."

I read the obits and worked the crossword puzzle and then went over the back page again. There was nothing remotely time-warp-related. The moon was at first quarter. Sunset would occur at 7:51 P.M. Road conditions for the Eisenhower Tunnel were snow-packed and blowing. Chains required. My horoscope read, "Don't get involved in wild goose chases. A good stay-at-home day."

Rosa no more knew where the Seven Cities of Gold were than her great-great-grandfather. According to the stuff I read in between moratorium jaunts, he had changed his story every fifteen minutes or so, depending on what Coronado wanted to hear.

The other Indian scouts had warned Coronado, told him there was nothing to the north but buffalo and a few teepees, but Coronado had gone blindly on. "El Turco seems to have exerted a Pied Piper–like power over Coronado," one of the historians had written, "a power which none of Coronado's officers could understand."

"Are you still working on that crazy Coronado thing?" Jake asked me when I got back to the *Record*. "I thought you were covering the hearings."

"I am," I said, looking up the Grand Canyon. "They've been postponed because of the snow. I have an appointment with the United Coalition Against Uncontrolled Growth at eleven."

"Good," he said. "I don't need the Coronado piece, after all. We're running a series on 'Denver Today' instead."

He went back upstairs. I found the Grand Canyon. It had been discovered by Lopez de Cardeñas, one of Coronado's men. El Turco hadn't been with him.

I drove out to Aurora in a blinding snowstorm to interview the United Coalition. They were united only in spirit, not in location. The president had his office in one of the Pavilion Towers off Havana, but the secretary, who had all the graphs and spreadsheets, was out at Fiddler's Green. I spent the whole afternoon shuttling back and forth between them through the snow, and wondering what had ever possessed me to become a journalist.

I'd wanted to travel. I had had the idea, gotten from TV, that journalists got to go all over the world, writing about exotic and amazing places. Like the UNIPAC building and the Plaza Towers.

They were sort of amazing, if you like Modern Corporate. Brass and chrome and Persian carpets. Atriums and palm trees and fountains splashing in marble pools. I wondered what Rosa, who had been so impressed with Cinderella City, would have thought of some of these places. El Turco would certainly have been impressed. Of course, he would probably have been impressed by the doughnut shop, and would no doubt have convinced Coronado to drag his whole army there with tales of fabulous, cream-filled wealth.

I finished up the United Coalition and went back to the *Record* to call some developers and builders and get their side. It was still snowing, and there weren't any signs of snow removal, creative or otherwise, that I could see. I set up some appointments for the next day, and then went back down to Research.

El Turco hadn't been the only person to tell tales of the fabulous Seven Cities of Gold. A Spanish explorer, Cabeza de Vaca, had reported them first, and his black slave Estevanico claimed to have seen them, too. Friar Marcos had gone with Estevanico to find them, and, according to him, Estevanico had actually entered Cibola.

They had made up a signal. Estevanico was to send back a small cross if he found a little village, a big cross if he found a city. Estevanico was killed in a battle with Indians, and Friar Marcos fled back to Coronado, but he said he'd seen the Seven Cities in the distance, and he claimed that Estevanico had sent back "a cross the size of a man."

There were all kinds of other tales, too, that the Navajos had gold and silver mines, that Montezuma had moved his treasure north to keep it from the Spanish, that there was a golden city on a lake, with canoes whose oarlocks were solid gold. If El Turco had been lying, he wasn't the only one.

I spent the next day interviewing pro–uncontrolled growth types. They were united, too. "Denver has to retain its central identity," they all told me from what it was hard to believe was not a prewritten script. "It's becoming split into a half dozen subcities, each with its own separate goals."

They were in less agreement as to where the problem lay. One of the builders who'd developed the Tech Center thought the Plaza Tower out at Fiddler's Green was an eyesore, Fiddler's Green complained about Aurora, Aurora thought there was too much building going on around Colorado Boulevard. They were all united on one thing, however: downtown was completely out of control.

I logged several thousand miles in the snow, which showed no signs of letting up, and went home to bed. I debated setting my alarm. Rosa didn't know where the Seven Cities of Gold were, the Living Western Heritage series had been canceled, and Coronado would have saved everybody a lot of trouble if he had listened to his generals.

But Estevanico had sent back a giant cross, and there was the "time-thing" thing. I had not done enough stories on psychic periodontia yet to start believing their nutto theories, but I had done enough to know what they were supposed to sound like. Rosa's was all wrong.

"I don't know what it's called," she'd said, far too vaguely. Nutto theories may not make any sense, but they're all worked out, down to the last bit of pseudoscientific jargon. The psychic dentist had told me all about transcendental maxillofacial extractile vibrations, and the time travel guy had showed me a hand-lettered chart showing how the PARTIAL LOAD setting affected future events.

If Rosa's Seven Cities were just one more nutto theory, she would have been talking about morphogenetic temporal dislocation and simultaneous reality modes. She would at least know what the "time-thing" was called.

I compromised by setting the alarm on MUSIC and went to bed.

I overslept. The station I'd set the alarm on wasn't on the air at four-thirty in the morning. I raced into my clothes, dragged a brush through my hair, and took off. There was almost no traffic—who in their right mind is up at four-thirty?—and it had stopped snowing. By the time I pulled onto Santa Fe I was only running ten minutes late. Not that it mattered. She would probably take half an hour to drag herself to the door to tell me the Seven Cities of Cibola had canceled again.

I was wrong. She was standing outside waiting in her red car coat and a pair of orange Bronco earmuffs. "You're late," she said, squeezing herself in beside me. "Got to go."

"Where?"

She pointed. "Turn left."

"Why don't you just tell me where we're going?" I said, "and that way I'll have a little advance warning."

"Turn right," she said.

We turned onto Hampden and started up past Cinderella City. Hampden is never free of traffic, no matter what time of day it is. There were dozens of cars on the road. I got in the center lane, hoping she'd give me at least a few feet of warning for the next turn, but she leaned back and folded her arms across her massive bosom.

"You're sure the Seven Cities will appear this morning?" I asked.

She leaned forward and peered through the windshield at the slowly lightening sky, looking for who knows what. "Good chance. Can't tell for sure."

I felt like Coronado, dragged from pillar to post. "Just a little farther, just a little farther." I wondered if this could be not only a scam but a setup, if we would end up pulling up next to a black van in some dark parking lot, and I would find myself on the cover of the *Record* as a robbery victim or worse. She was certainly anxious enough. She kept holding up her arm so she could read her watch in the lights of the cars behind us. More likely, we were heading for some bakery that opened at the crack of dawn, and she wanted to be there when the fried cinnamon rolls came out of the oven.

"Turn right!" she said. "Can't you go no faster?"

I went faster. We were out in Cherry Creek now, and it was starting to get really light. The snowstorm was apparently over. The sky was turning a faint lavender-blue.

"Now right, up there," she said, and I saw where we were going. This road led past Cherry Creek High School and then up along the top of the dam. A nice isolated place for a robbery.

We went past the last houses and pulled out onto the dam road. Rosa turned in her seat to peer out my window and the back, obviously looking for something. There wasn't much to see. The water wasn't visible from this point, and she was looking the wrong direction, out toward Denver. There were still a few lights, the early-bird traffic down on I-225 and the last few orangish streetlights that hadn't gone off automatically. The snow had taken on the bluish-lavender color of the sky.

I stopped the car.

"What are you doing?" she demanded. "Go all the way up."

"I can't," I said, pointing ahead. "The road's closed."

She peered at the chain strung across the road as if she couldn't figure out what it was, and then opened her door and got out.

Now it was my turn to say, "What are you doing?"

"We gotta walk," she said. "We'll miss it otherwise."

"Miss what? Are you telling me there's going to be a time warp up there on top of the dam?"

She looked at me like I was crazy. "Time warp?" she said. Her grin glittered in my headlights. "No. Come on."

Even Coronado had finally said, "All right, enough," and ordered his men to strangle El Turco. But not until he'd been lured all the way up to Kansas. And, according to Rosa, Colorado. The Seven Cities of Cibola were *not* going to be up on top of Cherry Creek Dam, no matter what Rosa said, and I wasn't even going to get a story out of this, but I switched off my lights and got out of the car and climbed over the chain.

It was almost fully light now, and the shadowy dimnesses below were sorting themselves out into decentralized Denver. The black *2001* towers off Havana were right below us, and past them the peculiar Mayan-pyramid shape of the National Farmer's Union. The Tech Center rose in a jumble off to the left, beer cans and trapezoids, and then there was a long curve of isolated buildings all the way to downtown, an island of skyscraping towers obviously in need of a moratorium.

"Come on," Rosa said. She started walking faster, panting along the road ahead of me and looking anxiously toward the east, where at least a black van wasn't parked. "Coronado shouldn't have killed El Turco. It wasn't his fault."

"What wasn't his fault?"

"It was one of those time-things, what did you call it?" she said, breathing hard.

"A temporal agitation?"

"Yeah, only he didn't know it. He thought it was there all the time, and when he brought Coronado there it wasn't there, and he didn't know what had happened."

She looked anxiously to the east again, where a band of clouds extending about an inch above the horizon was beginning to turn pinkish-gray, and broke into an ungainly run. I trotted after her, trying to remember the procedure for CPR.

She ran into the pullout at the top of the dam and stopped, panting hard. She put her hand up to her heaving chest and looked out across the snow at Denver.

"So you're saying the cities existed in some other time? In the future?"

She glanced over her shoulder at the horizon. The sun was nearly up. The narrow cloud turned pale pink, and the snow on Mount Evans went the kind of fuchsia we use in the Sunday supplements.

"And you think there's going to be another timewarp this morning?" I said.

She gave me that "How can one person be so stupid" look. "Of course not," she said, and the sun cleared the cloud. "There they are," she said.

There they were. The reflecting glass in the curved towers of Fiddler's Green caught first, and then the Tech Center and the Silverado Building on Colorado Boulevard, and the downtown sky-line burst into flames. They burned pink and then orange, the Hotel Giorgio and the Metropoint Building and the Plaza Towers, blazing pinnacles and turrets and towers.

"You didn't believe me, did you?" Rosa said.

"No," I said, unwilling to take my eyes off of them. "I didn't."

There were more than seven. Far out to the west the Federal Center ignited, and off to the north the angled lines of grain ele-vators gleamed. Downtown blazed, blinding building moratorium advocates on their way to work. In between, the Career Devel-opment Institute and the United Bank Building and the Hyatt Regency burned gold, standing out from the snow like citadels, like cities. No wonder El Turco had dragged Coronado all the way to Colorado. Marble palaces and golden streets.

"I told you they were there all the time," she said.

It was over in another minute, the fires going out one by one in the panes of reflecting glass, downtown first and then the Cigna Building and Belleview Place, fading to their everyday silver and onyx and emerald. The Pavilion Towers below us darkened and the last of the sodium streetlights went out.

"There all the time," Rosa said solemnly.

"Yeah," I said. I would have to get Jake up here to see this. I'd have to buy a *News* on the way home and check on the time of sunrise for tomorrow. And the weather.

I turned around. The sun glittered off the water of the reservoir. There was an aluminum rowboat out in the middle of it. It had golden oarlocks.

Rosa had started back down the road to the car. I caught up with her. "I'll buy you a pecan roll," I said. "Do you know of any good places around here?"

She grinned. Her gold teeth gleamed in the last light of Cibola. "The best," she said.

ABOUT THE EDITOR

Anne Devereaux Jordan was born in Pennsylvania, but grew up in Kansas. She is a graduate of the University of Michigan (B.A. and M.A.) where, in 1968, she received the Avery and Jule Hopwood Awards in poetry and short story. In 1973, she founded the Children's Literature Association and served as its executive secretary until 1976.

In addition to teaching on the college level, she was with *The Magazine of Fantasy & Science Fiction* for ten years, moving from assistant editor to managing editor during that time. She has published poetry in *F&SF*, *Isaac Asimov's Science Fiction Magazine*, and *Star•Line*, the magazine of the Science Fiction Poetry Association. In addition, she has reviewed books for the *New York Times Book Review*, published articles on both children's literature and science fiction, and written two nonfiction histories, *The Baptists* and *The Seventh-Day Adventists*. Her most recent anthology, coedited with Edward L. Ferman, is *The Best Horror Stories from The Magazine of Fantasy & Science Fiction*.

Currently, Anne Jordan lives in Mansfield Center, Connecticut, with her son David, where she works as a full-time freelance writer and editor, and teaches at Wesleyan University.